FIRST SKIRMISH

"Louisa?" The earl touched her chin, raising it.

"Yes?" she said, and saw his totally disarming, utterly charming smile.

No words of explanation were forthcoming. Rather, he bent his head to capture her lips. His kiss was all she had dreamed it might be. She felt on fire with a longing such as she had never known before.

The earl released her to hold her loosely against him. "My dear," he said, "how glad I am that you came into my life. I really do not mind anymore that your mother had an affair with my father. Let me have his letters and we shall burn them."

Louisa drew away from him. She was still burning, but now with rage. She had been mistaken. This was not love. It was war. . . .

EMILY HENDRICKSON lives at Lake Tahoe, Nevada, with her retired airline pilot husband. Of all the many places she has traveled around the world, England is her favorite and a natural choice as a setting for her novels. Although writing claims most of her time, she enjoys gardening, watercolors, and sewing for her granddaughters as well as traveling with her husband.

SIGNET REGENCY ROMANCE
COMING IN MAY 1990

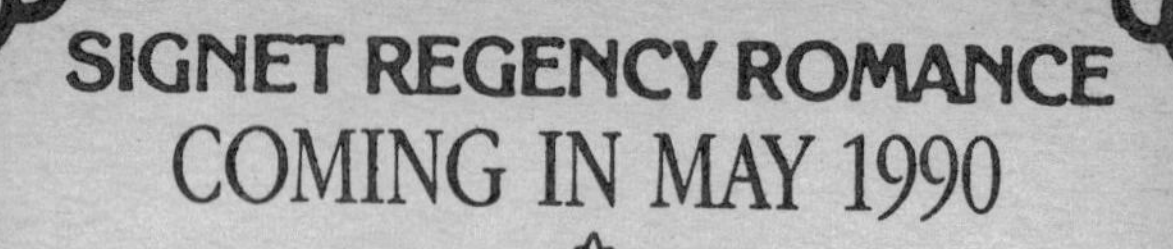

Dawn Lindsey
The Talisman

Dorothy Mack
The General's Granddaughter

Mary Balogh
The Incurable Matchmaker

THE COLONIAL UPSTART

by

Emily Hendrickson

SIGNET
Published by the Penguin Group
Penguin Books USA Inc., 375 Hudson Street,
New York, New York, 10014 U.S.A.
Penguin Books Ltd, 27 Wrights Lane, London W8 5TZ, England
Penguin Books Australia Ltd, Ringwood, Victoria, Australia
Penguin Books Canada Ltd, 2801 John Street, Markham, Ontario,
Canada L3R 1B4
Penguin Books (N.Z.) Ltd, 182-190 Wairau Road,
Auckland 10, New Zealand

Penguin Books Ltd, Registered Offices:
Harmondsworth, Middlesex, England

First published by Signet, an imprint of Penguin Books USA Inc.

First Printing, April, 1990

10 9 8 7 6 5 4 3 2 1

For Kirsten, my best assistant and dearest daughter

1

The first portmanteau dropped remarkably close to where he stood in the open courtyard of the Bear and Billet Inn. Lord Westcott brushed off an imaginary speck of dust from his impeccable dark blue Bath cloth coat, then looked about impatiently for the coachman to appear, quite ignoring the incident. His business in Chester finished, he was most anxious to return to his estate.

The second traveling case was more nicely aimed, from his point of view, for it landed further from where he stood. He didn't bother to glance up. After all, it was no matter of concern to the Earl of Westcott what unorthodox means a person used to move luggage about. A flash of frothy lace caught his eye when the soft case gapped open as a result of the impact. Very feminine and exceedingly expensive lace could be seen, even in the light of early morning.

It was the rope of sheets that finally captured his full attention. It cascaded down before his face like something from an East Indian fakir's show, undulating back and forth with a near-hypnotic sway. Now, *this* was too much for a man to tolerate. He looked up to see descending toward him a very shapely ankle above a trim little foot. A second foot could be seen peeping from the cloud of fabric that billowed about the woman, concealing her identity for the moment.

Glancing over to the exterior stairs that led to the courtyard, Westcott could see no earthly reason why the chit should take such a strange means of departure . . . unless she was trying to escape the payment of her bill. Then he noted that the rope was most conveniently short of the ground. With a roguish gleam in his eyes he obligingly positioned himself in such a place that he would be the one to catch the miscreant when it came time for her to let go her improvised means of exit.

He was most amused when the slight figure hanging in midair groped about for more "rope" with a tentative foot. That slender ankle was *very* trim, he observed with a connisseur's eye, perhaps promising a fetching armful. Her unorthodox descent came to an abrupt halt. In a flurry of blue muslin and white silk, the figure gasped a startled exclamation that sounded suspiciously like a muttered "Drat and blast!" and tumbled directly into the arms of Drew Shalford, the Earl of Westcott.

The earl looked down his aristocratic nose at the delightfully charming bundle he held, to take note of a pair of wary eyes the color of blue gentian. In an oval face of classical proportions a straight nose drew his gaze down to her full mouth, now in a stubborn line, above a resolute chin. Over a smooth brow, ebony hair could be glimpsed peeping from beneath a fetching little bonnet—a bonnet his sister could have told him was at least a year out of date. The scent of honeysuckle teased his nose, wafting up in a delicate whisper from the young woman he so carefully held.

"If you would be so kind, suh, as to place me on my feet, I should be glad of it." The softly melodious voice held a foreign accent, attractively intriguing.

Westcott found he was oddly reluctant to allow that fascinating morsel of femininity to escape his clasp. He slowly set her on her feet, watching with amusement as she brushed down her shirt, then set her bonnet at a becoming angle. She certainly appeared proper enough at this moment.

However, if he hadn't seen her rather strange mode of departure, he would never have given her a second thought. Well . . . taking another, longer look, he admitted he might have permitted his eyes to linger on such an entrancing view just a trifle more than good manners allowed. But the fact remained that she was highly suspect in her behavior. *Ladies* simply did not do such outrageous things.

Miss Louisa Randolph met his searching, assessing gaze with determined eyes. After going to such lengths to assure private conversation, even possible assistance, with the Earl of Westcott, she was not going to let a mere stare from those rich brown eyes put her out of countenance. When she had glimpsed his familiar-seeming face last night, she had hastened to the innkeeper to discover his identity. It had been a shock to find that his father, the old earl, was dead. Yet she needed help.

"Well?" she said with her usual forthrightness. She tilted her head while awaiting his verdict, then added, "I assure you, Lord Westcott, I truly intended no harm to befall you with my somewhat precipitate leave-taking. But I hoped to meet you, you see." Her voice was hushed, as though to prevent being overheard.

He didn't miss her anxious glance to the door of the room at the head of the stairs. Nor did he fail to note that she knew who he was. When she hesitantly motioned him to the area below the wooden gallery that led to the room on the second floor, he followed, out of curiosity as well as politeness. Given the young woman's genteel speech, it was obvious she was Quality.

"You have the advantage of me, it seems, for I have no clue as to your identity." He observed with approval that she clasped her hands discreetly before her, and now seemed to be all that was proper. So intrigued was he that he quite forgot to check to see if her abigail waited close by.

"I met your father while he yet lived. He visited our family home in Virginia. I am a Randolph, Miss Louisa Randolph," she stated with the confident air of one who is accustomed to recognition. "You resemble him quite strongly, as I suppose any number of people have told you. I will confess that when I inquired about you last night, I was dismayed to learn you are the new earl. It would have made things so much simpler for me were it otherwise, you see. Your father might have been able to tell me what I wish to know. However, the innkeeper explained that he is no longer among us."

"You would not have heard that he died shortly after his return from your country. If I can be of service to you in his stead . . . ?" Westcott observed his coachman pull up to the Bear and Billet to wait with obvious curiosity. While it was not too unusual for Westcott to be detained by a pretty face, it was a rare sight for him to pause to chat with one in a common open area.

"My family died as well, suh," she said softly, her gentle Virginian accent pleasing to his ear. "Yellow fever struck them all, I fear. Before she passed on, my dear mama begged me to seek my papa's relatives in England. Since there was no one left to run the farm, I decided to sell up and take my chances with my English family. Papa was such a kindly man, can they be less?" Her face revealed none of the pain she had suffered during the long hours and weeks of nursing the sick, seeing her family die one by one, or the grief of her departure from her beloved home.

Lord Westcott gazed down into the ingenuous face that now beamed a hopeful smile up at him, and thought that the young miss knew very little of the world if she truly believed such foolish words. "What optimism you reveal." He noted the worry that suddenly flared to life in her eyes.

"My papa warned me I must be careful on that account. I fear I am ever the optimist, suh, yet I trust I am not impractical. I had so hoped to locate your father—for Mama kept his kind letters—sure that he might know the identity of my English relatives. My papa abandoned his family name when he left for America, using a second name instead. Dare I hope that 'Randolph' is not too common?"

Westcott shook his head in wonder. Looking around, he failed to see so much as an abigail. Such independence would not be considered seemly in an Englishwoman. "I find it hard to believe he never spoke of his family remaining in this country. There were no clues among his effects?" Yet Westcott knew that there were emigrants who had little love for the relatives left behind. Younger sons, in particular. "I fear it may be a difficult task you have set for yourself." He paused, wondering quite how to phrase his next query. In his experience, Americans were a mite touchy on the subject. One never knew how they would react. "Was your father of the . . . nobility?" At her frown, he hastened to add, "I only ask because it does make the search easier, although I imagine most families keep excellent records.

There are also the church accounts, you know, weddings, deaths, and births, not to mention family Bibles."

Miss Randolph appeared to digest this information. "Mama said she suspected his family were of the peerage, but beyond that I could not say. Failing to locate your father, I had expected to hire a solicitor. Is there an honest one to be found in this city that you might recommend, suh?" Soft blue eyes gazed up at Lord Westcott with great trust and hope.

He glanced about the area, his air of calm confidence sitting easily upon his shoulders in spite of his concern. What could one possibly do with such a babe? While her blithe demeanor was delightful, such a romantic outlook on life was hardly practical. She would need more to sustain her through the difficulties that he could foresee lay ahead of her. "Is there no one to care for you?"

She gave an impatient shrug of her shoulders. "Jessy, my maid, was supposed to have traveled with me. But she jilted me and hired herself elsewhere. There was no time to seek another. I did not appreciate that, you can be certain. It left me open to all manner of disagreeable trials." She compressed her mouth in annoyance at what she had been forced to endure in the name of compassion.

Louisa glanced upward to where she knew the overly kind Hannah Moss slept in the room at the top of the stairs. For the many weeks of the crossing, Mrs. Moss and her tall, thin son, Aubrey, had been Louisa's constant companions. Mrs. Moss had declared Louisa in need of her protection, what with no maid along on the voyage to lend propriety. It had been given in a near-smothering quantity. Scarcely a moment had been Louisa's own from the moment she had observed poor Mr. Moss after he hit his head on a passage door. She had applied a lavender-water-drenched handkerchief to his bump. Apparently he mistook her polite concern for true interest, for he was ever at her footsteps from that moment on.

The voluble Mrs. Moss had pried—ever so gently—into Louisa's financial standing until Louisa was quite convinced that Mr. Moss was in need of a fortune. That his mother was determined to get her hands on the sizable one Louisa possessed was also apparent. The lady's concern was supposedly due to worry that Louisa would need help once in England. Louisa surmised otherwise. She strongly suspected that Mrs. Moss aimed at a marriage for her son.

All Louisa could think of at the moment was to escape the overpowering woman and her docile son before such a dreadful event came to pass. Knowing that dear Hannah, as she insisted Louisa call her, was an exceptionally light sleeper, Louisa had determined to escape her vigilance for once to see Lord Westcott without those eager ears close to hand. Now it seemed Louisa's efforts were in vain.

She clasped neatly gloved hands before her, giving a sign of resignation. Looking up at him, her anxiety clearly revealed in her eyes, she explained, "I have found the caring of some people to be a burden. There were two such souls on the voyage to England. I scarce had a moment to myself. I believe I should fare better were I to place myself in the hands of a good solicitor. If you could recommend one to me, I should be most grateful. I am finding it a troublesome thing to be alone in a strange country. As well as assisting me in locating my relatives, he might be able to advise me as to hiring a maid, for you must know I am in need of such immediately." She gave him a sunny look, her hope clearly revealed in her eyes.

Lord Westcott suddenly had an image of this sweet young woman being imposed upon by a pair of mushroom upstarts determined to use her for their own purposes. Who knew what their intent might be? If his own father had been a guest of her family, how could he then refuse to assist her? Why, it practically amounted to a duty. His duty. He gave her a reserved smile, placed one of her dainty hands on his arm, then offered, "I shall do better than that. We shall locate that gentleman, find you a maid, and then I will take you to my mother. She knows everyone who is anyone, and can remember more family trees than you would believe."

Louisa glanced at the still-closed door at the top of the stairs, a glance not missed by Lord Westcott, and smiled at him with patent relief. "I should be most grateful to you, suh. I had thought our Virginians to be fine examples of gentlemen. I see they shall have to look to their laurels. You are most kind to a poor stranger. But I really ought not impose on your mother. No. If you will but take me to the solicitor so I may place my case before him, then find a maid, that is all I dare ask of you.'' She gave him a tremulous smile, then added, ''I shan't wish to return to this inn, however. There must be another place where I can stay for the time being. If I might take those two portmanteaus with me, I could send for my trunks later on.'' She flicked another glance at the stairs, fearing she might see the gaunt figure of Mrs. Moss coming down the steps toward her.

''Is it that bad?'' he murmured, her statements settling the matter as far as he was concerned. Having had some experience with encroaching people, he doubted Miss Randolph possessed the ability to fend them off. With the thought that his father would have been most pleased with him, Westcott beckoned to a groom, gave him a few directions, then ushered Miss Louisa Randolph to the waiting carriage.

John Coachman raised an expressive brow at the sight of a pretty miss entering his master's carriage. Since 'twas no business of his, he flicked his whip and they were off.

Neither Louisa nor Westcott observed the door at the top of the stairs crack open to reveal the curious eyes of Hannah Moss.

Hannah watched the departure with rising anger. She had been so certain that little Miss Randolph would not escape her. It had taken a bribe to ensure that Miss Randolph got a room far down the gallery so Hannah could be certain not to miss any attempt to depart. That was gratitude for you. The girl obviously did not appreciate true kindness. Why, Aubrey had seen to it that Miss Randolph's every need was tended to from dawn to dark. They had made sure that the dear girl had not been left to insults from the other passengers for the entire trip. Aubrey, poor lamb, would be rendered heartsick at the thought that the wealthy young woman had been whisked away by some stranger. Unless . . .

Hannah's faded blue eyes grew thoughtful. There had been

some fancy crestlike design on the door panel of that carriage. Nobility? She placed a hand to her thin breast at the very idea. She envisioned an earl or even a duke.

Why shouldn't she and her dear worthy son be the ones to help poor Miss Randolph to locate her family? Doubtless they were to be found in some romantic castle or country estate, or, delight of delights, London. Hannah desired entrée to the topmost limits of English society. Her letters of introduction were well and good, but she suspected one could never have enough of that sort of thing.

Determined to get Miss Randolph from the clutches of that noble, whoever he was, she bestirred herself. Dressing hastily, she scurried down to her son's room, where an urgent conference was held. Aubrey was informed in no uncertain terms that he was to search the town of Chester until Miss Randolph was found.

"Check with the innkeeper. I want you to find out who that man with the carriage is. Poor Miss Randolph, Louisa, that is," Hannah moaned. "Such a dear girl, but most assuredly needing us to look after her. Go!" she ordered her bemused son. "I shall not rest until we have found the poor child and have her safely under our protection once again."

Louisa felt cushioned and protected as she had not since her dear papa died. It was truly gratifying to have found a gentleman who appeared to have Papa's attitude toward ladies. She was escorted to the solicitor's office with every attention. He accepted her commission to uncover her relatives, although expressing some doubt at the speed of inquiry owing to the small amount of information provided.

When the woman at the employment agency where they were directed first looked at the outmoded—though quite pretty—dress Louisa wore, her nose rose a trifle with evident disdain. Then Lord Westcott stepped forward. Louisa stifled the desire to laugh at the rapid change in the woman's expression. There had been nothing less than a gracious bow and an obsequious smile. Louisa had a suspicion that the applicant produced for her inspection was far superior to any she might have found on her own.

Outside the agency, Louisa faced her benefactor. "I thank you for your assistance, suh. I confess that without your help I would have found this morning a severe trial." While she had managed the farm at home during the siege of illness, that had been a series of familiar tasks. This had been altogether different. "That solicitor certainly asked a multitude of questions. I hope the answers I was able to give him will be of help." The search for her family had seemed such a simple thing back in Virginia. It was turning out to be far more complicated than she could have ever anticipated. She edged away from Lord Westcott, preparing to walk with her new abigail, Tabitha, to the inn she intended to patronize.

"I have the distinct impression that you are about to bid me farewell. May I suggest you reconsider?" asked Westcott with great circumspection. Between his sister and mother, he had learned a thing or two in handling women. "Why not take a stroll about the town and enjoy the rather interesting sights to be viewed? Not far from where we stand begin the famous 'Rows.' And you must see the cathedral. After we pause for biscuits and hot chocolate, of course."

Looking up at this gracious man, Louisa felt quite justified in sailing across the ocean to hunt for her family. If this stranger could be so kind, would her relatives not be even nicer? "I believe that would be just lovely," she replied in the soft, melodious voice that the Earl of Westcott clearly found enchanting. The three set off along the neatly paved walk to a nearby cake shop.

Over a selection of lovely biscuits and a pot of delicious chocolate, Louisa gave Lord Westcott a contrite look. "I fear I have overset your plans quite dreadfully. I am certain you wished to depart for some point this morning, and you have devoted yourself to my concerns for hours. That simply will not do. I declare, when I urged you to proceed about your business, I truly meant it. As pleasant as it might be to have you show me about the town of Chester, I would never wish to delay you on an important trip. You must have concerns of your own." The gentian blue of her eyes deepened as she gazed wistfully out of the cake-shop window. How she yearned for her own family to love and cherish.

The thought had crossed Lord Westcott's mind that he was impatient to head for his estate. He knew full well that his mother would be anxious for the parcels she had ordered, the lace and linen from Ireland, and a list of sundry other items. As well, there were other matters claiming his attention. Since his father's death, he had refrained from the petty delights of society, although he certainly felt he had not become a stick, as his sister avowed on her infrequent visits. Yet he refused to leave this tender bud of womanhood to her own devices. Anyone with eyes could see that she needed someone to watch over her. His normal cynicism evaporated in her cheerful presence.

At the look of worry on her face, he patted her nicely gloved hand in an avuncular manner. "Now, there, young lady, do not worry your head about a thing. I am certain you will get on famously with my mother, and she will be delighted to have such a project to undertake. Since my sister married and I have not, Mother has been often at a loss for something to occupy her time."

"How lovely for you to have a married sister. Does she have children?" Louisa softly smiled at him. She had sorely missed her dear brother and three little sisters since they had been taken from her by the yellow fever.

He frowned. "Two. Toby is seven and Pamela is five. I rarely see them, so I couldn't tell you much about them," he added as he observed the flare of curiosity in her eyes.

"I envy you," she replied, then finished the last bite of her crisp biscuit. "I expect we had better hurry along. I do feel quite guilty at keeping you, you know."

"I assure you that it is my pleasure. After all, I have the honor of English gentlemen at stake." He allowed an amused smile to escape at this small sally, then escorted her from the shop.

Louisa was enchanted with the "Rows." At street level, shops crowded together in usual fashion. Above these was an open-sided roofed gallery overlooking the street, with more clever little shops to be found. The covered gallery provided an attractive walk, and Louisa delighted in peeping into shop windows to see interesting displays, some similar to home, some vastly different. Wine merchants, jewelers, and goldsmiths, together with toy shops and other merchants, rubbed cheek by jowl along the walk.

"You must enjoy purchasing toys for your niece and nephew," she declared as they looked at the colorful display in a toy-shop window.

"Hadn't given it much thought," he admitted. "My mother usually sees to that sort of thing."

"Oh." She impulsively placed a hand on his sleeve. "Do let us go inside. I should be right pleased to buy a gift for them. Your mother can direct it to their home." Louisa left Lord Westcott's side to hurry into the shop. Once there, she debated between a French puzzle and a Noah's ark complete with every animal imaginable. She settled on the ark for the boy, and then turned to select a beautifully dressed doll. Glancing at the stern gentleman at her side, she said, "Every little girl wishes for such a doll. You notice I prudently overlooked a drum. My brother had one and drove my mother nearly wild with the noise of it."

A bemused Lord Westcott nodded, watching as she confidently walked to the shopkeeper to pay for the purchases. He had intended to intervene, to pay for them himself. She had mentioned living on a farm; perhaps she was not well-to-do. Yet she looked charming and was so eager to please. Too eager? a small voice whispered. He pushed that cynical thought aside and approved the transfer of parcels to the short, rather plain Tabitha's capable arms.

Their stroll took them along to the lovely old cathedral. Lord Westcott first insisted she walk along the old city wall for a good perspective of the church.

Louisa was charmed with the sights to be seen from the wall, especially the many examples of old timbered buildings. Then she stiffened as a familiar figure came into view. Mr. Moss. He appeared to be searching for someone or something. Louisa had a sinking feeling that she knew full well who it was he sought. Herself.

"Is something the matter?" Lord Westcott noticed her intent stare. He permitted her to withdraw from him and into the shadows cast by a tree. He caught a glimpse of a tall, thin man who appeared to be looking for someone. Could there be some manner of connection?

" 'Tis nothing, I assure you. I thought I saw someone I know. Please, let us continue, suh." Resolutely she turned away from the sights of the town to face the cathedral.

Lord Westcott worried that whoever Miss Randolph had fled from would appear to create trouble. From what little she had said, it was apparent these people were encroaching types, the kind to make more than a spot of bother. He detested people who created scenes in public. It was so . . . common. He felt it beneath his dignity to engage in argument. Cynically, he also felt it achieved nothing.

The tour of the cathedral was brief. Louisa made no demur at the hurried viewing. She dutifully noted the portions of the building that she was informed were Norman in origin, then murmured appropriate comments on the intricacy of many of the wood carvings to be seen.

" 'Taint fittin'." Tabitha gave a wide-eyed look at a small image of an old monk with the devil tipping up his tankard. Louisa quite agreed with her whispered remark.

If Lord Westcott heard that small observation on the decoration of the cathedral, he showed no sign. Instead he propelled both women out the tall wooden door and hurried them along to where Louisa had chosen to stay.

Louisa was relieved to escape into the pleasant interior of the old inn. The danger outside made it imperative that she remain hidden. But would Mr. Moss come searching for her in here? She turned to Lord Westcott, wishing that it was his jovial father rather than this somewhat reserved young man.

"I fear detection, Lord Westcott. I confess I am at a loss as to what I had best do." Running the farm back in Virginia was a great responsibility, but it hadn't prepared her for the present situation. Now, if someone was needing a recipe for preparing a tasty dish, or instruction on housewifely matters, Louisa was happy to oblige, for she had been well taught.

"I believe we ought to proceed with my plan. The solicitor has my direction and will send any communication to my estate. I am certain my father would wish you to travel with me to reside under my mother's protection." Westcott's mien of modest assurance served to convince Louisa. Although he seemed to be somewhat the cynic—she had caught those expressions that flitted across his face—he also appeared to be a dutiful son. And she trusted him. He had that aura about him of utter respectability.

Louisa capitulated. She knew when to quit gracefully.

"Suh, if I may change my mind, I believe I will do as you suggest. Since my luggage has not been unpacked, it should not take Tabitha and me long to be ready. It is but for you to appoint the time."

Lord Westcott quickly considered where they might stop overnight should they leave within the hour, and nodded decisively. "Immediately."

Thus it was that within an incredibly short time the elegant carriage bearing the noble design that Hannah had observed early that morning drove out through the east gate of the city of Chester, bound for Westcott Park.

Westcott had taken pains to avoid mentioning their destination in the hearing of the ostlers at the inn. The innkeeper knew nothing, either. Only the solicitor knew where Miss Louisa Randolph had disappeared to, and he was as mute as a fish when Mr. Moss came to inquire if he knew the whereabouts of a Miss Randolph.

For all intents and purposes, Lousia Randolph had vanished from the face of the earth.

2

He was most dignified, Louisa decided as the three of them rumbled along in the traveling coach. She rather liked his brown eyes. Almost a tobacco-brown iris, she thought, with hints of gold and ringed with black. His hat sat most correctly over that luxuriant brown hair that she now only glimpsed on the sides of his head. She supposed one could describe his lean face with that longish nose as aristocratic. But it had character. A sculptor would find it pleasing, with its beautifully modeled planes and hollows. Then he smiled at her, and Louisa found she had lost her breath somewhere. As a smile, it would be classified someplace between enchanting and staggering.

"I trust the journey is proving not too difficult for you, Miss Randolph. My mother finds traveling wearying. She might enjoy the Season in London but for the length of the trip." His smile had brought a faint twinkle to his eyes. Louisa's heart gave an odd lurch.

"I marvel at your roads, Lord Westcott. This road is as smooth as if rolled. And the graciousness of the inn where we stopped last evening was greatly to be admired. I had not expected to be treated in such elegant fashion, nor to find such excellent food. Everything is decidedly English." She laughed, and added, "I expect that sounds a bit foolish to you. But I do find a difference in the atmosphere and the cooking. A charming difference, however." She felt her cheeks grow warm at his returned nod of approval. It was not unlikely that their reception was owing to the earl's rank, she surmised.

Back home in Virginia there was a social order of sorts. Her family had been of the first consequence of society, mixing with the elite of the county. There, one's position had to do with family ties and wealth, rather than nobility.

She had a cousin who was poor, in spite of Louisa's desire to help, yet she was everywhere received. And a man could raise himself in the world by dint of hard work and saving, his wealth and position the key to society. Possibly it had more to do with a person's character. Yet, casting an appraising glance at Lord Westcott, she also knew that were he to present himself to Virginia society, the hostesses would fall over one another to capture such a prize for their drawing rooms.

Her thoughts winged to Mr. Moss and his overwhelming mother. He appeared to want social elevation by way of marriage to a wealthy Randolph. At least she felt his mother did, and with those two, that amounted to the same thing.

She was startled from her thoughts as the carriage gave a lurch and she was thrown against Tabitha. The little maid shrank against the squabs, wide-eyed with fear. Louisa impulsively patted her hand in reassurance. "I gather I spoke too soon about the excellent roads." She tossed an amused glance at a puzzled Lord Westcott.

"One of the ostlers at the last inn gave my coachman a report of a hard rain along this route. It seems we may be in for a rough go."

Westcott stuck his head out the window of the coach and called a question to the groom who rode alongside. Evidently not pleased with the answer, Drew turned to look at Louisa. "It is as I feared. Bear with us for the next few miles. I believe we shall have a spot of trouble."

A "spot" was putting it too mildly, Louisa decided within a short time. The coach rocked and lurched as though riding over boulders and ruts. Tabitha clung to her hand, not saying a word, though trembling with fright. To tell the truth, Louisa was glad enough for her closeness. At times like this, another woman's presence was welcome.

It was silly. Louisa had sailed from New York to Liverpool and never known a day of illness or concern. Later in the summer one might expect to find icebergs lurking in the waters, or serious fog. Her ship had been blessed with fair weather and favorable winds. Moments had been spent watching porpoises gambol in the water, or reading, when she wasn't being pestered to death by Hannah or her son and his endless tales of mercantile interests.

And now Louisa felt as though her poor stomach was about to commit mutiny. Surely she must appear as green as she felt. She swallowed with care and was about to suggest that she and Tabitha—who looked equally ill—be permitted to get out and walk for a bit when the coach found smooth ground once again. It came as they turned off the main road onto a graveled lane.

"Could we pause for a few moments? I declare, I feel as though I have passed over the mountains in a handbarrow. I see some lovely flowers from the window. I wonder if their fragrance might not be a welcome restorative."

"Dear lady, allow me to beg your apologies," said Lord Westcott, a rueful smile on his face. He tapped his gold-headed cane on the roof and the carriage drew to a halt with remarkable haste.

She was handed down with all courtesy, and strolled away from the instrument of her torture with a feeling of relief. Louisa was disappointed to find that the poppies and clustered bellflowers along the verge of the road had little scent. How she had dearly loved her gardens at home. A wave of longing swept her as she thought of the masses of honeysuckle that would soon be blooming beneath her window. Or the window that once was hers, she amended. She had distilled the essence of their fragrant flower to bring with her, so that she might have some small memory of Virginia at her new home. But then, it was far too late to turn back at this point. And glancing to where Lord Westcott stood conversing with his coachman, she was not certain she would return even if she could. From this aspect, she noted Westcott's broad shoulders and erect carriage. No need for excessive padding there, she surmised. He was no dandy, either. His dress was quiet elegance, almost to the point of plainness.

He caught her look and crossed to her side with flattering speed. "Do you feel able to continue? It is not far from here. We are on Westcott Park land even now."

"Oh," said Louisa, feeling slightly foolish. "I truly believed I could not last another moment, but I am certain

I can drive on now." She placed a hand to her bonnet, wondering how disheveled she might be following the tumbling about in the coach. She brushed off a bit of dust from her pelisse, then decided that restoration was a hopeless task. Accepting his arm to return to the carriage, she hoped his mother was an understanding soul.

The remainder of the trip was uneventful from the standpoint of the roads and Louisa's stomach. The parkland was lovely. Every turn of her head brought her views of beauty such as she had not expected to see once she left her beloved Virginia.

A sudden turn in the graveled drive brought an edifice to view. Louisa gasped in awe and pleasure. A magnificent house of red brick trimmed with white loomed before them in stately splendor. Turrets with ogee cupolas stood at each corner, and at the entrance rose six columns of white marble to create a portico of impressive design. As the coach came closer, she could see that the work was distinctly that of Adam, the noted architect and designer. His influence was to be found even in America.

She managed to exit the coach without disgracing herself as a bumpkin. After all, her plantation home had been elegant as well, not quite as large or grand as this, but well enough. Her father, perhaps with a touch of nostalgia, had seen fit to have a Georgian style for his home, filling it with the finest-quality imported furniture and trimmings as he had prospered.

But what about the woman who presided over this home? How would she react to an upstart from the colonies, as Louisa had heard her homeland referred to more often than once since her arrival. Smoothing her soft kid gloves with nervous fingers, Louisa joined Lord Westcott to walk up the final steps of this phase of her journey.

The double doors were swung open by unseen hands; then an elderly butler moved forward to bow to his master. "Your mother awaits you in the drawing room, milord."

"Very good, Newton. If you would see to Miss Randolph's belongings." He waved a hand toward the pile of portmanteaus and trunks being removed from the coach. Taking several small parcels from the footman who had followed them inside, he turned to Louisa. "Come with me."

She might have preferred to make herself more presentable. As it was, she handed her pelisse to the butler, then smoothed down her dress. But her ire at this trying situation prevented her from being overwhelmed with the distinction of the entrance hall. Here Adam's influence was clearly seen in the white stucco designs on soft gray background. It was a touch austere for her taste, and she comforted herself that she need not feel quite so in awe of the place. They crossed the gray slate floor to a tall set of oak doors. Newton was there to open both with a grand flourish.

"Drew! I had begun to wonder if you had been swept off to sea in that deluge we endured these past days." Setting aside a large piece of needlework, a plump, yet elegant woman rose from the sofa to hurry toward them. Her pale blue gown fell in soft folds, and a neat lace cap sat atop graying hair. She smiled at her son, happily noting the parcels in his arms, then turned to face Louisa, sobering, her aristocratic brows rising faintly in question.

"Mother, may I present Miss Louisa Randolph, lately of Virginia in America. Father was a guest in her home while in that country. Her family has passed on, and now she is in England to locate her father's relatives."

Louisa dipped what she hoped would be an acceptable curtsy to the lady. The Countess Westcott. Louisa admitted to a slight feeling of trepidation. Generations of breeding stood revealed in the gracious and dignified woman. Louisa suspected that hidden beneath that ample exterior lay a thread of steel. There was just something about her. In a way, she was like Louisa's mother. Helena Randolph had prided herself on never raising her voice, yet had always managed to get what she wished. Louisa wagered the countess achieved no less.

"I am charmed to meet you, ma'am. I declare," Louisa offered in her soft, sweet Virginian accent, "I do not know what I would have done had your son not come to my rescue. He is quite the hero. Things are very different from what I expected. But then, nothing is ever as simple as it appears before you commence, is it?'' Louisa's smile held more than a trace of ruefulness. Yet her cheerful acceptance of her own lack of foresight could not be taken amiss.

The countess smiled, her dignity not receding before the delightful personality of the young lady. ''I am pleased to learn my son has such noble qualities. A mother always hopes, you know.'' She cast a glance at the tall slender man who stood quietly holding the parcels. ''Oh, do put those on the sofa, Drew. I shall attend to them later.''

Louisa caught the note of anticipation in the countess's voice and hesitantly spoke. ''I daresay you are longing to open those packages. I simply do not know how you could bear not to. I had a glimpse of some linen in a shop window that Lord Westcott said was similar to what he had bought for you, and, ma'am, it was frightfully pretty.''

The countess smiled a bit more warmly, then nodded. ''I shall open them soon. How lovely to have another woman in the house. But first, what is this about locating relatives? Do explain, please.''

They strolled down the large room to where a comfortable-looking group of chairs clustered by one of the sofas. At a gesture from Lady Westcott Louisa thankfully sank down on a chair, mindful to keep her back straight as her mama had taught her.

''Well, ma'am, my papa left England as a young man. All I know is what Mama told me, that he was a younger son of an English peer and had changed his last name when he arrived in America. He took one of his other names, Randolph. My mama's parents are dead, and her brother . . . well, Mama did not wish me to importune him.''

Louisa knew that while her mama had never uttered a word against her brother, she had detested the parsimonious skinflint. Louisa knew full well that living with him would have relegated her to the position of a sort of housekeeper, in spite of the wealth she possessed. He believed in the ''no-work, no-eat'' philosophy. At least, for others.

''Since Papa was the dearest of persons, I just knew his family must be lovely as well. I suppose that is not a very practical view, as your son hinted, but I am ever the optimist,

I fear. I expect that one day I shall have a most rude awakening." Louisa shared a look of feminine understanding with the countess before continuing. "Thanks to the kind direction of your son, I put my quest before a . . . solicitor in Chester. Then Lord Westcott insisted I journey to his home. To place me under your protection, I believe is how he phrased it."

"Miss Randolph has had a difficult trip to England, Mother. I felt since your husband, my father, had been a guest of her parents' and there seemed to be a friendship there, the least I could do was to bring the young lady to you."

He gave that utterly enchanting smile again and Louisa held her breath. Dear heaven, did the man have any idea how appealing he was when he smiled like that?

"Quite right. How was it that your parents knew my husband? Was your father involved in the government? Just before he left for home, Edward had viewed the inauguration of your President Madison. As head of the trade delegation, he had contact with a great many of your countrymen."

"I believe they met regarding matters to do with trade between America and England. I really cannot tell much more than that, as Papa never discussed business within my hearing. However, I have all the charming letters Lord Westcott, your husband, that is, wrote. My mama kept them all in a packet, tied with blue ribbon. She said it was unlikely that she would ever receive letters from so distinguished a gentleman again."

Louisa twinkled a smile at the countess, thus missing the frown that briefly settled on the noble brow of her host.

Drew leaned back in his chair, a thoughtful expression crossing his face. Letters? From his father to Miss Randolph's mother? Just what was afoot with the little Virginian miss? Odd that his father should have corresponded with a married woman in Virginia. To his knowledge, his father had not been the sort who made a mistress of another man's wife.

A stir at the door brought an affectionate expression to

the countess's face. Louisa turned her head in that direction, to be amazed by the sight of two gentlemen dressed exactly alike. She had seen twins dressed thus as children, never as adults.

"Miss Randolph, may I present my brothers, Cecil and Cosmo Tewksbury."

The twins beamed a good-natured look at Louisa. Their hair was dressed so they appeared for all the world like a pair of startled owls, with large brown eyes adding to the illusion.

Louisa nodded, murmuring something that seemed to be accepted as proper, while she absorbed the glory of their attire. It seemed they did not share Lord Westcott's fondness for restrained garb. Gray velvet coats hung open to reveal waistcoats of clear blue satin embroidered with a trellis of tiny roses. Over the pocket flaps the vines formed the initials of the wearer, and the border had bits of green glass beads sewed in a fine design. Quite impressive. Their smallcothes were deep gray, and Louisa supposed they were dressed very elegantly. She vastly preferred the quiet, understated look of Lord Westcott. Before returning her gaze to Lady Westcott, she caught sight of the gentlemen's stockings, pale gray with delicate rose clocks on them. She stifled a smile at this touch of daintiness.

"A guest! What a delight. We did not expect you to be so obliging, Drew," the one introduced as Cecil said. "We feared to be at our wits' end for entertainment. It is to be devoutly hoped that Miss Randolph will join us in our little games?" He gave Louisa a hopeful stare, brows raised above his wide eyes, mouth puckered.

Louisa turned to meet Lady Westcott's gaze. "Games?" she softly echoed.

"My brothers are sad rattles, I fear. They enjoy games of cards and such," offered the indulgent lady.

"Must keep the pot boiling, y'know," said Cosmo.

Cecil, with a wary glance at Lord Westcott, added, "However, we know which side our bread is buttered on. Shan't wish to make a virtue out of necessity."

"Nor make bricks without tools," piped up Cosmo.

"But make on the swings what one loses on the roundabouts," countered Cecil.

"And always seek that *ne plus extra*," declared Cosmo, with the obvious satisfaction of one who has topped another.

Louisa had tried to follow this bewildering flow of banter with no great success. She felt as though she had tumbled onto a whirligig.

Seeing her confusion, Lord Westcott wryly inserted, "My uncles delight in such conversation, I fear. While you remain with us, you will undoubtedly become used to it."

"And that brings us back to the reason for your journey to England, my dear," added Lady Westcott, her brown eyes dark with concern. "Your father used one of his middle names, Randolph, rather than his rightful name. Not uncommon among younger sons, I suspect. However, it does cause complications in attempting to trace your family. First we must try to list all those with younger sons who left England for America about the time your father did. Do you know the precise year?" At Louisa's nod, Lady Westcott continued to think aloud. "Cecil and Cosmo can help me draw up the information we shall use. I have a copy of the peerage someplace around here." She looked vaguely about the vast room as though expecting to see a book pop up.

"I should try the library if I were you, Mother," said Lord Westcott in his quiet way.

It seemed to Louisa he had withdrawn when the twins entered. Although she was certainly as aware of him as she had been from the very first. He was one of those who command attention by mere presence. He had no need to spout nonsense to draw the eye.

She allowed her gaze to slip about the room while the other four engaged in speculation about her family. Since that was a path she had trodden full many a time, she would await their conclusions.

The ceiling of the drawing room must be all of ten or eleven feet high and the room was quite large. Yet in spite of its size, it appeared a comfortable, livable place, with a profusion of sofas, chairs and tables of all sizes, books, pictures, and a pianoforte as well. It seemed as well-filled as a small room might. She attributed this clever management to the countess, a woman she sensed ought never be underestimated.

"My dear," Lady Westcott broke in on Louisa's musings, "you must be desirous of seeing your room. I ought to have remembered your need to refresh yourself after that journey from Chester. Do forgive me. I travel all too seldom, I fear. One forgets. I shall place the blame entirely on my curiosity."

"We did not make it in one day, Mother," Lord Westcott reproved gently.

"Nonetheless, I shall ring for Newton to find some maid to take her up to her room. You have your own abigail?"

The question was sharply put, and Louisa was thankful to be able to nod agreement.

"Good. We shall see you at dinner, then." Lady Westcott turned to the pile of parcels at her side with an enthusiasm that caused guilt in Louisa's sensitive heart. The dear lady must have been pining to open those intriguing packages all this time, and had been wonderfully patient.

Louisa followed Newton from the gray hall, down a passage, then up a fanciful staircase. The walls were light green and decorated, like the entrance hall, with a white stucco plasterwork of Greek vases and classical swags. She glanced up at the ceiling to take note of the colorful painting. Some mythological tale, she supposed.

At the landing she was handed over to a calico-dressed maid. They went down the passageway to where a door stood open. As they entered the room, Louisa fully grasped what elegance she was to know in the following days.

The walls of the room were hung with delicate pink taffeta. The bed was draped with the same pink taffeta that had been painted in the Chinese fashion with flowers and foliage. The window curtains were done in like manner. Satinwood chairs were painted with green ornamentation, and a satinwood chest and Pembroke table matched the design of the bed. Above the fireplace mantel hung a misty Chinese landscape.

Louisa recalled the set of Canton dishes her mother had

prized, and which Louisa had so carefully packed. They would of a certainty fit in with the taste of this house.

She turned to thank the young maid, then as an afterthought inquired, "When ought I come down for dinner?"

"There are two calls for dinner, miss. Come at the sound of the second gong." The girl curtsied and left.

Once the door was closed, Louisa drifted across to the window to stare at the parkland beyond. She had escaped from Mr. Moss and his mother. That was a blessing. But now she found herself in a slight pickle. When she accepted Lord Westcott's kind offer of asylum with his mother, she had not figured upon an attraction to that gentleman. And it definitely existed.

Taking one of the drapery tassels in hand, she worried the silk cords while she considered the expression on his face when she had left the drawing room. He had been more than reserved. He had looked coldly upon her.

A swish of soft fabric caught her ear as Tabitha removed a lilac lutestring from the wardrobe. Louisa turned to face the frowning maid. "Is something the matter?"

"I expect you shall want to wear this gown, miss. It is the most up-to-the-minute you possess. I take it you were in mourning for some time before you left America."

"And you rightly remind me that I had best see about ordering new gowns now that my period of mourning is past. Though I shall never forget them, you know." It was as well that the maid took pride in her mistress's appearance. Louisa knew that she would need help to gain a modish appearance. She had no desire to look like a frump.

"I am certain you are all that is right, miss." Tabitha was subdued and almost colorless when viewed. Yet Louisa sensed there was a story hidden behind that mien of demure silence. She sighed with the knowledge that she best keep her curiosity to herself. Somehow, she had the impression that the relationship between employer and servant was slightly different here than back home.

She heard the first gong for dinner. Quickly she changed into the lilac gown trimmed with discreet touches of Antwerp lace and purple riband. The fabric was of the finest quality, as were the trimmings. Yet she presented a simply dressed figure when she went to leave her lovely pink room for the lower regions of the house.

Pausing by the door, she looked back at her quiet maid. "You have a decent room and will get a good meal, I trust?"

Tabitha was obviously startled at her new mistress's concern. "Yes, miss. I have a room for myself, and shall eat with the housekeeper. This is a good place." Seeming to feel she had said more than she ought, she firmly closed her mouth, looking meekly at the floor.

Shaking her head at the overly humble maid, Louisa retraced her earlier path to the lower floor, where she espied Newton in the large hall.

"Ah, Miss Randolph. The family have gathered in the drawing room before dinner. Allow me." He crossed with deceptive speed to open the doors for a bemused Louisa.

Four pairs of eyes focused upon her caused her to be most thankful that Tabitha had thought to place out her best gown. The countess was dressed with exquisite simplicity in mauve taffeta trimmed with knots of cream ribands. The pearls at her neck were of the finest quality. Louisa reflected that she had no need to repine on that score. She wore her mother's bridal pearls, an example of the excellent nature of the goods her father had lavished upon his beloved wife.

Seeing her hesitation, Lord Westcott stepped forward to greet her. "I trust you are getting settled?"

"Yes, I thank you. 'Tis a lovely room and the view is enchanting." Once again she noted his reserve, greater than it had been prior to their arrival. Did he now wish himself rid of her? Was he sorry he had invited a stranger into his home? Or was he merely the sort of man who became more restrained when at home and with family?

"As you may guess, we have been discussing your plight and how best to achieve success in locating your relatives."

"Wish to come off with flying colors, don't y'know," explained Cecil, or was it Cosmo?

Louisa looked from one to the other. They were now

arrayed in plum coats with silver waistcoats embroidered with voilets and ivy, black smallclothes and hose. There appeared to be no difference between them.

"It is our hair that gives the clue. Cecil parts his to the right, I to the left," said Cosmo.

Blushing that she was so patently confused, Louisa nodded. "I shall endeavor to remember."

Ignoring her brothers, Lady Westcott said, "I have begun a list. The Beauchamps had a younger son who left for America. Likewise the Bedingfelds."

"Do not overlook the Conesford and Dalmeny families," added Cecil.

"I seem to recall talk that a Derwent emigrated," commented Cosmo.

"Did you not say the youngest Feversham boy had gone, Mother?" offered Lord Westcott.

Louisa listened as name after name was offered to the list that grew longer and longer. She was most relieved when Newton opened one of the doors to announce that dinner was served.

The countess was escorted by her two brothers, while Louisa placed her gloved hand upon Lord Westcott's austerely covered arm.

During the meal, her head whirled as names such as Thynne, Pomeroy, Northcote, Kingsale, Gower, and Waldegrave sailed past her ears. It seemed to her that a great many families must have lost a member to the lure of the Americas. Some sailed off to Canada. But a goodly number settled in places such as Boston, New York . . . and Virginia.

The debate as to whether a family did or did not have someone who had departed the shores of England for greener pastures continued through dessert.

Finally Louisa, embarrassed that her dilemma had kept them occupied all through the meal, coughed, then spoke. "I hope this is not going to prove too much of a task. I ought to find myself a place to rent, where I can await the investigation without putting you to such bother."

"Heavens, no!" declared Lady Westcott. "I have not had

such an interest in an age. You know, I am quite pleased that my memory has held up so well. Is that not right, Cecil? Yes, I daresay I could hold my own with the best." She smiled with a complacent air before continuing. "No, dear girl, you shall remain with us." Lady Westcott had noticed the tension in the air whenever her dear—and still single—son was close to the young American. While the girl's clothes needed updating, from their quality that would be no problem. She mentally rubbed her hands together with anticipation, but merely bowed her head with regal aplomb, saying, "We can order some new clothes for you if you wish. You shall be so busy, you will not have time to think."

Louisa wondered why that was considered desirable. Another look at Lord Westcott's face convinced her there was something amiss. She missed his smile. What had happened?

3

The Tewksbury twins chattered away all through dinner, with the countess teasing them in a regally charming manner.

Louisa tried to study their hair partings in a way that would not be noticed. The solution to their identities did not help much, given the wild direction of their hair. How was she to tell whether the part was to the left or the right when she couldn't see one? The best thing to do was listen for the inflection of voice. Cecil's was a trifle higher in pitch than his brother's.

Louisa glanced at Lord Westcott. How thoughtful he appeared, as though sunk in the mire of a problem. It certainly could not be the meal. The food was surprisingly hot. Most kitchens were a distance from the eating room, and the food grew correspondingly cold as it traveled the corridors to the table. She popped another morsel of chicken in her mouth, thankful that she had dared to escape the clutches of the Moss pair. While her descent upon Lord Westcott was certainly not ladylike, it had achieved her desire. She now had help.

"Ah, he is a man of parts, he is," said Cecil with appreciation.

Glancing at him, Louisa wondered what she had missed.

"To make one's mouth water," said Cosmo with a wistful sigh.

"You shall not lure him away from me, no matter what. He is quite devoted. Besides, Drew pays him better than you would." Lady Westcott gave her brothers a sly look and chuckled at their obvious chargrin.

"Many a time and oft have I said Drew pampers his servants, especially his chef." Cecil shot a challenging look at Lord Westcott.

Lord Westcott was at last roused from his introspection to counter his uncle. "Not to put too fine a point on it, but you never pay enough. And that is why you shall not lure my good chef from my employ."

Cosmo placed his hand against his chest in a dramatic flourish. "And you would nip in the bud any attempt we made, wouldn't you?" He lifted both hands in a shrug of despair. "I shall leave it in the lap of the gods. It is an open secret that we adore the food in this house."

"Thank your sister. She has the running of it." Westcott's stern expression had softened as he glanced at his elegant mother in her mauve dress.

"Runs in the family," said Cosmo with a smirk.

"Well, enough of that," said Lady Westcott. "Miss Randolph will think we talk of nothing but food in this family."

"But 'tis one subject that never bores!" countered Cosmo.

"Careful, dear brother, or you shall put that to ruin," cautioned Cecil, his eyes sparkling with humor.

Lady Westcott waved her brothers to silence. "You have been very quiet, Miss Randolph. I hope these sad rattles have not overwhelmed you. That is a lovely dress you are wearing tonight. I had no idea that the colonies had such up-to-date fashions."

At Louisa's barely perceptible stiffening, Lord Westcott said in a chiding manner, "They are no longer the colonies, Mother. We lost them, remember?"

"I know, I know." She waved a hand about in a vague gesture of bewilderment. "I never could understand what that tea business was all about."

"It had to do with local self-government and individual rights, ma'am. They complained about taxation without representation. I believe they wished to have a say in how the monies were collected and spent."

"And do we not all?" inserted Cecil slyly.

Lord Westcott glanced at his uncle, then turned to face Louisa. "You will find divided feelings about America in this country. How do you feel about the current situation?"

"America was my home, and as such I have a loyalty to it. However, I expect that I can come to feel affection for a lovely place like England, especially if I meet charming people like you all. I can only hope that the present strain between our countries will not increase."

"Nicely put, Miss Randolph." The countess rose from the table, motioning for Louisa to follow her while the gentlemen remained for their port.

Slippered footsteps whispered on the gray slate of the hall as Louisa and the countess crossed to the drawing room. The butler silently opened the door for them, leaving it ajar at the countess's request.

"May I return to the subject you brought up just now? The problem of clothes?" Louisa tucked a pillow, as she had observed the maid do earlier, behind the countess while she settled on the sofa. Then Louisa glided across to hesitantly seat herself on a rather imposing chair.

"But as I said then, you look charming." The countess managed to appear properly erect, yet relaxed, an enviable achievement.

"This is the newest gown I posscss, purchased before I sailed. I have barely left off wearing my blacks. As you can well understand, I should like to appear more the thing." Louisa gave her a pleading look.

"We shall remedy that situation quite simply. I shall call for the seamstress." Lady Westcott gave a pleased nod.

"I have ample funds, ma'am. No need to stint." Louisa desired the lady to know that her guest did not seek financial aid, nor scrimping in any manner.

The countess glanced toward the door, then back to Louisa. "Tell me what you can remember of my husband."

Her expression softening, Louissa smiled faintly. "I ever enjoyed his visits. He had such wit and charm. You must miss him sorely, ma'am. He was all that was correct while at our plantation, but wrote the most droll letters. Mama was used to read them at the dinner table for our pleasure. I have brought them with me, somewhere in my trunks. I thought that perhaps if I were so fortunate as to find you both, you should like to have them. They give his impressions of my country. He had quite amusing encounters with American Indians, which we fully appreciated. He esteemed their intelligence and sought friendships with them to learn more about their culture. He was a very wise man. I even thought to put the letters in a book."

"What a clever idea," said the countess with no sign of her inward reaction.

Her words were lost in the entry of the three men. Lord Westcott had heard the final sentence spoken by the little American and wondered what had been said during his absence. His mother appeared controlled as usual, but she had ever been an excellent actress. He crossed the room to choose a chair close to Miss Randolph.

"You are having an enjoyable evening?"

Louisa nodded. "Your mother is the most charming of hostesses. She has made this visitor feel most welcome."

"You were deep in conversation when we entered." He wondered if she might be artless enough to reveal to him what she intended to put into a book.

"I mentioned to your mother that I hope to find a local dressmaker who can bring me up-to-date. I fear it takes a while for the fashions to drift across the ocean to America. We are sent the latest designs from France and England, but often they are several months old before they reach our shores. And then they must be passed from hand to hand. I was fortunate to obtain this gown before I sailed, or you would find me sadly out of vogue. I declare, I believe the dressmakers conspire to see how quickly they can change the mode of dress." A rueful moue curved her lips.

"I cannot believe you ever looked other than lovely, Miss Randolph." He studied the attractive picture she made, seated in her pretty gown on the imposing chair. Lawrence should paint her like that, he thought suddenly. The soft, clinging fabric revealed a pleasing figure. The lilac color became her, and her poise was most artistocratic. One could think she had been raised on a country estate rather than a mere farm.

She inclined her head slightly, giving him an amused look that told she little believed his words, and it made him think better of her. Yet what of that book she wished to write?

"You must know that *La Belle Assemblée* is quite popular in America," she continued, as though he had not complimented her. "My little sisters begged for the old copies so as to cut out the figures, which they used as dolls of paper. Mama enjoyed the stories and poetry. I always looked forward to reading the literary reviews."

"You are a writer?" He was glad for the opening that presented itself. What would she say?

Louisa blushed a becoming rose. "I should like to write for children, Lord Westcott. I have had many occasions to read the stories available at present, for it was usually my task to see my sisters to bed. Most of the tales were quite boring. Improving, I had no doubt. But I felt the girls' imaginations might be better stimulated." She saw his arrested expression and shook her head in dismay. "Oh, do forgive me for chattering on so. Mama always said it was my besetting sin."

"You were close to your mother?" Perhaps she knew what was in those letters from his father.

Smiling with fondness, Louisa agreed. "True. She was a very special lady, my mama. I shall ever remember her with happy thoughts."

He nodded, then tried a different tack. "Surely you do not disapprove of Mrs. Sherwood or Hannah Moore? They have printed books of stories for children, you know."

The countess edged forward on the sofa, proving to Louisa the lady kept track of all that went on in her drawing room while she was present.

Clasping her hands together in sudden concern, Louisa tried to think of a way out of the trap her impulsive tongue had set for her. As inclined to daydreaming as she was, she forgot there were practical people who expected every item in existence to have a meritorious value.

"They are both all that is proper. I feel sure their tales of morality with the rewards and punishment contained in them are quite noteworthy. I am told *Goody Two-Shoes* is an exemplary book, yet I find the character an insufferable little prig. I prefer the more traditional stories. I grew up on Jack the Giant-Killer and Cinderella. There is a moral to be found in these tales as well, if you look for it." At the surprised expressions on the faces about her, Louisa sighed and shook her head contritely. "Dear me, I do not usually go on so."

The countess gave a strained smile. "Mrs. Sarah Trimmer has stated that fairy tales are vicious books, giving children improper thoughts. She feels there is much harm done by placing such books in the hands of children."

Louisa's eyes flashed briefly at the thought of her darling little sisters urging her to read "Cinderella" for possibly the hundredth time and treasuring every word of the story. Louisa sat straighter in her chair, replying in a stiff little voice, "I shall read fairly tales to my children, if I am so fortunate as to have any. In lieu of that felicitous event, I will write."

But, mused Lord Westcott, she did not say precisely what she would write, did she?

Recalling her duties as a good hostess, Lady Westcott clapped her hands and cried, "Tea, I believe. Newton?"

Louisa was distressed to be so lost to propriety as to have voiced what was in her heart. She turned to Lord Westcott, hoping to regain some of his esteem. "I fear I forgot myself, sir. When it comes to writing and children I am apt to state precisely what I think. And I am inclined to be somewhat the romantic, as well."

"And you find the tale of Cinderella to be romantic?"

She smiled, relieved at his seemingly softened attitude. "I expect it is. For does not every little girl desire to find the prince of her dreams?"

"Is that what you seek in this country? A prince of your dreams? Little colonial farmgirls rarely make such eligible connections," he said wryly.

Flushing witih repressed anger, Louisa countered, "I come from a respectable family, suh. I need make no apology." Then, wishing she had not accepted his kind offer of hospitality, she added in a cool voice. "I ought to seek a residence in London. I have no desire to impose upon you."

He realized that if Miss Randolph were to leave this house, he would never know about the letters she had mentioned. What had she said to his mother? He had best mend his fences. Really, it was quite unlike him to argue with a guest, especially such a lovely young woman. Before he could speak, Cosmo intruded.

"Good to see a young woman who don't beat around the bush. Most gels in society act as though they have no thought in their heads save getting a husband," he said with a sly look at Westcott.

"I fear it is not *comme il faut* to speak out on such matters, Mr. Tewksbury," replied Louisa gently.

"I don't care a fig for that nonsense. Rather have a decent conversation any day," that gentleman answered, amused at the high color staining his nephew's cheeks.

"Always did like a good give-and-take," added Cecil, also noting the expressions on the faces about. He dearly loved to stir the pot and keep things aboil.

"In all conscience, I must say I rather liked the story 'Jack the Giant-Killer,' " murmured Cosmo.

"Now, I thought 'Little Red Riding Hood' to be a fine tale. Teaches us to beware of wolves dressed in finery, what?" Cecil chuckled, nudging his brother, who joined in the quiet laughter.

"You two are not to be borne," said Lady Westcott dryly. She understood her dear brothers and their notion of wit.

"I say, we ought to be spending our efforts in the direction of locating Miss Randolph's family. Can you not think of anything your father or mother might have told you that would be of assistance?" Lord Westcott flicked a glance at his irrepressible uncles and his mother before turning his attention to Miss Randolph.

"I fear not. As I said before, they never spoke of his family in England. I do not know why. It was not until Mama was so sick that she told me to seek them out, else I doubt if she would have said a word to me. She was far too ill to explain anything other than to mention that connection to the peerage." Louisa thought of those pain-wrenching days when the last of her family lay dying from the yellow fever. Striving to retain her countenance, she almost missed the disturbance in the entrance hall.

"The Lady Bromfield is come, my lady," announced Newton to his mistress. "Along with Master Toby and Miss Pamela."

Lady Westcott rose from the sofa to float across the room. "Felice? Whatever are you about, girl, to be traveling so late in the day?"

A pretty young woman, her face revealing the ravages of coping with two fractious children for several days, entered the room. She curtsied stiffly to her mother, then the others. "I cannot survive another day. The children's nanny has left. I have lost count as to how many that makes in the past year. Really, Mama, it is too tiresome."

Behind her a footman entered the room carrying a tray holding all the makings of a truly excellent tea. Cecil perked up and crossed to the tea table to select a plate of the pastry cook's delectable dainties and a steaming cup of bohea. Cosmo followed, seeming to believe he would not be needed in the family reunion.

"Where are the children?" Lady Westcott peered into the entrance hall, and failed to see any sign of them.

"I instructed Newton to have them carried up to the nursery. One of the maids can look after them. I . . . I know not what to do or where to turn." The pretty young woman pulled a scrap of cambric from her reticule. It gave evidence of much use.

Lady Felice dabbed at her eyes in a way Louisa could only envy. Did all the ladies in this country show such refinement of manners as to cry so beautifully? Louisa was given to great gusty sobs that tore her apart.

"We shall have our tea, then you and I shall go to your room, Felice. We have company." With that dire warning, Lady Westcott ushered Lady Felice to the sofa, drawing her down next to her with a firm, no-nonsense hand.

"Oh, I do beg your pardon." Lady Felice fluttered impossibly long brown lashes at Louisa, never raising an eyebrow at the sight of a stranger in the drawing room. "What must you think of me." Turning to her mother, Felice added in a low voice, "It is Bromfield, Mama. He is to take off soon . . . without me, I fear. Since I have lost that nanny, there is no one to oversee the children. And I do not trust him to go alone."

"We shall discuss this later, my dear," intoned the Countess Westcott with all the warmth of one of the icebergs Louisa's ship had avoided on her sail across the Atlantic.

Cecil contemplated a second cup of tea, looking as though he mentally rubbed his hands together with relish.

"She seems more frayed than hurt, I believe," commented Cosmo softly to his brother.

"Most likely much ado about nothing, if you ask me," replied Cecil in an equally gentle tone, not to be outdone.

"A minor matter," agreed Cosmo. "No doubt a mare's nest. Felice has not changed, in spite of marriage and two children."

"Most likely *because* of marriage and two children," said Cecil with a knowing look. "I always did think Bromfield to be a queer fish."

"Well to grass, however," added Cosmo. "Shall be interesting to see which way the cat jumps."

"If she has set her heart on going with Bromfield . . . well, I expect we shall hear the pitter-patter," reflected Cecil, nudging his brother once again.

"Hardly pitter-patter. More like thump and bump," declared Cosmo, with a woeful shake of his head. His gaze strayed to where Felice sat, then wandered over to Louisa. His face brightened, large brown eyes growing speculative. "I have an idea."

"As long as you do not intend to bestow a toy horn upon our grandnephew, I shall listen." Cecil placed his cup on the tea table, then walked with his brother to the far end of the room, where the two stood in soft conversation, regardless of the rules of polite society.

Louisa accepted a cup of bohea from the footman, then selected a dainty biscuit from the tray he offered. Not knowing what the custom was in this house regarding breaking the fast come morning, she had best be fortified.

"This is a most unexpected turn of events," said Lord Westcott. He was seated once again in the chair that matched the one where Louisa had taken refuge. "I wonder what it is that Felice wants this time." The latter comment was spoken more to himself.

Louisa stifled the desire to answer.

He must have noticed something, however. "What do you think?"

"Not knowing your sister, it is difficult to say. Offhand, I should expect she plans to leave her children here. Should you mind overmuch?" At her question, Louisa took the opportunity of looking at him directly. That reserve she had noted earlier had altered to something else, but she wasn't quite sure as to what. He wore a pleasant expression and seemed more at ease.

He murmured a soft denial while looking at his sister on the sofa. Louisa turned her attention as well. Lady Felice had tossed aside her smart chip bonnet to reveal a luxuriant mass of brown curls shaped closely to her head in what Louisa presumed was the latest mode. Her high-collared velvet pelisse had been taken by a hovering Newton. Now she perched on the edge of the sofa like a wren about to take flight. Her delicate brown muslin was a clever design. High-waisted, with a cambric frill at the buttoned neck, it was vastly becoming. Brown half-boots peeked from beneath the tucked hem of her gown. Louisa noted that although she seemed calm enough, she nervously worked at the York tan gloves she wore. It seemed she was not quite as sanguine about leaving her children as first appeared.

"Your sister's husband travels a good deal?" Louisa felt it only proper to make a mild inquiry.

"Umm," Lord Westcott murmured in reply. "With the government in diplomatic circles. He is off to Denmark unless I miss my guess."

Since Louisa had developed a certain amount of respect for Lord Westcott and his perception, she merely nodded her acceptance of this information. From the little that Lady Felice had said, it seemed she did not trust her husband in a far-off location. Given the pretty blonds that might be found in the Danish court, Louisa placed her sympathies with Lady Felice. Why they simply could not take the two children along was undoubtedly owing to the lack of a nanny.

"What think you, Miss Randolph?" Lord Westcott asked in a soft aside. "Ought my sister to remain sensibly to home, and permit her husband to get on with his task? Or should she trail along?"

"If it were my husband, I would pack the children up and trust to providence a maid could be found." In one thing she was united with Lady Felice. "A husband ought never be left to his own devices for long." A roving eye might catch something that could lead to trouble. "Besides, I believe a wife's place its at her spouse's side. We women do like to feel we are needed. Or do you believe in the utmost freedom for husbands, Lord Westcott?" She didn't know what possessed her to be so outspoken. Mrs. Moss would have had a spasm—at the very least—at Louisa's daring words.

"That all depends . . . on the wife." He slanted her what Louisa thought a wicked look, but failed to reveal what qualifications that wife would need. Since she hadn't quite forgiven him for his somewhat snide remark about colonial farmgirls, she ignored further discussion of the subject. Farmgirls, indeed!

The uncles strolled back to join the group around the sofa where Lady Westcott now held firm control of the conversation, inconsequential chatter for the most part. Louisa wondered what manner of plot they had been hatching between them. They had the look of mischievous schoolboys on a lark.

"I expect we had all best get a good night's sleep," the countess commented. "I know Felice must be exhausted, and I expect Miss Randolph has had a tiring day as well. You will find the night candles by the stairs, Miss Randolph," she added in her imperturbable manner. "Going up now, Cecil and Cosmo?"

"I believe I shall," replied Cecil. "Don't want to miss a moment of tomorrow, you know." He exchanged a mysterious look with his twin, and the two headed out of the drawing room, past the stoical Newton.

Louisa excused herself and whisked around the corner.

Suddenly she couldn't wait to get to her room and the undisturbed peace of her bed. Taking a dainty holder with a tall candle, she made straight for the staircase. A large oil lamp illuminated the landing above.

"Sleep well, Miss Randolph. We shall make progress on the morrow, once Mother is organized." Lord Westcott had suddenly appeared at her elbow, disconcerting Louisa no end.

"There is the solicitor in Chester, Lord Westcott," she reminded him, gathering her skirts in one hand and preparing to hurry up the steps. The candle holder was firmly grasped in her other hand, the candle's flame wavering in a slight draft.

"I wouldn't depend too much on his services," replied Westcott with a cynical lift of an eyebrow.

Determined to give him no opportunity to further tease her, Louisa gave what she hoped was a superior smile and gently replied, "Then we shall have to hope that your mother is monstrously clever. For I feel certain that you will not wish to house a stranger for long, even if I did know your father."

With the knowledge that she had discommoded him just a little, Louisa walked up the stairs, each step a deliberate defiance of the man who stood below. As she turned at the landing to continue her way up, she looked back at where he watched her. "Sleep well, suh."

She managed to sleep well, at any rate. Once tucked in bed by the quiet Tabitha, instead of turning and tossing, she had slept immediately.

The breakfast room was vacant despite the insistence by Cecil and Cosmo that they intended to rise early. Tabitha had wanted to bring Louisa something in her room, but she had felt uneasy for some odd reason. Better to brave the world, she decided.

Choosing coffee and toast, she wandered to the tall windows that looked out upon the back view of the house. From here she could see across a vast lawn, neatly scythed, to the stable block. Swallowing the last bite of toast, she was about to replenish her coffee when she observed two children stealing away from the rear stairs.

They looked like dear little tots. She decided it might prove interesting to chat with them. Children were undoubtedly much the same here as in Virginia. However, it would be helpful to know precisely what they were like, if she were actually to pursue her notion to write stories.

Placing the cup on the table, she slipped from the pretty yellow room to the rear door. Espying Newton in the hall, she obtained direction from him.

The air was fresh with the fragrance of the early morning—summer flowers, newly cut grass, and animals. She quickly followed the footsteps left on the dewy grass to the stables, where she discovered the two culprits animatedly discussing the merits of a dog. A medium size white-with-black-spots dog, unlike any she had seen before.

"Hello. What a very nice dog you have there. Does he have a name? Let me guess. Freckles?" She gave them both her most beguiling smile and walked closer to where they stood in wary silence.

The boy gave her a reproving look and shook his head shyly. "No, miss. He is a coach dog and his name is Spot."

"How . . . how very original," was Louisa's faint reply as she struggled not to laugh at this sober little man.

"Why do you talk so peculiar?" asked the girl, lisping slightly, undoubtedly because of a missing front tooth.

"Because I am from America. I came to this country to look for my relatives after my parents died. I knew your grandfather, you see. And now your uncle has kindly offered to assist me in my quest."

"Do you have any children?" demanded the lad.

"I do not. However, I took care of my little sisters. We used to have ever such good times. Every night I made up stories for them." Louisa marveled at the cautious reserve of these children. Though they were free of the nursery, they showed no sign of high spirits.

The little girl edged closer to Louisa, finally tugging at her blue cambric round gown above the two rows of worked trimming. "I love stories. Would you tell me one?"

"If it pleases your mama, I shall." Louisa reached out to stroke the soft blond curls that tumbled in an uncombed riot over the child's head. "Could you tell me your names? Mine is Louisa Randolph."

"I am Toby Kemsley and my sister is Pamela." He watched as the dalmatian walked over to sniff at Louisa's clothes, then her extended hand.

Captivated by the unusual dog, Louisa crouched down to pet his back and fondle his ears as her little dog in Virginia had so loved. The dog aptly named Spot placed his head confidingly against her, sitting nearly on her feet.

"Busy charming the whole lot, are you? We shall have to put it to use," drawled a voice from the door of the stable. It was a voice Louisa would recognize anyplace. Lord Westcott. What did he mean by that curious remark?

4

"How do you do, Uncle Drew?" said Toby with almost adult politeness.

"We are very pleased to see you, Uncle Drew," lisped Pamela, dipping a rather good curtsy for one so young.

The spotted dog trotted over to sniff at Lord Westcott, then sat back to give him a happy grin.

Only Louisa was silent for the moment, assimilating the meeting with surprise. She rose from where she had crouched while fondling the dog to give Lord Westcott a wary look. Brushing down her skirt, she studied the children with curious eyes. So they were Lady Bromfield's children. But did Lord Westcott intimidate them? Or was this stifled behavior typical of English children? She thought of her little sisters. While they were polite in society, they were fun-loving, happy children, given to pranks and rollicking good times. These young ones didn't appear to know what that was.

Sensing she must take things in hand, Louisa turned to Lord Westcott. "What an interesting dog. I have never seen one like it before. What breed is it?"

"It came from the country of Dalmatia on the Adriatic Sea, hence the name: Dalmatian. They make excellent watchdogs. Quite useful, as well. They can be taught to hunt, but better yet, they are good companions for the horses. Silly dogs like to run between the wheels of coaches, though." He bent to give the dog a fond pat.

"I told you he is a coach dog," said Toby, daring to speak up, even with his tall, imposing uncle nearby.

"Is that not dangerous?" Louisa snapped her fingers, and Spot obediently trotted over to his new friend. While she patted his head, she observed another dog slowly approach. It was a female, well along toward having pups. "How lovely, the children shall see the puppies, if they visit here long enough."

"Really, Miss Randolph. I was unaware that young women were accustomed to speaking of such things, even in America." She thought the look he gave her a rather toplofty one.

Louisa flushed, but stood her ground. "You forget, suh. I helped run a farm. It would be rather silly to pretend I have never observed what is about me."

"Not within Lady Bromfield's hearing, I think," he said with a dry expression in his voice.

Ignoring a subject she now felt better left alone, Louisa inquired, "And what is the other dog named?"

"The groom told me he calls her Dot," offered a helpful Toby.

Lord Westcott was afflicted with a spate of coughing. Louisa beckoned to the female while she gave a soft, endearing chuckle. "Dot and Spot. How utterly delicious. I fully expected some wonderfully pretentious names, like Horatio and Clementine."

"Do you think us such a pretentious lot, Miss Randolph?" His expression was a blend of curiosity and something else she found disturbing.

"Of course not," Louisa denied promptly. "But you all do seem to have a fondness for things . . . antique, and elegant, and imposing." She held out her hands to the children, beguiling them with a smile that Lord Westcott found most appealing. "Come, Toby and Pamela. I will wager that neither of you has had a proper breakfast yet this morning. I believe Cook made gem muffins for us. I have grown rather fond of them. "And," she said with the air of a conspirator, "I have a parcel for you each."

The three left the stable block to stroll up the path to the house. Miss Randolph kept up an animated chatter with them, laughing and bringing smiles to their small faces. Lord Westcott watched them until they disappeared into the house. His sister had complained about fractious children. "Disobedient and willful brats" were the actual words used, he recalled. Miss Randolph either had an ability to charm like no other, or his sister exaggerated a trifle.

He nodded to the groom who suddenly appeared, then discussed the health of the two dogs. He had thought it would be novel to have a pack of dalmatians to run about his coach. Then he had found what great companions they were for his horses. It was odd to see the affinity between the two animals, one so large, the other so relatively small.

As he watched the female slowly wander back to the bed of clean straw she claimed as her own, he wondered if Miss Randolph had second sight. As sure as the sun came up in the east, Felice would find a way to convince his mother to house her children while she traipsed off to Denmark with her husband.

With his usual calm confidence shaken just a shade, he turned to follow the others to the house. Children underfoot? Perhaps he would leave for London and a change of scenery? Then he chided himself that that would be a chickenhearted thing to do. But would there be an acceptable nanny or governess to be had? If Felice told the truth, that she had an impossible time keeping a nanny for the children, chances were that not one agency in London would have a suitable candidate willing to accept the post. Word did get around.

Yet Miss Randolph seemed to get along well with the tots. Mulling over this seeming inconsistency, he entered the house to find his two uncles bearing down on the breakfast room, dressed, as usual, in identical fashion.

Four unusually large brown eyes surveyed him before Cecil spoke. "Been for a walk so early? We want to see how the chit fares with the children. Have a wager, you know. I say she will do well enough. Cosmo says she won't make a dent in those offspring of your sister's. Plaguey children, she says."

"I believe you have already lost, Cosmo. The last I saw of the trio, Miss Randolph had them completely in her power. Telling them fairy tales, no doubt," Drew added wryly.

"I'll have my money now, if you please," chortled Cecil with glee. "Next time, pay attention to what goes on under your nose."

Cosmo dug into a red leather purse, then handed his brother the gold coins. "I ought not pay until I see for myself. Westcott might be making the thing up, y'know." They strolled down the hall until they reached the door of the breakfast room.

Here, the three paused. At the table, Louisa sat between the two children, buttering muffins with seeming goodwill. She was talking to them in her soft musical voice, its accent quite delightful.

"Then Martha climbed up in the plum tree, and before she could reach it, the naughty kitten jumped down all by itself. Jane and Esther laughed until Mama said they would have to mend Martha's dress to look just like new where it got torn. I fear they did not find that at all amusing, as neither of them liked to ply a needle."

"You mean there are other little girls who do not like sewing?" said Pamela, much taken with these sisters who appeared to have had a great deal more fun than she had ever known. Her hazel eyes were large and wistful as she took a dainty bite from her muffin while swinging her feet back and forth, a usually forbidden thing.

"Did your brother really have his own pony?" asked Toby with an awed voice.

"He did. Parker rode him out every day until he was old enough for his own horse." She handed another buttered muffin to Toby, then added, "He wanted to be an explorer and go off to Tennessee and beyond, for he longed to climb in the mountains." There was a tightness in her throat when she remembered that her sisters would never climb another tree nor would Parker ever see his mountains.

"Miss Randolph lost her family to the yellow fever a year or so ago," Westcott informed his uncles in a low voice.

"I want to be an explorer too," declared Toby. Why couldn't their nanny have told such interesting stories to them? Then he espied his uncle and great-uncles and his face fell in a near-comical manner. He moved closer to Miss Randolph, as though he instinctively knew that she would protect him from everyone and everything.

Pamela swallowed the last of a muffin half and piped up in her high voice, "Good morning."

"Good morning, uncles," added Toby in a stiff little manner. He rose and executed a bow of sorts.

"I believe we are near finished with our meal. Children, shall we investigate the donkeys I observed from my window?" Louisa supervised the final bites of food, sipping the last of her morning coffee before rising. "We shall save the parcels for tea."

"Yes, please," whispered an enchanted Pamela. In all her days, she could not recall an adult making an effort to entertain her so. Usually she was made to do things like sewing on a sampler and working at letters and being quiet like a good little girl.

"Does either of you know how to spell 'donkey'?" inquired Louisa. "Jane could never get it right, you know. Then Parker told her to think of 'monkey' and change the M to a D. Only then she had trouble spelling 'monkey.' "

Toby thought that prodigiously funny and laughed, stopping abruptly as he caught sight of his uncle's face. He tugged the interesting Miss Randolph out the door as fast as he could.

"I believe I won fair and square," said Cecil in a thoughtful voice.

"I believe you did," Cosmo replied, equally distracted.

"I believe I shall die if I must allow Bromfield to go to Denmark by himself," announced the Viscountess Bromfield as she entered her mother's bedroom. She crossed the soft Oriental carpet to stare out the window before seating herself on a chintz-covered chair near the bed.

"Do you feel so uncertain about him?" asked the countess, wishing she dared probe more closely. Her own marriage had been much like a good many others, she supposed. Once she had provided an heir as well as their daughter, her husband had gone his own way, off to London, then later to America. She felt she had scarcely known him, for all the years they were wed.

Avoiding the question for the moment, Felice forged ahead

with the largest problem on her horizon. "I have had the most abominable luck with finding a proper nanny. It seems they turn out to be either tyrants or thieves. I suppose what I really need is a good governess for Toby and Pamela, but where to find the pargaon to cope with my angelic scamps is more than I can imagine."

She rose from the chair to pace about with restless steps. Hands behind her, she came to a stop beside the bed, studying her mother in an assessing manner. "What am I to do? Gilbert has a roving eye. I have been forced to cope with the children through all this coming and going, and he finds comfort elsewhere, I know he does. Although no one is so impolite as to actually *say* anything to me, they hint. Oh, my, they hint a great deal." She gave a deep sigh, then arranged herself on the little chintz chair once again to give her mother a hopeful look. Always in the past her mother had found solutions. Why not now?

"Of course you must leave them with me, dear girl. Whether or not I can locate a good governess for them remains to be seen." The countess gave her daughter a doubtful look, then decided she was doing the best thing possible. Perhaps if she herself had gone with her husband, their lives might have been different . . . and more pleasurable.

Satisfied that her desires would be achieved, Felice toyed with a handkerchief in her lap, then asked a burning question. "And what of this Miss Randolph, Mother? Who is she, really? What is her background? Do you credit she actually believes to find her father's family after all these years?"

A mask fell over Lady Westcott's face, concealing all from her daughter. "She knew your father. He visited her home in Virginia, apparently involved in talks with her father to do with trade between our countries. Had your father lived, I believe we would not see the deteriorating situation between England and America. At any rate, she seems to be of a good family, and she refers to their plantation. I surmise that means a farm of goodly size, something like our estates."

"But English relatives!" Felice sputtered.

"While it is true we have little to go on other than a name

and a year of sailing, I believe that a thorough search will bring them to light."

"But . . . ?" prompted her daughter, hearing the note of hesitancy in her mother's voice.

"I fear that once she finds them, either they will reject her or she will find they are not to her liking. It has happened before." The countess exchanged a concerned look with Felice before going on to discuss the children's routine and how long her daughter estimated she and her husband would be gone.

"Are the donkeys gone?" asked Pamela, not seeing a single one.

"I suspect they are playing a game with us. There"—Louisa pointed to the corner of the barn—"I believe I see a pair of very long ears."

Pamela laughed delightedly and clapped her hands as the donkey caught sight of the carrots in Louisa's hands. It was but minutes before he and two others had ambled over to the fence to nose about for a treat.

A groom passed by on his way to the stables, and Louisa inquired if the donkeys might be ridden.

"They be gentle enough, miss," he replied before hurrying on his way.

In short order, Pamela and Toby were seated atop the fat little animals, blissfully hanging on to a scrubby clump of mane. Pamela was pleased to sit as though on a sidesaddle, feeling terribly grown-up. Toby manfully sat astride, thinking himself to be a very fine fellow. Had there been a need to adore Miss Randolph, the muffins and promise of parcels might have served well enough. The donkeys were icing on the cake.

Never in their short lives had Toby and Pamela been treated like this. It wasn't that the lady wasn't firm with them. They were immediately given to understand what was pleasing behavior and what she would not tolerate. But she actually seemed to enjoy their company, and that utterly enchanted them.

"Busy as the proverbial bee, I see. You do have a way

of getting around, Miss Randolph." Lord Westcott looked down his aristocratic nose at the children, who suddenly found the day a bit dimmer.

"Do not spoil it for them, please," she whispered, not taking her eyes off the children. "The groom said the donkeys are safe, and indeed, they seem placid animals. But Toby and Pamela are having the greatest of times. Life is so short, surely they can have this little treat?"

She had turned to face him at that last sentence, beseeching with those blue eyes of hers. It would take an entire field of gentian to duplicate the color. And he could detect the honeysuckle scent again, in spite of their proximity to the barn.

"You smell like honeysuckle," he said. The non sequitur brought forth a smile from her, the one he had noted before and admired.

"I distilled the essence last year. It was a blessing, seeing as how I had to leave. There was a mass of honeysuckle right beneath my window, and I would wake up in the morning to inhale that delicious fragrance. To me, it is home and Virginia."

His look was sympathetic. "You will not be happy at the news, then. Relations are worsening between our countries. Should you change your mind, you may find it too late to retreat. I suspect we may find a blockade of trade."

"Again?" she said with dismay. "I had hoped that when the embargo was removed last year it would last. If only your country would not continue to impress our young men into your navy. It is a terrible thing to do, you know," she said soberly, before turning to the children.

She lifted Toby to the ground before plucking Pamela from her donkey's back, continuing to hold the girl in her arms. "I shall see you later, I expect." She paused when he cleared his throat and seemed about to speak further.

"Miss Randolph, will you give some thought to the notion of assuming the role of governess to the children? Things might get a bit touch-and-go for you. This would give you an income for the nonce."

"Is that a condition of your help, my Lord Westcott? I

shall consider it." With head held high, Louisa stalked off to the house. Toby trailed behind her, giving wistful looks back to the donkeys by the fence.

The next day Louisa sat with Lady Westcott after offering to draw some new embroidery patterns for her. Like Louisa's mother, the countess had lamented the lack of new designs for her needlework.

"I found nothing to my liking in the last issue of the *Ladies' Magazine*," Lady Westcott said quietly. "I would have a pretty design for a lappet," the countess stated, referring to the piece of fabric that formed the streamers of caps and tied under the chin.

In the far corner of the drawing room Cecil entertained Toby and Pamela with his watch. Louisa had peeked at it when she went to fetch drawing paper. It was an automaton such as she had never seen. As music played, the scene on the watch front portrayed dancers who turned and moved slightly about the ballroom, while a conductor waved his baton and a harpist strummed—a bit oddly, to be sure.

Composing herself at a table close to Lady Westcott, Louisa smiled tentatively. "Sprays of flowers, you said?" Trained to be of assistance to her mother, it was unthinkable for Louisa not be occupied in productive occupation.

"One can never get enough designs, can one? Yes, I believe I should like some sprays of dainty blossoms. Perhaps you can draw me some of your honeysuckle, child. I find I quite like the scent. Mayhap you could tell our housekeeper just how you manage to achieve such delightful results with your distillation. She does well enough at lavender, though lately we have been buying it. There always seems to be so much to be done about the place."

" 'Tis a shame your son has not found a wife to ease the burden from your shoulders. My mama always said she looked forward to the day when Parker should bring him home a wife," said Louisa earnestly.

"Yes, I know what she meant. 'Tis not as simple a matter as it might seem to you. The girl must be of good birth and acceptable fortune." The countess looked over to where

Toby leaned against his great-uncle, then continued. "You do well with the children. It seems that Felice has as much ease with her two as I did with mine," she said with a wistful note in her voice.

Louisa glanced up from her paper that was rapidly being covered with delicate designs of honeysuckle and butterflies. She wasn't quite certain how to reply to this comment, if indeed she was supposed to do so.

"I have at times regretted the lack of closeness such as you have described in your family. But then, it seems your parents' marriage was a love match." Countess Westcott spoke absently, concentrating on threading her needle with embroidery silk.

"Yes, indeed it was. According to my mama, Papa came courting her sister; then, once he got a glimpse of his Helena, all other ladies disappeared into the mist. It sounded most romantic." Louisa was surprised that the seemingly reserved countess would discuss a subject so private.

"I expect it does to a young girl like yourself. It does not always work out so well, I fear. Although an arranged marriage often turns to love, so they say." Lady Westcott gave a tiny sigh, then gazed out the window, an unhappy look in her eyes. Seeming to recall herself, she turned to face Louisa. "You have a magical quality, miss. I cannot remember so forgetting myself as to chatter away in this manner. Assign it to distraction over my daughter's difficulties." It was evident that the countess believed her revelations indelicate, and she was not normally given to that sort of talk.

Louisa smiled in her charming way, nodding in sympathy. She had pieced together a great amount of information in the time she had spent at Westcott Park. Perhaps it was because she missed her own dear family so much, or maybe it was normal curiosity. But Louisa had found the situation at the Park utterly fascinating. She wondered that any gentleman would neglect so entrancing a lady as the Viscountess Bromfield. Lady Felice, with her lovely brown eyes and lively manner, was a wife any man ought to have considered desirable.

Louisa's compassionate heart went out to the young wife and mother. Believing in prompt action to remedy a bad situation, Louisa fully supported Lady Bromfield in her wish to join her husband.

"Your son suggested that I ought to support myself by taking the position of governess to your daughter's children," commented Louisa in her soft, pleasant voice.

"Since we seem to have reached a high degree of confidentiality in a short time, perhaps you would not mind revealing if you have a need for such employment?" The countess had been curious to see if her own observations were true. "I would be happy to assist you."

Louisa chuckled, then slowly shook her head. "I am pleased to say that I have no need for such, ma'am. I had a considerable portion before my papa's death. With everything sold, save for a number of keepsakes, I am an heiress of no small standing. I could with ease use my competence to set myself up in my own household. It is merely my strong desire to know my papa's family that brings me on this quest." Cheerful optimism rang in her voice.

"You wished to leave your home, feeling as you do about your country?" The countess forgot her sense of propriety so far as to pry a little.

"There was a stout gentleman a goodly number of years older than myself who professed himself willing to take on the management of our plantation . . . and me as well. I confess I found that not at all appealing, dear ma'am. And then I found myself pursued by Mr. Moss and his mother. It is difficult to say who desired a union the more, Mrs. Moss or her son." She shared an amused look with the countess. "I have no need to seek a moneyed husband. Indeed, I fear it may be the other way around."

Lady Westcott studied the young woman carefully inscribing a spray of delicate blossoms on the crisp paper. She was quite pretty, with her black hair and blue eyes, and she was extremely feminine in her ways. She certainly had the sort of assurance that came with a comfortable situation. How could Drew have been so muddleheaded as to think Miss Randolph needed employment?

"Do I appear the sort you might hire, ma'am?" asked Louisa with a cheerful grin.

"You read minds as well? Dear me," chuckled Lady Westcott. Miss Randolph's lighthearted spirits were contagious. The house had never seemed so agreeable.

"I confess I took affront for a moment, mind you. But," Louisa continued with a blithe look, "I decided I had possibly invited the suggestion by my behavior with the children." She glanced over to where Toby and Pamela sat quietly opening their parcels. "They are assuredly delightful."

"Only if you have the stamina to cope. The maid I have assigned them does well enough, but we must see to obtaining a governess." She gave Louisa an assessing look before a mischievous expression crept into her eyes. Drew had become terribly stuffy of late. He really deserved to be taught a lesson. Would Miss Randolph participate?

Louisa completed the drawing, handing it to Lady Westcott for her inspection. She observed the naughty gleam in her ladyship's eyes and wondered a little at the cause.

"Miss Randolph, you desire my assistance in finding your relatives. I wonder if you might help me in return? I think it too bad of Drew to fail to note your obvious gentility, and I think he needs to be taught a wee lesson. 'Tis harmless, surely. I do wish he were not quite so tedious at times, much as I depend on the dear boy."

Puzzled, Louisa tilted her head to one side, nodding her encouragement. This house had contained one surprise after another. What would come next?

"Let us play a little trick on my son." The countess smiled with great charm. "Accept the job of governess, then proceed to do just as you please with the children. I have observed you with them, and wonder if they might not benefit from a bit of your American freshness. They are too restrained, I believe."

"Accept the job?" echoed Louisa.

"What a wonderful solution to my dilemma," caroled Lady Bromfield, sweeping into the drawing room in a cloud of pink muslin. "Do say you will accept. I shall pay any amount you wish. Only agree, and I can be off to Denmark."

Upon hearing their mother's words, Toby and Pamela ran to lean against Louisa's side, knowing better than to say anything, but pleading with eloquent eyes. They had never found such an agreeable adult, and the notion of having her around for a while was extremely delightful.

About to thank the countess and her daughter kindly for the offer, Louisa stiffened as Lord Westcott entered the room. "I could not help overhear your suggestion, Mother. I think it an admirable solution to poor Miss Randolph's situation. With the embargo in force, she will be in no position to return to America. If she does not find relatives to take her in, she will have a reference from Felice to assist her in establishing herself."

Louisa took one look at his overconfident demeanor, glanced to where his mother sat, eyes twinkling with surprising charm, then to the two children.

"I shall be most happy to accept, with the stipulations you set forth, Lady Westcott."

5

"Oh, and, Drew, do see to it that she gets some more up-to-date clothes. Every stitch that poor girl owns is sadly out of style, save one or two. Even if she serves as a temporary governess to the children, she ought to be dressed more becomingly." Felice pouted at her brother's expression before turning to leave the breakfast room. "Besides," she tossed over her shoulder, "should her relatives actually decide to claim her, I would not wish them to think we have kept her in a dungeon all the while."

Her brother gave Felice a glowering look. "She appears quite fine to my eyes." Lovely, he might have gone on to say if he hadn't known his sister.

"Fiddlesticks. And what do men know about the style of new gowns?" Felice grinned at him, much as she had as a girl, before slipping from the room. She could be heard in the central hall giving orders to a footman.

As he slowly joined the family by the house entrance, Lord Westcott considered the apparel of the new addition to the household. Her clothing seemed attractive to him, the lavenders and pale blues she favored most appealing. Not once had she been garbed in what he would deem an inappropriate manner. It seemed Felice wanted to see Miss Randolph decked out in the latest mode, as though her present turnout was sadly lacking. Well, he might not agree with his sister—for he felt Miss Randolph a taking thing—but he knew full well that no one could hold a candle to Felice when it came to the current trappings. If she said new gowns were needed to be up to snuff, they were definitely required.

Toby and Pamela clung to their newfound friend while they watched the departure of their mother's coach. When the dust had settled back down on the graveled lane, they tugged at Louisa's hands to venture away from the house. Since they had never seen all that much of their harried mother, they felt little sense of loss at her going.

Lord Westcott observed the trio head for the stables. The donkey pasture, he would wager.

"Felice says Miss Randolph needs new gowns, Mother. What say you?" Westcott clasped his hands behind his back, looking uncommonly like his father as he strolled back and forth before the spacious entry to the house.

Placing her hand on his arm to halt his perambulations, Lady Westcott gazed thoughtfully at her son. "I believe she is dressed well enough for a governess. After all, we would not wish to have people think she attempts to rise above her station." Her face was remarkably placid as she pronounced this plumper.

Westcott gave her an amazed stare. "But she is quality! Why, Father visited her home in Virginia, had dealings with her parents." That had bothered him a little over the past few days as he considered precisely what those dealings might have been. "You yourself said she is most genteel. Besides, when we locate her family, she will wish to be presentable. I believe I agree with Felice. I shall send to London for a dressmaker and all the folderol necessary. The London Season is coming to a close, so they ought to be glad enough for a large order. Who is the dressmaker you patronize?"

"Rose Bertin is the best, but I doubt she will travel into the wilds of the country, even for you." Lady Westcott prudently omitted the interesting fact that she herself merely called the local modiste for the making her own gowns. Since she didn't mingle with the *ton* at London parties, she was not concerned with the very latest mode. But she knew that Louisa desired the very best. And that was not easy to find out on a country estate. But hardly impossible. One could obtain the latest in fashion journals, fabrics, and trimmings, along with an accomplished seamstress, if one set her mind to it.

"Have her abigail take her measurements and I will see to it that Madame Bertin handles the order," Westcott announced in a decisive manner. "I will not have it thought that we considered her beneath us merely because she is a colonial. She shall have the best to be had."

The Countess Westcott glanced at her lordly son and smiled to herself. Life of a sudden had become quite fascinating in this quiet backwater. As they entered the house, Westcott headed for the library and a spate of letter writing. The countess walked up to her pretty sitting room, where she made out a list, a very long list. Then she had words with Tabitha, after which the countess wrote a number of letters. Pot-stirring was turning out to be jolly good fun, as Toby might say.

"This is jolly good fun, Miss Randolph," pronounced a delighted Toby as he clung to the donkey with firm control.

"I want to ride a donkey too," lisped Pamela, holding tightly to Miss Randolph's soft hand. With the absence of a familiar figure, she sought reassurance from a solid and friendly person.

"We shan't wish to have you ride until you can have a proper sidesaddle, love. No reason for all the world and his wife to view your petticoats," said Louisa quietly.

"Toby wears skirts and he is riding," said Pamela with a sound childish logic.

That Pamela was correct was irrefutable. Louisa thought the practice of dresses for little boys not too bad for infants. But for a boy the age of Toby to be kept in skirts was utterly ridiculous. To be sure, his nankeen trousers covered his sturdy legs under the dark plaid dress tied with a bright crimson sash. However, Louisa resolved to effect a change as soon as possible. He ought to be at least permitted to wear a skeleton suit such as she had seen while in Chester. The ankle-length one-piece article of clothing looked far more practical and a good deal more comfortable to her eyes than the fussy dress and trousers.

Setting the wiggling Pamela on the ground, Louisa led Toby's donkey around the paddock which the groom had permitted them to take over for the practice session.

Pamela was garbed as usual in tucked white muslin sashed

in blue satin. Her white pantalets were decorated with rows of lace. From under the brim of her blue bonnet her wee little face peered with great longing at the donkey her brother rode so nicely.

Louisa hoped that it would not be long before someone found the small saddle upon which Lady Felice had learned to ride. If this estate was run anything like her plantation, nothing was ever thrown away, but stored in some attic or cupboard until needed.

"This be it, miss," exclaimed the groom. Louisa turned to discover that the man she had sent off on the search was followed by a curious Lord Westcott.

"Find an animal," she murmured vaguely, wondering why this elegant lord persisted in coming upon her when she just knew she looked a fright.

"I see you have taken your new duties to heart. Toby appears to have a good seat. Why is little Miss Pamela hiding behind your skirts?" He was in a jocular mood this day. Felice was gone, things were returning to normal. With any luck, his two uncles might take their nonsense and wagers off to London. Then, after the children left, the house could doze in peace once again. That sounded rather dull, put so baldly. But he desired a well-regulated household. Miss Randolph disturbed his peace greatly.

"The groom will have her mama's old saddle on a donkey presently. I felt it improper to have her riding bareback. My sisters did such at home, but I sense it is different here." Actually the horrified look that crossed the groom's face when she mentioned Pamela riding that way had told her the truth of the matter.

Westcott really didn't care about his niece and nephew all that much. It was the enchanting Miss Randolph that drew his presence to the paddock today. "No news as yet regarding your relatives," he cheerfully relayed.

Louisa wondered at his tone. Did he sound pleased because he wished her company, or was he merely revealing his opinion of her scheme to locate her family? She gave him a dubious look.

Changing the subject, she inquired, "Might I have the

ordering of a few garments for the children? I saw a clever little outfit in Chester while there. It is called a skeleton suit and seems ever so practical for Toby."

"Nonsense." Westcott bristled at the very idea of change. "What's wrong with what he has on? I wore the same as a boy. We all did." Like many a man, he resisted until forced, and then found change distasteful.

Louisa observed Toby's compressed lips and downcast eyes. "My brother was so happy when he was allowed to go into long trousers. Soon Toby will be wearing pantaloons, you know. Children have a habit of growing whether we like it or not."

"Do you intend to revolutionize the dress for both of the children? What do you propose for Pamela? I suppose you will put her in trousers as well!" All this talk of change was not to his liking.

He looked down that aristocratic nose of his and Louisa longed to punch him. What a pompous, starched-up person he was.

"What a marvelous notion, my lord," Louisa said, her voice revealing her views to the truly astute. She bestowed a cool look on him before turning back to the donkey now bearing an ecstatic Pamela seated on the very saddle her mama had used as a child. " 'Tis a pity I am not clever with my needle in that way. I could devise such wonderful changes." She noticed he seemed to wince at the mere sound of the word.

"I will not have you upsetting the running of things."

"Heaven forbid a woman should express an opinion of her own," replied the outraged Louisa, her drawl more pronounced in her anger. "Yet I feel that the children will be the better for any efforts," she went on, with an attempt at her more customary cheerfulness.

"Why do I doubt it?" Westcott muttered in his usual pessimistic manner. In his experience women were forever desirous of alteration. His mother persisted in moving furniture about the house. It had gotten so that he always checked before he sat down, lest his favorite chair have been relocated during his absence. He had learned to accept a certain amount of movement. But if things continued apace here, he would be forced to seek his club in London. There, nothing ever changed.

Louisa watched his departing figure with mixed emotions. He had been such a charming man while in Chester. She had not missed that roguish gleam in his eyes when she had daringly dropped into his arms that first day. All during the journey to Westcott Park he had been the soul of courtesy, and most refined in his manners.

Now he was as a good many other men she had observed. Older, more settled friends of her parents' had been inclined to this same stubborn resistance to any modification in their living. But to discover it in a young, handsome gentleman of the very highest *ton*, as Felice declared him to be, was discouraging. Were all the gentlemen thus in this country? How depressing.

The lesson over, the children bade a fond adieu to the donkeys, then strolled along with Louisa until they reached the barn, where they espied the dogs.

She watched the children gently play with Spot. The female dog withdrew into the shadows of the barn upon hearing the piping voices come near. Louisa surmised the dog's time was nigh, and cautioned the children they must leave her in peace.

Returning to the house, Louisa handed the care of the children over to Annie, their nursery maid. After washing the dust from the paddock and barn from her hands and changing to a better gown, she joined the countess in the drawing room.

"See what you think of this list I have drawn up," said an enthusiastic countess. "Knowing you to be unfamiliar with the latest in fashion, I consulted with Felice before she left, then checked the pile of fashion journals remaining in her room. I have made page references for each item on the list." The countess offered a strip of paper covered with a neat list of garments. The stack of magazines at her side seemed rather daunting to Louisa. But delightful, she added to herself.

"How terribly efficient," said an admiring Louisa. She had not failed to notice the attire worn by the fashionable

Felice. If that young lady pronounced a gown to be the thing, Louisa felt she might trust her judgment.

The list was longer than anticipated, but since each article of apparel was entrancing in design, and such delightful fabrics had been suggested, Louisa was quite of the opinion to approve all of them. She met the countess's hopeful gaze with a smile. "I believe the entire lot should be ordered. But how?"

"Drew mentioned something about having to attend to a matter in London. I propose to send this list, along with your measurements, to a dressmaker there. With the Season drawing to a close, she ought to welcome our patronage. And you may trust this woman implicity."

"I had best give him instructions regarding payment. I recall my money has been placed in Hoare's Bank. That is an acceptable establishment, is it not, ma'am?"

"That it is," responded the countess a bit dryly. "But wait awhile. Allow Drew to handle the bills, then give you the final reckoning. You can settle with him later."

Louisa gave her a dubious look, then nodded. "Very well, if you say so. You know him best."

The countess gave a small sigh. "If I only did," she murmured so softly Louisa was not sure she had heard aright.

At that moment the butler entered, followed by two women, one middling in years, the other quite young. Never had Louisa seen a more plain and proper female.

"Lady Dunstable and Miss Ann. How lovely that you could come for tea. I would that you meet our colonial visitor, Miss Louisa Randolph." The countess gestured to Louisa with the pleased expression of a magician who has just pulled a rabbit from his hat.

Louisa was thankful that she had worn the prettiest gown she possessed, to make a good impression on these neighbors, as they turned out to be.

Over tea, she tried to quiz—ever so gently—Miss Ann about her life in the country. It was rather heavy weather, as Parker might have said. Miss Ann apparently believed that one should save words much as one would hoard coins.

It was quite fascinating to observe Lord Westcott enter the

room, to stop in his steps at the sight of the visitors. He bowed exquisitely, then politely joined in the conversation. Miss Ann had little to say to him either. Louisa had a vision of her in the years to come with that patient, closemouthed expression on her face. Doubtless she would open her mouth to say, "I do," and that would be the last to be heard from the woman. Her mother was far more voluble.

Fluttering her scant eyelashes at his lordship, Lady Dunstable coyly stated, "We are here to inquire if your good mother, and your guest," she added graciously, "would care to join us in the new Ladies' Royal Benevolent Society undertaking of seeing to the Poor." Her tones were dramatic as she made the pronouncement. It was evident she thought she was bestowing a great condescension upon the Westcott household.

Louisa darted a glance at the countess, to see a bland expression. No clue there.

Cosmo and Cecil had entered the room, probably in search of a comfortable cup of tea and several of Cook's biscuits. Louisa watched, fascinated, as they studied the guests.

Cecil made a leg, followed by his brother. "Greetings, fair ladies. Setting out to do your bounden duty, I see."

Cosmo added, "Cast one's bread upon the waters, so to speak?"

His brother cast him an eloquent look, the said, "It is to be devoutly hoped that we can be of assistance, that is, the household," he added at his nephew's dark glance.

"For those of us in fine feather, the fate of the less fortunate is to be deplored. The fleshpots of Egypt are ever to be despised," Cecil concluded piously.

"Dear me," said Lady Dunstable faintly.

"Do you join your mother, Miss Ann?" inquired Lady Westcott, seeking to smooth over her brother's words.

"Yes. I am ever at my mama's command," replied Miss Ann obediently.

"I am certain Lord Westcott would wish to do the right thing. Perhaps Louisa shall join me in visiting our tenants?" Lady Westcott cast what Louisa interpreted as a beseeching look at her young houseguest.

"It is not merely your tenants, for I am sure they are better off than most. It is the poor in the village we seek to help," clarified Lady Dunstable, the feathers in her bonnet bobbing about with her vigorous nods.

Lady Westcott thought of the neat cottages in the village and wondered what the Dunstable woman hoped to achieve. Although there were many places that showed the effects of hardships, Westcott was not among them. Oh, it might be there were one or two that needed salvation. But most were good enough.

"Yes," Miss Ann volunteered, "we intend to read the Bible to them, inspire them to live better lives."

Louisa stared at the earnest young woman with a degree of surprise. While it was a praiseworthy goal, it seemed to Louisa that they would listen better had they food and a decent job.

Cecil and Cosmo suddenly discovered they had forgotten something of importance in the library and disappeared with great haste. Lord Westcott excused himself to follow his uncles. Louisa looked to Lady Westcott, who sat with serene grace at the tea party.

"Such admirable intentions, I'm sure," she stated in her clear, sweet voice. "I shall do as we deem necessary, you may be certain."

The prescribed time for a proper visit being expired, the Dunstable ladies rose to leave, with much fluttering upon Lady Dunstable's part. From Miss Ann there was a surreptitious peek in the direction Lord Westcott went.

When they were again alone, Lady Westcott sat quietly, a considering expression on her face. She brightened when her son returned to the room. Ignoring Louisa, he walked to stand near his mother.

"I will not have you driving about the area preaching to the poor souls who dare not turn you away," he pronounced gruffly. "If you wish to bring food for those in need of help, that is well and good. They can look to the vicar for their divine salvation. You set an example by attending church every Sunday." He paused a moment, glancing at Louisa before continuing. "I have never heard a more prosing pair of women. No, I stand corrected. Miss Ann doesn't look as though she could say boo to a goose. However, her mother says enough for two. I pity the man who weds that girl."

"As you say, dear." Lady Westcott sighed, then offered him the list that had been drawn up before the Dunstable ladies had arrived.

"What's this? The list I requested?" He started to read, then raised his eyes to look at his mother. "I know I suggested a few garments, but I believe this is an entire wardrobe."

"I shall pay for everything, suh," said Louisa in that soft musical voice that always delighted his ear. "Your mother kindly suggested what she felt necessary for me. I know that when I find my family I will want to appear to my best. That cannot be too soon. I fear I impose on you."

The realization that Miss Randolph might be whisked from his life very shortly did not please Lord Westcott. Consequently, when he spoke, it was in a stiff, gruff voice that Louisa found utterly odious.

"As much the visionary as ever, I see. You may build castles for yourself if you wish. Do not attempt to instill that quality in the children. I do not desire any trouble from those two while they are here."

Rising from the chair where she had sought refuge after the departure of the Dunstable ladies, Louisa clenched her fists as she faced the man she admired and disliked. "I do hope your country is not universal in the suppression of all individual rights."

"Rights? Pray tell, what have rights to do with anything?" The two combatants totally ignored the clearly fascinated Lady Westcott as they faced each other across the room. Drew was most annoyed with the pretty colonial.

Louisa thought of how Toby desired to explore, to have adventure. "Did you not do anything exciting as a child? I would not keep young Toby under my thumb." She turned away from that haughty gaze to look out of the window. Best not reveal her plans for the children while she was here. "However, as I feel sure that word will soon arrive of my family in this country, it is a moot point. Are you to leave for London soon, Lord Westcott? I hope so. Otherwise I should wish to send an express to the fine dressmaker your mother has promised me. I imagine that if I send a letter of instruction to my banker, all will be in hand regarding payment."

Turning to face her antagonist once again, Louisa lifted her chin in a manner Lady Westcott silently applauded, and added, "Pray do not tell me I am not fit to oversee my accounts and investments. I have been doing it for some time. My father thought every woman should be capable of keeping household accounts. I listened to his wise words on investments many a time in our evening conversations. *He* believed that women have brains."

Looking down, she studied her clasped hands before she spoke once again. "That is one reason I wish to write my little stories . . . to prove to his memory that I am capable of being creative and independent. And to prove to myself that I have a contribution to make to society, or at least to children."

Raising her gaze to meet his eyes, she was puzzled at the expression she saw there. She stood absolutely still, waiting, wondering how he would respond to her little speech of independence.

Drew was again reminded of the letters she had mentioned, letters from his father that her mother had kept. He glanced to his own mother, seated with proud grace on the sofa. What would she think of those letters? Might they contain something which would upset her tranquil world? That could not, must not, be permitted. He knew nothing of the relationship between his parents, had no real desire to know. It was none of his affair. But he would not permit this little upstart to harm his mother in any way. Even if Miss Randolph was beautiful and charming, in her colonial manner.

True, she had Pamela and Toby, children his sister declared to be fractious and disobedient, eating from her hand. Pamela said Miss Randolph told them stories. He was going to have to investigate those tales. He wondered what was discussed between them. Instilling some of her notions of colonial independence?

He tucked the list in his coat pocket, bowed slightly to his mother, asking, "Are there any other commissions I may perform for you while in Town? I believe I shall leave directly." Looking at Louisa, he added, "I shall endeavor to return with as much of your order as I may. Perish the thought that you might not feel well-dressed while leading donkeys about the paddock."

Louisa sat in puzzled silence at the tartness of his words. What had she done to deserve such harsh treatment? Surely her few words did not merit such.

Hearing nothing from either woman, Drew walked toward the door, then paused. "If I might see you in the library for a moment, Miss Randolph?"

Louisa took a step, then glanced to Lady Westcott for her approval. Why, she wasn't sure. Receiving a nod, Louisa continued out the doorway into the hall, marching across the gray slate with the peculiar feeling that she was going to get a lecture. She recalled the feeling from many years ago, when, as a child, a scolding came her way.

The butler was there to open the door for them. Louisa met his eyes, surprised to see curiosity and perhaps sympathy in them.

She decided to sit. If her senses were correct, she might have need of a chair's support. "You wished to speak privately with me, Lord Westcott? May I say first that I appreciate your hospitality and the kindness you and your family have shown to me. And I am very grateful that you personally will handle my request for new clothes. If there is anything I might do for you . . . please say so."

He gave her what she could only describe as a fulminating look. What she had done, at least in the past few minutes, to earn his censure, she couldn't imagine.

"Well, now, that is to say . . ." He seemed at a loss how to begin. "Perhaps you might keep a curb on my mother regarding that expedition to the tenants and village. She is inclined to be overly generous. They have good conditions, for I firmly believe that healthy people are more content and work better."

"Very well." She knew Lady Westcott would do precisely as she pleased on any matter. Her son might think he had some influence over her, but Louisa suspected he didn't know the half of it.

He ran his finger inside his elegantly tied cravat, looking a bit uncomfortable.

Louisa sat quietly, not wanting to create a distraction. "And?"

"About those letters. The ones you mentioned from my father to your mother." He began to pace back and forth along the wall of books that rose from floor to ceiling behind him.

Louisa opened her mouth to inform him that the letters had been addressed to both her parents, but was given no chance to speak as he continued.

"I should like to know what you intend to do with them. I have no desire for my mother, or anyone else, to know of any indiscretions my father may have committed while in your country. If there was a, er, closeness between him and your mother, it might be concealed. You mentioned writing children's stories. I do not accept that that is what you really have in mind. Children's tales? Unlikely subject when you have a much more interesting matter to hand. I want your promise that you will not write about any liaison between my father and your mother."

Louisa was thunderstruck. She sat as carved from stone while mulling over his astounding words. Could he actually believe she would do something so horrid? Especially after meeting his charming mother? And being a guest in his home? What a low opinion he must have of her! And to think that her darling mother would have an affair with his father. Well!

Feeling as though the sun had just disappeared behind a gigantic cloud, never to return, she nodded mutely.

In seconds he was at her side, lifting her chin so he might gaze into her eyes. "You promise?" His beautiful brown eyes were dark; no amusement lit them now.

"I do." What else need be said? Would he believe in her

innocence if that was the awful view he held of her? And she had thought he liked her just a little. Had those warm looks meant not one thing?

"Very well. I shall hold you to that. And now I had best be off to London. I expect I shall return in a week or so. Perhaps you may hear from the solicitor that he has found your family, but do not raise your hopes too high. I deem it unlikely. Good-bye, Miss Randolph."

He left the door ajar when he went out. Louisa sat in the chair, feeling as cold and as lost as she had after the funerals of her family. Alone, unwanted, rejected.

Suddenly she heard the children's voices and her heart rose. A thin ray of sunshine shot across the room, lighting a path to where she sat. She had friends, and there were worthwhile things to do. But the ache now in her heart would persist for a long time, she knew.

6

"*I* believe I shall change the furniture around," said the countess in a thoughtful voice. "I do so enjoy a rearrangement of things. The only room that is sacrosanct is the library. Drew put his foot down and I daresay it would be a trifle difficult. I have no patience to move books about on shelves, and the furniture in there is sadly lacking in interest. Stuffy old sofas and chairs that are more for comfort than looks. I wonder that he can bear to spend so much time in there. Wants imagination. But in here I can exercise wondrous changes."

"I had the feeling that your son does not precisely care for such," offered Louisa hesitantly. She bestowed a concerned look on her hostess, who was standing in the drawing room with a decidedly calculating look in her eyes.

"Quite so," pronounced the countess with a sly smile creeping across her face. "I considered the matter at great length and decided that if things are too comfortable for him, he will never seek a wife. I have noticed of late that he is becoming more and more set in his ways. That leads to dullness, you know. If something is not done, he will turn into an old stick."

"I see." Louisa turned aside, ostensibly to study the placement of a chair. The vision of Lord Westcott walking down a church aisle with some blond beauty was not exactly pleasing. Of course Louisa was well aware that he must marry and provide an heir for his estate, but yet the notion brought gloom to her usually cheerful heart.

"Your fragrance is delightful, dear girl." The countess inhaled with appreciation as she walked past Louisa. "It brings back such pleasant whispers from the past. As I recall, honeysuckle means 'sweetness of disposition.' Did you know that? Most appropriate." The countess motioned a husky footman to place a chair on the far side of the room, then turned to face her guest.

"In Virginia it came to mean 'bonds of love,' or so I found in a little book my mama had. It has truly bound me to my home and family with happy memories." Louisa had a wistful glimmer of a smile on her lovely face.

"Precisely so. Fragrances can be so evocative, can they not? Roses, gillyflowers, and peach blossoms—so many scents have come to have meaning down the years." The countess sighed before instructing two footmen to move one of the sofas. Her sharp-eyed gaze missed nothing. She directed the men with the precision of a general.

"Roses and gillyflowers I know, but peach blossoms?" Louisa backed out of the way of the second sofa as it appeared to float past her, carried by two stalwart footmen. Louisa had observed that all of the footmen in the house were sturdy lads, though not necessarily handsome. Now she thought she knew why. If the countess made a practice of rearranging the furniture frequently, muscular staff must be a necessity!

"Peach blossoms?" echoed the countess in a rather vague manner. "It means 'I am your captive,' my dear. What a pity the Season is past." She crossed the room in a flurry of skirts, her bright red turban a spot of busy color as she directed the changes in the room.

The non sequitur caused Louisa to stare after the countess for a moment before its meaning came through. It seemed the dear lady wished her son to be captive to the charms of a woman, the one who would be his wife.

With the last of the chairs set down in a new location, the countess surveyed the room with a satisfied nod. "It will do . . . for this week, at least." She brushed her hands together as though she had been the one to actually help position the furniture, instead of merely directing. "Now, dear child, sit down and tell me what you think."

Louisa gingerly perched on the deep blue sofa that now faced its mate before the Adam fireplace. "Quite lovely, dear ma'am."

"Tea, I believe. Hard work always makes me thirsty." Lady Westcott pulled the bell rope next to the fireplace while she studied Louisa. Observing the sad droop of the beautifully shaped mouth, she crossed to sit by her guest.

"You had words with my son before he left yesterday. I am terribly sorry if he rang a peal over your head. I gather he did, for he looked as black as a thundercloud when he left, and you were nowhere to be seen. I made certain you would have wished to give him final instructions regarding your list. What happened? if you will forgive an old woman's curiosity."

Louisa studied her clasped hands a time before lifting her gaze to meet the countess's soft brown eyes. "Do you recall that I mentioned some letters your husband wrote?"

"Yes, I do remember. You offered them to me to read. I should like that, I think. Although I confess my first thought was one of concern. My husband and I saw very little of each other the years before he died." Her eyes grew misty as she gazed off into the distance. She cleared her throat after a few minutes, then continued. "That is another reason I desire Drew to wed. But I do not mean for him to marry where there is no affection. No, indeed! There must be some means to get what is best for him." She stared off again before recalling her manner, and turned to Louisa, a question in her eyes.

"But what about these letters? What do they have to do with Drew?" That she was puzzled was clear. That Louisa found it difficult to reply botherd her even more. "Tell me," she commanded gently.

"Somehow or other, your son has the ridiculous notion that your husband and my mother . . . Oh, it is too bad of him, really." Louisa came to a halt and gave Lady Westcott an unhappy, beseeching look.

"Drew thinks the two of them had an affair?" For a moment the countess had a pained expression on her face before she realized that if that were the case, the girl would hardly have brought the letters here, would she?

"I fear that is precisely what he believes. And he has some maggoty idea that I intend to expose the 'liaison' between them to hurt you. As though I could do such a thing." Louisa gave the countess an indignant look. "Of course it is far from true. Had he given me the opportunity, I could have revealed all. The letters were written to both of my parents and read to all the family at the dinner table. Your husband had such charming wit and described things with delightful humor.''

Countess Westcott appeared to breathe more easily and nodded graciously as Newton brought in the tea tray to place on the low table that now stood between the two sofas. ''What *are* we to do? It is really naughty of him to behave in such a disgraceful manner toward you, our guest.''

Somewhat mollified, Louisa nodded. ''He was but trying to protect you, ma'am. No mother can feel that to be totally without virtue.''

''I am quite of the opinion that he needs to be taught some manner of lesson,'' stated the countess in a very firm voice. ''It simply is not done, you know. To accuse without proof is not quite the thing. I cannot understand Drew to behave in such a manner. No, I shall teach him a lesson. And I believe I shall combine it with my effort to reduce his bothersome tendency to stuffiness.''

''Lord Westcott?'' replied Louisa, clearly dismayed at what her tale had brought about.

''What about Drew?'' Cecil inquired from the doorway as he and his brother entered the room.

Louisa had decided they could detect a cup of tea from an incredible distance. Biscuits, as well.

The twins resembled a pair of marigolds today, with golden-yellow coats over green breeches. Rust-colored vests were embroidered with *fleurs de lis*, as were the clocks of their cream stockings. They were elegant to the top of their frizzed heads. Slightly protruding brown eyes stared at Louisa as though in alarm. She knew full well it was quite normal for them to look like a pair of startled owls, yet it never failed to surprise her.

''What have we here?'' Cosmo inquired coyly as he patted his stomach. ''Cook's biscuits! I declare, I believe I am famished.''

''You are always famished, dear brother,'' said the countess with a wry but fond smile.

''I want to know what Drew has done to deserve your ire,

sister mine." Cecil had all the tenacity of a donkey who will not budge. He accepted a cup of tea from Louisa, who had been pressed into service by a suddenly harried countess.

"Yes, well . . ." She capitulated gracefully. "Louisa brought a packet of letters—I have not read them as yet, but I shall—written by Edward to her parents while he was in America. She declares they contain the most amusing stories. I find that difficult to believe. I did not realize he possessed a sense of humor, you know. At any rate, Drew heard of these letters and jumped to the silliest conclusion."

"What?" demanded Cecil, determined to ferret the tale from his sister. Life in the country tended to be dull at times. He enjoyed a bit of gossip.

While Louisa gazed into the bottom of her cup, the countess assumed an insulted air. "Drew indicated he believed Edward had a liaison with Louisa's mother."

Cosmo gave a snort of disgust. "I could have told him it was all a hum, that. Edward never did an improper thing in his life. Dull dog. I told you he would be, before you married him. Wouldn't listen. Never do," he grumbled.

"Was there anything else? I fail to see how that could bring such an absence of manners to our oh-so-proper nephew." Cecil fixed his gaze upon Louisa, pinpointing her to her place on the sofa. "What other matter was brought up, child?" Seeing her reluctance to speak, he added gently, "We merely wish to help you."

"Well, as a matter of fact, there was another trifling thing." Louisa placed her cup on its saucer, then clasped her hands in her lap.

Cosmo joined her on the sofa, munching a biscuit while he gave her a sidelong glance that fair undid her.

"He does not accept that I plan to write children's stories. For some odd reason, he feels I shall tell the world the tale of his father and my mother. A tale, mind you, that does not even exist outside of his imagination." Her voice rang with her indignant reaction to the entire situation.

She popped up from the sofa to wander about the room. "I confess I do not like to speak of this. It seems unfair and disloyal to Lord Westcott that we talk while he is not here to defend himself." She turned away to look at the view outside the drawing room.

Cosmo gave his brother a nudge, and made an approving nod toward Louisa, and the two turned to Lady Westcott for her evaluation.

"I said he ought to be taught a lesson," she said softly.

"Indeed," agreed Cosmo.

"You might be able to fish in troubled waters, sister dear," offered Cecil with a sly glance at Louisa.

"Profit by the disturbance? I do not see quite how." The countess gave him a frown; then her brow cleared. "I see what you mean." The trio gave a very considering look at the slim figure near the windows.

"I have a great mind to tell him what I think of such Turkish treatment," declared Cosmo softly as he reached for another biscuit.

"It's a bit like helping a lame dog over the stile, you know. Look at the child. You can tell she was terribly hurt by his charges." Cecil sipped his tea, then glanced at his sister. "We shall think of some way to stir the pot."

"I am not certain whether that is good or not," replied the countess, giving her brother a rueful smile.

"Hope springs eternal," said Cosmo, for no apparent reason.

Louisa had espied Toby and Pamela sitting properly on a bench. A glorious summer day was being totally ignored while the two children were watched by a frustrated-looking Annie. Pamela was obviously being scolded by the nursery maid for fidgeting.

"I shall spend the afternoon with the children, if it is acceptable with you, dear ma'am." Louisa dropped a graceful curtsy to the three still watching her from the sofa. At the countess's answering nod, the young woman escaped from her most uncomfortable hour since her interview with Lord Westcott.

An odd peace of mind settled over Louisa. She reflected, as she crossed the lawn to where the children still sat, that perhaps it was a sense of relief that Lady Westcott knew the whole of the story. Later on the letters could be found in the bottom of one of her trunks and given to the dear lady. It was incredible that she had not known the wondrous charm and humor of her own husband. Louisa prayed that she would not have the sort of marriage the countess had endured.

Yet it appeared Lady Westcott was content enough with her life. She enjoyed her brothers, obviously adored her grandchildren, and seemed to love her son and daughter. But the lack of a loving husband could not be dismissed.

''Hello, Miss Randolph,'' Pamela lisped, a huge smile lighting up her face. Hazel eyes danced with delight when what she perceived as a rescuer came toward them.

''Must we sit here?'' demanded a disgruntled Toby. ''That Annie says so.''

Louisa greeted the nursery maid, then dismissed her, saying, ''Lady Westcott gave me the custody of the children for the afternoon. I shall return them to you later.''

The obviously relieved Annie slipped off to the house before the young miss could change her mind.

''Now, what shall we do?'' Louisa longed to remove the stiff pink bonnet and ruffle the pretty blond curls of the little girl sitting so properly beside her.

''Ride the donkeys,'' replied Toby with promptness.

''We did that this morning,'' countered Pamela, mindful that Miss Randolph seemed to invent amusing things to do aside from donkeys.

''Well,'' mused Louisa, ''if you want to sit here like two lumps of coal, we could play conundrums, or do you not like riddles?''

Toby jumped off the bench. ''I am *not* a lump of coal.''

''Me either,'' added Pamela, wiggling to the ground.

''Then let's go.'' Louisa held out her hands and the three wondered off in the general direction of a stream that crossed the estate.

It was a clever little stream, curling back and forth through the meadow in the most cunning manner. Clumps of reeds and tall grasses made wonderful places for frogs and field mice to hide. Louisa watched a dragonfly hover over the still surface of the water where, below, a small fish seemed to consider the possibility of an afternoon snack. The dragonfly soared away as the fish rose to the surface.

"How would you like to sail a boat down our little river?" Louisa plopped herself down on the grassy bank to watch the clouds in the distance as they lazily floated along in a pale blue sky.

"Capital!" declared Toby, always ready for adventure, no matter how small.

"But we don't have a boat," added the ever-practical Pamela.

"I have some paper," offered Toby, disappointed in Miss Randolph. His heroine ought to have magically produced a magnificent boat of which he could be captain.

"Let me have it, and I shall see what we can do." Accustomed to making toys for her sisters, Louisa took the little squares of paper. She rummaged about for a few sticks and pods, and shortly held up several small boats of a fashion. Square paper sails had sticks for masts, and pods formed ingenious craft.

"Good show, Miss Randolph," Toby said, admiration ringing in his young voice.

"I fear you had best remove your shoes and stockings," Louisa declared, not wishing to bring back evidence of the improper afternoon events.

Toby and Pamela accomplished this with a speed that would have astonished the nursery maid. Louisa rolled up the trousers beneath Toby's dress and rolled Pamela's pantalets as high as she could.

She then sat back to watch as the children waded into the shallow stream to blissfully sail the little pod-boats into the perils of the water. Actually, the tranquil flow of the stream offered no danger that she could see. They pottered along the bank, poking the boats about and having imaginary trips to faraway lands.

"We shall have a war," declared Toby after some time had elapsed and he looked for other interesting things to do with his craft.

"I do not like a battle," replied Pamela. Turning to Louisa, she said, "Tell Toby we must not fight. My boat might sink."

Louisa sensed that, as is often the case, they had begun to tire of the boats. Dismayed, she noted they had splashed water on their clothes and they were otherwise wet and in need of a bit of sun to dry off.

"I could tell you a story if you have a mind to listen." She offered a hand to Pamela and permitted the girl to curl up next to her on the sunny bank.

Toby resisted for a moment, lip thrust out in a stubborn way, until he realized his sister might hear a tale he would miss. He flopped down on the grass in a boyish manner that Louisa found endearing. And terribly normal.

"There once was a dragon who lived in a large cave in the furthest-off forest, far, far from the castle," Louisa began.

"Did he have to eat his beans?" demanded Toby, thinking of his most hated vegetable.

"Dragons do not eat beans, silly. Now, be still, or I shan't continue. He was a very sad dragon because he had lost his fire," said Louisa in a confiding voice.

"Stupid," inserted Toby, forgetting the requested silence. "A dragon cannot forget a fire."

Pamela punched her brother with all the effect of a feather against a stone, and he grew quiet.

Without further interruption, Louisa wove the tale of the fat little dragon, so woebegone, and in great danger because he could no longer defend himself, except for a good lashing of his tail. The young lad who came to fight him sounded remarkably like a slightly older version of Toby. When the lad befriended the dragon, proceeding to solve the problem of the fire, Toby was heard to whisper, "Good show!"

The boy and his dragon were about to set off on an adventure when Louisa realized the day was getting on. Smoothing out the clothes as best she could, she hurried them back to the house, wondering if she was to face the countess's wrath.

Instead, she was met with smiles and the suggestion they

follow Miss Randolph's schemes for the following days. And they did.

Louisa offered the packet of letters to Lady Westcott and the dear woman disappeared for hours, to return with faintly pink eyes, as though she might have been crying. No comment was made about the letters, but they remained with her, safely in her desk.

Discovering that a quite adequate skeleton suit might be purchased in the village, Louisa ordered several for Toby. Sighing at the proper little Pamela, she decreed that while they were out by the stream, the little girl might omit the pantalets. They had a tendency to get wet and dirty. Thus Louisa not only acquired the devotion of the children but also earned the affection of Annie, who had found the pantalets dreadfully hard to wash.

The tales of the boy and his dragon friend were added to each day. They were balanced by the stories of a little girl who was very lonely and found friends in her garden.

They had great fun. Toby became faintly tan and his cheeks were a healthy rose. Pamela was naturally protected by her bonnet from such danger, but her bonnet was a simple affair, as were her clothes. No frills, Miss Randolph decreed. Simplicity was the order of the day. And how the children loved it.

And then the puppies arrived.

Toby and Pamela were enchanted. Even Lady Westcott deigned to take a look at the new members of the household. She agreed the children ought to have one of the litter.

"We had best wait until Lord Westcott returns to decide which it will be," commented Louisa to the countess while they watched the children, wide-eyed with wonder and delight.

"Perhaps. Although the man assigned to the dogs most likely knows which would be best," came the dry reply.

As the days grew into a week, then two weeks, Louisa wondered what Lord Westcott was doing in London. Why didn't he return? Had he escaped from the children and other guests? Or was he involved with a lady? He knew his mother desired him to find a wife. That last thought was hastily buried in a seldom-explored part of the Louisa's mind.

It was one of those sunny days in England when it seems there cannot be anyplace on earth quite so lovely. The air was fresh and scented with flowers, wee unthreatening clouds dotted the distant sky, and they were having an absolutely smashing afternoon.

Toby had carefully rolled up the legs of his skeleton suit so he might better sail his new boat. This one was from the toy shop in the village. It had three sails and a flag and was carved in wondrous detail. Pamela was content to putter along the sandy bank, sailing a yellow-painted duck that bobbed up and down in a fetching manner. Even Louisa had kicked off her slippers and removed her stockings to permit her feet to dangle in the refreshing water.

Pamela squealed with delight as she wiggled her toes in the water while Louisa commenced the latest edition of the tale of Robert and the dragon. When informed that Robert was Toby's middle name, she agreed that it was admirable for the boy in the story. She had just reached the dangerous part of the adventure, with Robert scaling the rocks to reach a castle, when a disdainful voice came from behind them.

"Do my eyes deceive me? What can be the meaning of this? I could not imagine what was going on when I looked from the coach window. At first I thought someone had fallen into the stream and there was a rescue party at work. Miss Randolph, explain yourself." Lord Westcott stood behind the guilty trio with a condemning look.

Terribly conscious of her bare feet, Louisa quickly tucked them beneath her gown, succeeding only in getting the hem wet. Toby seemed to sense that trouble was afoot, for he hastily left the stream, taking his lovely boat with him to show his uncle.

Pamela had forgotten how very daunting her uncle could be, and ran to him, holding out her duck with happy hands. "See, Uncle Drew? Miss Randolph bought this for me at the toy shop. I can sail it, and it never sinks to the bottom."

Not to be outdone, Toby—the legs of his skeleton suit now unrolled and shoes and stockings hurriedly donned—came forward. "And this is my new boat. Miss Randolph has been telling us the most famous stories, all about dragons and heroes."

"And a little girl who has flower friends," piped up Pamela, not to be left out.

"This is how you teach?" asked Lord Westcott in a dangerously quiet voice.

"I have learned how to spell ever so many flowers, Uncle Drew," said Pamela, coming to the aid of her friend.

"Miss Randolph has been teaching me the globe. I know where all the explorers went on their voyages. Just look at my ship!"

While Lord Westcott managed a brief inspection of the new boat, Louisa hurriedly put on her stockings and slippers, careful to keep this effort from his sight. She was not so lost to propriety that she cared to flaunt her bare feet to him thus.

"We saw the new puppies. Grandmama said we may have one if you let us," said Toby urgently. "Will you come and look at them?" he demanded politely. "After you greet Grandmama, of course," he added, recalling his manners.

"Why don't you go on up to the house and tell her I am come? I shall be along directly." The children took one look at his expression, glanced to where Louisa stood, eyes downcast, then fled across the parkland.

"I had hoped to return to a tranquil household. I ought to have known better. You gave me reason to doubt before I departed for London. I should have paid more attention."

Not understanding in the least what annoyed him so, Louisa merely said, "I trust you have had a good journey. Was your stay in London productive?" Now, why had she said that? She did not wish to know if he had settled upon some young lady to wed. That other things probably had transpired had not registered.

"I stayed at my club. It is very tranquil there, Miss Randolph. Silence reigns, and peace is the order of the day."

It sounded horridly dull to Louisa, and she must have conveyed that thought to her host in her expression.

"I quite like it. Most restful," he insisted.

Really, it was too bad of Miss Randolph to look so delectable. Her ebony curls framed a face flushed rosy with indignation she could ill conceal. Those gentian-blue eyes were snapping with an anger that became her. In that simple India mull of blue and gray, she seemed terribly appealing to him. Tempting. He had been required to firm his resolve. She would not soften it.

The domestic scene he had come upon had been tranquil, in a way. Toby had played with his little boat by the shore while Pamela had been cuddled up to Miss Randolph in a charming manner. Dash it all, he had envied them. He could not recall a single instance from his boyhood to match.

"I recall my grandfather desirous of peace and rest . . . before he died," she said in her soft voice that carried a touch of acid in it.

Ignoring that provocative remark, he went on. "I gave your list to the modiste my mother recommended. The bills are in my case. Shockingly dear, all those clothes and fribbles. I have brought a goodly number of the items with me." He stood watching, wondering how to make his point clear to her.

Louisa took a step toward the house, anxious to see her new clothes as well as escape from this intimidating man. He attracted her, yet he made her so terribly angry. As glad as she was to see him, she wished nothing more than to push him into the water. How she would relish the sight of this vile-tempered man with the enormous reserve cooling off in the stream! "I shall instruct my banker to handle the expenses, suh." She dipped a mocking curtsy before again turning to leave. At the sound of his voice she paused.

"In regard to the children, I count myself their temporary guardian while my sister is away. Things must change." He took a step toward her and was satisfied when she hastily backed away from him. Let her know that he was not one to fool. If intimidated about the children, she would be more tractable about the letters. "You are turning them into heathen savages, with improper clothes and nonsensical games and stories. I will not have it!"

7

"*A* billiards table?" the countess said faintly.

The Earl of Westcott shifted slightly in his chair as though uneasy with the knowledge he had brought home an entertainment that might not please his mother. "I thought your brothers would enjoy it."

"I see," said the countess, feeling lost at sea. Drew had never sought the approbation of her brothers in the past. She brightened at the very thought. Perhaps Drew was not so averse to their company as she had feared. She could give him the news of their prolonged stay with no hesitation. It seemed their last stab at gambling had depleted their pockets to an alarming degree and they needed a place to rusticate.

"Where?" she wondered aloud. Several of their friends had placed billiards tables in entry halls, for want of space. Still others had put them in the corners of libraries. One never knew where one might come upon them, it seemed.

"In the long gallery. We have nothing but portraits there and it could cheer the place up a bit." Westcott wondered if other men his age still felt like schoolboys when sitting like this. Perhaps his mother was right and he needed a wife. As long as she didn't make him feel the lad, it might be fine.

"I saw Miss Randolph with the children when I arrived," he said in his most repressing tone, ignoring the leap from the subject of wife to Miss Randolph.

Never would he admit how often his thoughts had lingered on the blue-eyed, black-curled miss while in London. Whenever he had been out and about and had spotted black curls peeping from a bonnet, or caught sight of a pair of flashing blue eyes, he had paused in his steps. Louisa? But of course it had not been she.

At the modiste's exclusive shop he had presented the list to Rose Bertin with all the hauteur he possessed, impressing her with the necessity for speed. When he was asked to describe Miss Randolph's coloring, Madame Bertin had watched him carefully. She appeared to draw conclusions which could be forgiven if they were fancifully colored. Drew's eyes had softened, his mouth become tender as he spoke of the exquisite charms of the slender Miss Randolph.

He now brushed his memories of the sweet Louisa aside to concentrate on his anger. After all, the girl came from heaven knew where. A Virginia farm? And what was that, pray tell? The more he thought about it, the more it seemed to him that she might be on the search for a husband. A wealthy husband. It stood to reason that she was arraying herself in expensive clothes for some reason. That must be it. He totally ignored, or forgot, that his sister and mother had been urging new garments on Miss Randolph. He also forgot that she was standing the expenses.

Why had he been so impetuous as to invite her home? Because of his father's association with her family? His visage darkened at the mere thought.

"She was permitting scandalous behavior," he snapped. "The children are allowed to behave like the veriest urchins. I found them in the stream!"

Lady Westcott gave him an amused look. "Scandalous? I hardly think so, Drew. She has been utterly wonderful with them. They were always such stiff little ones in the past. Pamela now laughs with the charm of a pixie and Toby is becoming quite the young man. He has ever been fascinated with ships, you know. She has encouraged him to study the globe and learn his oceans and continents. Like many boys, he is intrigued with faraway places. She makes it fun to learn."

"Learning was never intended to be a game, Mother. My tutor certainly never treated so important a subject in such a manner." He gave his mother a forbidding look while wondering how anyone could make learning fun.

"Pity," mumured Lady Westcott as her brothers entered the room.

Cecil noted the expression on Drew's face, the one that

plainly said: "Are you still here?" "Welcome home, dear boy. Have a lovely flutter in town?"

Not quite as astute an observer, Cosmo added, "We have enjoyed ourselves in your absence. Indeed, it has become a very pleasurable stay. Miss Randolph is a most accomplished young lady. Her playing on the pianoforte bests most of the rubbish we have had to listen to in our day. Good at cards too," he reminisced, thinking of their game of last night. Miss Randolph had beaten them all quite soundly over whist. He could not wait for another chance to play against her.

He failed to note the rather daunting expression on his nephew's face, turning instead to inquire of his sister, "Are the arrangements for our little boating party all set? I vow the thought of rowing Miss Randolph along the shore is entrancing."

"What is this about a boating party? Is it not bad enough that she puts Toby in some outlandish rig, allows Pamela in the park without her pantalets, and goes without proper attire herself? Now we are to have boats?"

"'I have never observed Louisa improperly dressed. What did you see?" demanded Lady Westcott, the twinkle in her eyes hidden as she suddenly studied the handkerchief in her hand.

Drew rose to pace back and forth before the windows, vividly recalling the scene that had met his eyes. "She was reclining on the bank of the stream, her skirts pulled up to her knees, her bare feet dangling in the water! And . . . she had Pamela doing the same thing, while Miss Randolph related some nonsensical tale to them. Toby was wading along the shore with a boat."

"Serious, indeed," said his mother softly.

"Sounds like jolly good fun for a summer day," mused Cosmo, his gaze meeting that of his sister.

Mischief sparkling in his eyes, Cecil added, "I should have liked to observe that. Does she have pretty limbs, my boy?"

"Uncle!" said Drew, reminding them all of his father when he was young. Drew turned aside to stare out the window. Miss Randolph had presented an attractive picture when first seen, he remembered. The view had seemed a French painting come to life. "It was most improper for her to be so arrayed outside of her room."

"Or the plunge bath," added Cecil in a wicked little aside.

Ignoring that, Drew took a deep breath and returned to the subject which interested him. "You mentioned a boating party?"

Lady Westcott smiled indulgently. "Tomorrow, late in the morning, we are gathering down by the lake. There will be an *al fresco* lunch along with the boating and archery. I have invited a number of our neighbors and their guests for the occasion. We are all looking forward to it."

Since there seemed little to be said on the score, Drew left the room, his absence marked by soft chuckles from Cosmo and an exchange of glances between the three.

Louisa was nervous when it came time for the boating party to assemble. She had been safe enough during dinner last evening and had sought refuge in her room this morning to break her fast. Now it seemed her hours of respite were over. Lord Westcott approached.

"Drew, dear, would you present yourself here?" caroled his mother in her pleasant voice.

Louisa sighed with relief as she saw her nemesis turn aside to join his mother and two other women. When she had met the Dunstable ladies, she thought them plain. And now these two. It was to be marveled at, how many plain-faced women there were in England. Although Louisa had not had the felicity of a great number of parties, the ladies present today were exceedingly . . . ordinary. Her charitable heart would not permit her to think they were homely.

The younger of the two women had drab yellow hair that peeped from beneath a gay yellow bonnet. Her orange jaconet dress was simply cut but much flounced at the lower edge of the skirt. She was an unprepossessing sight, but Louisa had decided that Englishmen were a rather dull lot, with water in their veins—blue water, she supposed.

"Agnes Turner and her mother," commented Cecil in Louisa's ear. "Come," he insisted in his amused way, "I propose to test out one of the boats. I was once very good with the oars.'' He guided her along the path to the shore of the ornamental lake, where a number of pretty little shell boats were lined up in a row.

''It is so lovely that Lady Westcott thought to have such a charming party and invite such . . . er . . . interesting ladies,'' said Louisa, taking another glance at the Turners.

''M'sister wishes to see Drew wed,'' offered Cecil, his keen eyes watching the lovely face of the young woman he had seated in the rowboat.

''So I surmised,'' replied a subdued Miss Randolph.

''Heard nothing from that solicitor as yet, I gather,'' went on Cecil, seemingly oblivious of her downcast mien. ''Plaguey lot, those solicitors. M'sister has been going through all her books and letters to hunt for clues. If anyone will find your relations, it will be her, not some gent up in Chester.''

''I had so hoped that I might have had news by this time. I vow it would be comforting to know they exist. I feel I am a great imposition on Lord Westcott's hospitality.'' She darted a glance to where she had last seen him.

''Nonsense. You shake him up, and that is good for his liver. Always did say a man needs a good shaking to his liver now and again,'' pronounced Cecil in his heartiest tone.

Louisa glanced from the hands she had been clenching in her lap to the face of the gentleman who rowed the boat. He leaned on the oars, smiling at her like some wispy imp.

''You are a great tease, sir.'' She shook her head at him most playfully. He noted ruefully that her pretty black curls were confined beneath a neat cottage bonnet loaded with enormous flowers and bows.

''I gather Westcott brought you some of your pretties from Town when he came. You know, my dear, it is sometimes difficult to understand the why and wherefore of a thing. Better just to go along the best you can.''

Louisa gave him a confused look and nodded. There were moments when she found the two brothers totally incomprehensible.

She could see Lord Westcott strolling along the edge of the lake with Miss Agnes Turner at his side. He seemed much taken with the lady, so she must be exceedingly proper and well-bred. Breeding. Wasn't that what Lady Westcott said he required in a wife? His choice would scarcely sink to an upstart colonial who raised her skirts to her knees while dangling her feet in a stream!

Cecil returned Louisa to the shore with no mishap. Cosmo was there to assist her from the little boat with old-fashioned gallantry. Strolling along with the two vividly dressed gentlemen, she found the day improving with every step and the amusing tale they wove for her benefit.

The twins were arrayed in plum velvet coats and old-fashioned satin smallclothes with lavender satin waistcoats embroidered with seahorses. Cosmo had explained that the design was in honor of the boating party, never mind that the little lake had not seen nor ever would see such creatures.

They seemed much taken with Louisa's ensemble of pink-and-white cambric with surplice sleeves and a vandyke border around the hem. Her cheeks soon matched the pink of her dress with their many compliments. She twirled her pink parasol, and found it possible to eliminate the sight of Lord Westcott if she took special care.

Toby and Pamela walked decorously, with Annie right behind them. Louisa observed that Toby was once again wearing a tartan dress with white pantalets as fancy as Pamela's. He looked miserable as he fingered the vibrant red sash. Pamela seemed unhappy and gave Louisa a be-beseeching look of appeal, as though their friend might save them from this party that held no delight for them. Louisa suspected they would far rather be poking along the banks of the stream with their little boats and listening to stories. However, she was helpless to come to their rescue.

The activities appeared to charm all others in attendance. Many of the neighbors sat about on chairs beneath the spreading branches of the oak trees, conversing and sipping of the various beverages provided. Several of the gentlemen and one or two of the ladies vied in a bit of archery.

Cecil looked on as one young lady raised her bow and took aim. "Reminds me of a cupid I once saw," he commented, casting a wicked glance at Cosmo, who chuckled.

"Cupid is a bit late this year," observed Cosmo to no one in particular. "But when one is born with a silver spoon in one's mouth, things may take longer."

Louisa frowned at this odd remark and let it pass. She found that the more she listened to them, the more confused she got.

"I believe we are supposed to eat about now," urged Cecil, guiding them off the path.

"It is one's bounden duty to oblige, y'know. Let me see, chicken pastries and fruit compote, sliced ham and cheese. Enough to stave off the direst pangs of hunger." Cosmo led them to where a table had been set out on the freshly scythed lawn. Crisp white linen served as a background for the colorful array of edibles.

"Very little for me, thank you," cautioned Louisa.

"You scarcely ate a bite last night. Shouldn't let him put you off your food, you know. Give as good as you get, is my motto. Here, permit me." Cosmo heaped a plate held by Cecil, until Louisa laughingly protested.

The three were merry as grigs while Toby and Pamela obediently sat with their maid. Louisa took note of the miserable tots, bemoaning her inability to help. Lady Westcott paused to chat a moment before going on to look after her special guests, the Turner ladies.

Louisa was most careful to position her chair so that she would not have to see Lord Westcott with the plain Miss Turner. The sight did something to her. She wasn't quite sure whether to laugh or cry.

Lord Westcott and Miss Turner passed the shaded area where Louisa sat with the uncles. Louisa observed that while she might be unattractive, the young lady possessed a fine figure and colorful taste in garments.

Not far from where Louisa was perched in uncomfortable silence, Westcott and Miss Turner met up with Toby and Pamela.

"Oh," cooed Miss Turner, "what dear little ones. Your niece and nephew, I do believe. How noble of you to give them a home while their parents are far away." She batted sparse dun-colored eyelashes at Westcott, then turned to Toby, patting him not too gently on the head. "Such a pretty little infant. Are you having a lovely time?"

"Yes, ma'am." Louisa noted Toby's face turn a red to match his sash, and mentally congratulated him for not kicking the lady.

"And what a sweet little girl. Are you having a treat today?" inquired the lady in her high, thin voice.

Most uncharitably, Louisa thought the sound of it called to mind a mewling kitten.

Agnes Turner deemed it necessary to make a display of affection, so she bent over to give the child a brief caress. Pamela backed away, looking most confused.

Apparently even the dense Lord Westcott noticed that all was not well, for he quietly said something about showing Miss Turner some particularly fine roses, and the two departed.

"I had best see to the children," murmured Louisa, forsaking her interested escorts.

Not waiting for a reply, she walked as quickly as she dared, given the proper tone of the party, which had seemed somewhat dull to her eyes.

"Toby, what happened?" She knelt at his side and was surprised when he threw his arms about her and began to cry.

"Is she going to marry Uncle Drew?" demanded the ever-sensible Pamela.

"Say it ain't so," sobbed Toby. Manfully he backed away and wiped his eyes on the back on his hand. "I do not like that lady. She patted me on the head and called me her pretty infant. I am not an infant."

"Of course not. But you must know that your uncle, Lord Westcott, owes it to his name to marry and have an heir." Louisa understood that. Even in America it was desirable to have an heir to the family fortune.

"Did your brother have to?" demanded Toby.

"Had he lived he would. Families expect these things."

Toby appeared to digest this while Pamela tugged at Louisa's skirt. "Yes, dear?"

"She hugged me," the puzzled little girl explained. "But she was not soft like my mama. She was all hard."

From this Louisa surmised that the homely Miss Turner wore a bust improver such as was advertised in the magazines. "I am sure she is a very nice lady, Pamela. Come with me and we shall find you a treat." Louisa hoped the child would forget the possibly embarrassing fact of the bust improver. Miss Turner would not thank them for the revelation. But children were apt to say and do the most unpredictable things.

Toby plumped himself down at the water's edge, appearing to be satisfied with watching the boaters. Louisa, with a misgiving or two, decided to leave him alone. She towed Pamela, happy now to be with her beloved Miss Randolph, off to where a crumpet was found among the array of goodies. Smeared with cherry jam, it proved a delicious distraction.

At that shore, Toby stared at his uncle. He had left the rose garden and was strolling toward the lake. What a crabby old man he was. And that Miss Turner was even worse. Uncle had spoiled everything by coming home and scolding poor Miss Randolph. No more stories about Robert and the dragon. No more happy tales about the little girl and her flowers. Toby hated to confess it, but he liked to hear even those.

And his globe and maps were on the shelf again. He must await a "proper" tutor for his lessons. Toby picked at the grass; then a crafty look came to his eyes. He would fix everything. He rose and headed for the stables. The maid, distracted by demands from one of the guests, missed Toby's departure.

Lord Westcott assisted the coy Miss Turner into one of the boats, then reached for the oars. The morning was quite lovely. And if Miss Turner did not have eloquent blue eyes and curly black hair, she possessed a lovely figure and excellent manners. She was as proper as he could wish, allowing him to hold her hand only long enough to help her into the boat. *She* would never climb down a rope made of sheets to drop into a gentleman's arms.

Drew banished the memory of how delectable Louisa had felt while snuggled up against his chest, and how well she had fitted in his arms. Her delicate muslin gown and pelisse had hidden little of her basic anatomy from his detection. That she was well-endowed with womanly curves had not missed his senses. Soft and yet firm, pleasantly scented, and somehow . . . memorable.

Instead, he concentrated on the estimable Miss Turner. If his mother had invited her and her mother to visit, it must be with the intention of allowing Drew and Miss Turner to get better acquainted. And he knew well her purpose.

Lord Westcott had rowed around the lake and was returning to shore when Toby appeared carrying a puppy in his arms. Beside him trotted the proud papa, Spot. "Uncle Drew," called Toby. "See what I have!" He ran down the gentle slope until he reached the boat, now at the shore, with Miss Turner preparing to exit.

Drew was never certain afterwards, how the disaster occurred. Miss Turner gave a terrified squeal as Spot jumped into the boat to greet her. The boat rocked violently while Drew tried to rescue the lady. His efforts were to no avail. She sailed over the rim, to land in a foot of muddy water.

Drenched, the white feather on her yellow bonnet sadly drooping and her lovely orange jaconet dress filthy, she rose to glare at Toby. Then she realized that much worse had happened. Her bust improver had gone askew and was at a horrifying angle. Even more awful was the knowledge that the disaster was clearly visible, given the delicacy of her gown's fabric and the firm wax of the improver.

Lady Westcott had caught sight of Toby as he neared the boat carrying the puppy, and was drawn to the scene by an instinct mothers seem to possess. Now she hurried forward to offer her cashmere shawl to the chagrined Miss Turner.

Fussing over the poor girl in a satisfying manner, she hustled her from the lakeshore toward the house.

The incident was observed by a few, but closely only by Westcott and Toby. Westcott looked at the lad, wondering what was going on behind those guileless brown eyes.

"What a peculiar lady, Uncle Drew. I do not believe she is made at all like my mama," observed an innocent-faced Toby before he turned to seek out Louisa.

Westcott stood there a moment before pulling the boat up on shore. Spot sat nearby, looking as though he had enjoyed the situation hugely. "I have the oddest feeling about this scene, old boy," commented Drew to the dog.

"Sad state of affairs, nephew. In my day gels were not so missish as to be overcome with the appearance of a little dog. Now, if it had been one of those creatures we saw while in Switzerland, it might be understandable. Named the breed after some saint, did they not, Cecil? Interesting dogs."

"Bernard, I think. Sorry that had to happen. 'Twas quite a revealing accident. I mean, what gentleman wants a lady so lacking?" He coughed against the back of his hand while giving his nephew a knowing look.

Westcott then realized that a few more had observed Miss Turner's plight than first believed. He murmured something to his uncles, then turned to seek the elusive Miss Randolph. He had been trying to see her alone ever since coming home yesterday. He wondered if the entire family was conspiring against this happening. If she was not near his mother or the children, she was being shepherded by his uncles.

Espying the pretty pink bonnet he recalled selecting at the millinery shop in London, he quickly headed in that direction.

Behind him, Cecil nudged his brother.

"Quite so," replied Cosmo to the unspoken comment.

"Miss Randolph, I would seek a word with you."

Westcott looked down at his niece, who decided to heed the expression in her uncle's eyes. Pamela walked decorously across to where the nursery maid searched among the milling throng of guests for her young charge.

Louisa brushed down the skirt of her dress, hoping her

bonnet would hide her face until she had composed it. "I must thank you for bringing so many of my ordered gowns and bonnets from London, Lord Westcott. 'Twas most kind of you to take the trouble." She dared to meet his eyes, noting the warmth she had found that first day had *still* not returned.

"No matter." He offered his arm to her, indicating they stroll along the shore of the lake.

"I gather Miss Turner met with an accident. I am sorry your guest had such befall her. Toby ought not have brought Spot with him, but the boy is so very fond of the puppies, and Spot *will* tag after. I believe Toby hopes to persuade you to allow him to have one of the puppies. Might it be possible? I believe it would be a very good thing for him."

Louisa took a tiny skip to keep up with his lordship. He usually was more considerate. There must be something on his mind, and she was afraid she knew precisely what it was.

Westcott wondered why it was that every time he sought to speak with Miss Randolph, another subject was introduced to complicate matters. "You do seem to believe quite a number of things regarding the children. Tell me, Miss Randolph, were your little sisters permitted to behave in such a manner as I observed yesterday upon my return?"

"My sisters?" she echoed. Deciding to attack rather than defend, she smiled bravely, then replied, "Why, yes, they were. My mother had firm notions of propriety, you may be sure. But when we were by ourselves on our own property, we were allowed to relax and just be children. I feel it is good for Toby and Pamela to be allowed to explore a bit. I have been reading to them from a most unexceptionable book. I found it in the little shop in the village. It is called *Rhymes for the Nursery*. There is one poem in particular that Pamela has found comforting. She is afraid of the dark, you know. Or perhaps you did not? At any rate, the little poem is quite charming. It goes:

"Twinkle, twinkle, little star,
How I wonder what you are!
Up above the sky so high,
Like a diamond in the sky.

"And it continues with a kindly sentiment:

"In the dark blue sky you keep,
And often through my curtains peep,
For you never shut your eye
Till the sun is in the sky.

"Pamela needs a bit of reassurance, I believe, sir. And this paints such a lovely picture of a benevolent star shining through the night. I wonder that even Hannah Moore might object to such a sweet little poem. Whoever wrote it knew what delights children, you may be sure. I hope I can do as well."

Westcott was thankful that at last he could get to the subject he desired to discuss. Her writing.

"Have you begun your literary efforts?" he inquired smoothly. It was difficult to consider that this fetching young woman could be so devious as to write what he suspected she intended to write.

"No, I fear I have had little time, what with keeping Toby and Pamela company during the day and your mother in the evening. They are all such dear people. Your mother has most graciously made many efforts to discover my relatives. I doubt there is a family tree she has not checked in her enthusiasm."

"And you have not heard a word from the solicitor in Chester?" Drew found he was not eager to hear the news of her family, although it was to his advantage, he supposed, to have her gone from here.

"Nary a line. And now it seems that a passage home must be forgotten for the time being, what with this blockade. I must resign myself to spending the duration here, I fear. Will I experience any difficulties, I wonder?" The blue of her eyes deepened in her concern, and Drew found himself floundering a moment before he could reply.

"I stopped by while in Town to check up on things for you. I have left your direction with your embassy."

"That is small comfort, but I thank you nonetheless. What must I do when I change my address? For you must know that I cannot remain here much longer, imposing upon your kindness. You have done far more than I had any right to hope." Lousia gazed up at him, her present gratitude shining forth from those gentian eyes in a most disconcerting manner.

Drew decided it was better that she remain right where she was, under his nose, so to speak. If she was going to write anything, it might as well be where he would be the first to know about it. At least, that is what he told himself.

"Do not worry about the matter. Pamela and Toby would undoubtedly have my head were you to depart."

Louisa gurgled a little laugh and slipped from his side at the beckoning gesture from his mother.

Drew stood staring after her, wondering what in the world had possessed him to speak to her thus. He wanted her gone, did he not?

8

"I believe I have found a clue," reported the countess. She sat ensconced on a delightful papier-mâché chair near a small table upon which sat a faded blue box full of old letters. She and Louisa were in the cream-and-blue sitting room where the countess preferred to spend her mornings.

"A clue? How very delightful!" Louisa glanced up from her sketchbook with hopeful eyes and an eager smile.

The countess studied her lovely guest. If what she suspected was true, Louisa might soon be gone. She would be greatly missed. And not only by Toby and Pamela.

"At least I hope it is such," Lady Westcott continued. " 'Tis a letter from my cousin Lady Eudora Bellew. She is one who writes such very fascinating letters one can scarcely bear to part with them. Hence my collection." The countess gestured to the yellowing pile. "I cannot think why I did not consider her letters earlier."

"Do explain, dear ma'am. I am most eager to learn anything." Louisa jumped up from her chair, placing her sketchbook and pencil on the table before crossing to stand by the side of her hostess.

Countess Westcott scanned the faded writing on the paper in her hand. "She writes here that the youngest son of the Duchess of Emmerton refused to marry a young woman of their choice, and the duchess banished him from the house. The girl was one of those platter-faced heiresses, and they had no real need of her dowry. Poor lad. He gathered what money he could and set sail for America. The time that she wrote this letter is very close to the date you estimated your father's sailing to be." The countess studied Louisa a few moments, then added, "And I believe you have something of the look of the family, come to think of it. Further investigation will reveal if there was a son named Jason Randolph. I shall write to Eudora at once."

"The Duchess of Emmerton?" Louisa gasped faintly. "That sounds terribly grand. Could I really be related to a duchess?" Louisa walked to the window to stare sightlessly at the view of the beautiful gardens beyond. A duchess!

"Why ever not? The old tartar is still alive, the last I heard. Her eldest son married quite well. As I recall, they have six children. Their estate is quite far to the south of us, a country home in Kent. The children stay there with the duchess while her son and that featherheaded wife of his spend most of their days in Town."

Louisa absorbed every word the countess said, wondering if this might actually be her family. She had hoped and prayed for what seemed like such a long time. All during the voyage, while plagued by the attentions of Mrs. Moss and her precious son, Aubrey, she had thought of this day.

After the unpleasant episode of yesterday, when the plain, quiet Miss Turner revealed her nasty temper while drying her clothes, it seemed wise to leave here. It had not been amusing in the least, of course, to hear the tale from Tabitha. Louisa had been very conscious of the dark look cast her way by Miss Turner, as though Louisa would have anything to do with such a scheme. She wondered just how much Master Toby had had to do with the event. But then, he could have had no idea that Spot would jump into the boat, or worse yet, that Miss Turner would take a fright. She had looked quite bedraggled, even sheltered beneath Lady Westcott's cashmere shawl.

When Tabitha had reported the show of temper, she had given a pointed look at Louisa's nicely endowed figure, then commented unfavorably on those who try to improve on what the good Lord has given them.

Discreetly Louisa had feigned a deaf ear. But if the countess was determined to see her son wed, Louisa wished to be as far away as possible. She did not examine her motives. Lord Westcott possessed the oddest notions, and Louisa had no desire to be connected to that exasperating man anyway. Yet Louisa recalled those warm brown eyes and the delight of being held close to him in those strong arms. It was not the kind of memory to bring a peaceful and tranquil heart.

And now to be close to finding her new family brought such hope. The duchess was a tartar? Mayhap she was merely bitter over the past. Louisa had dealt with such before. With the supreme confidence of youth and of one who has not been fully tested in such regard, she decided she quite looked forward to meeting the old lady. Her grandmother!

"I believe we shall invite her to tea."

Louisa turned to face the countess once again. "I fear I missed your last remark. Who shall come to tea? The Duchess of Emmerton?"

"Belinda Selwick. She is a cousin of yours, if the connection should prove real. Lovely girl. I should like you to get to know a few young women while you stay with us. I shall arrange for you to meet several I know." Louisa missed the speculative look that crossed the countess's face.

At that moment Cecil came into the room, crossing to where Louisa stood by the table. "Good morn, dear lady. I see your day in the sunshine did you no harm. And you, Cordelia, what are you up to with that musty pile of letters?"

"I believe I have found Louisa's family. The Duchess of Emmerton?" The countess raised her eyebrows in question.

Cecil gave Louisa an assessing stare. "Could be. Has the hair and the family look about her, come to think of it. Particulars?"

"Cousin Eudora wrote to me that the youngest son refused to marry an heiress and decamped to America. The letter is dated the same month Louisa mentioned to us that her father sailed to America. Then, there is Louisa's strong resemblance to the family. I ought to have noticed it before." The countess gave a vexed frown.

"It seems he was an impetuous boy." Cecil glanced at Louisa.

"Are you implying, good sir, that I favor that trait in him? If so, I suspect you are right. I have discovered all manner of pitfalls in my simple plan." Louisa picked up her sketchbook and pencil from the table and walked to the door. "If you will excuse me, I shall see where Toby and Pamela might be."

After Louisa's footsteps faded away, the countess rose from her chair and stood looking at her brother. "I have mixed feelings about this. You do not know how close I came to hiding that letter at the bottom of the pile, or simply not revealing the contents. The duchess will eat her alive."

"No use to kick against the pricks, m'dear." Cecil patted his sister's shoulder affectionately.

"I know. 'Tis difficult to resist facts. But we do not have all of those, as yet, do we?" She gave him a hopeful smile.

"The long and the short of it, in a nutshell. What do you intend to do now?" Cecil was quite fond of his sister, Cordelia. He knew full well what her plans had been and how this news affected them.

"I shall write to Eudora, of course. She has an excellent memory, not to mention that diary she has kept for years. I have always wondered what was contained within that enormous leather-bound book . . . precisely." Her mischievous glance at Cecil brought forth a chuckle. "And I expect I had better write to the Duchess of Emmerton as well. She will not answer, naturally. But someone ought to read the letter and do something."

"But what?" mused Cecil as he left the room in search of his brother.

Once alone, Lady Westcott gave a sigh, then sat down at her desk and picked up her quill. Eudora first, then the duchess. Lady Westcott was not one who believed in doing the disagreeable first and saving the best for last. At least, not always.

"This is the best puppy, Miss Randolph," Toby said with great earnestness. "I have named him Pepper. Do you like that name? Do you think Uncle Drew might permit me to have him? He is a very good little fellow, is he not?"

Louisa crouched next to where Toby gently fondled a mostly white puppy. Only a few little specks of black might be seen on his silky coat. Toby had explained that the groom had suspected the other spots would show up later on.

"I like him," Pamela crooned softly, holding out a finger for the pup to sniff. "I hope Uncle Drew is not angry anymore."

Toby glanced up with a guilty look on his face.

"Your uncle was not best pleased yesterday." Louisa wondered what might be swirling about in Toby's head. "To have a guest fall in the lake was distressing. I would hope I see nothing like it again." She covertly glanced at Toby, to see a very thoughtful frown on his brow.

"I will not bring my puppy anywhere near the grown-ups again. If I am allowed to have him. Have you seen my uncle this morning?" asked an anxious Toby.

"If you are wondering whether you might ask him now, I cannot say." Louisa had made a point of avoiding Lord Westcott at every turn. She just knew he would issue a scold over that stream affair. As though there was something wicked in cooling her feet in the water!

"You may try. My answer will depend on what the question might be." The deep voice that came from over Louisa's shoulder startled the trio.

"Lord Westcott!" exclaimed Louisa rather breathlessly.

"Uncle Drew," Pamela crowed with pleasure.

"Sir," said Toby with a touch of nervousness. "I was hoping, that is, I wished . . ." Words failed the boy as he faced his elegant uncle, so toplofty in appearance.

Westcott looked at the small lad, of a sudden recalling himself as a boy, wanting a pony and being denied one by his nurse. He firmly believed his request had never reached his parents. "You wish for a puppy or a pony?"

Toby's small hand paused in its caress of the pup. It was clear he was torn. Raising hopeful eyes to his uncle, he dared say, "Both?"

Louisa raised her hand to cover her mouth and a chuckle that threatened to escape.

The movement did not elude Westcott's eyes, and their expression softened. "You shall have the dog, Toby. And I believe I know of a pony to be had. I gather you have selected a puppy already?'' He knelt to inspect the assorted litter nuzzling their mother.

''He is a clever one, and I promise to take ever such good care of him.'' Toby held out the chosen pup to show his uncle. ''Oh, that is jolly good of you, sir.'' Toby made a manful effort to contain his joy. Louisa knew he was wishing he could whoop and dance.

Pamela so forgot herself that she ran to her uncle to give him a generous hug.

Startled, Westcott slowly brought an arm up to gently hold her, meeting Miss Randolph's approving gaze over the top of his small niece's head. A warm glow radiated through him at the sight of her admiring smile, and he glanced down at Pamela. ''And what about you, missy?''

''I like you, Uncle Drew,'' she lipsed softly, ''but I do not want anything . . . except a ride on a donkey,'' she added shyly.

His smile faded. ''I'll wager that will change in a few years.'' He set her aside to stand looking down at the three.

Louisa's smile altered into a look of concern as she noted his stern expression. She slowly rose to face him, hands clasped before her lest she betray her trepidations.

''If you would walk along with me, Miss Randolph?''

She glanced to the worried little faces at her side, then smiled. ''Lord Westcott, I am pleased that you remembered that you promised to show me that special rosebush.'' She was rewarded by hesitant smiles from Toby and Pamela.

Drew gave her a puzzled look, but was far too much a gentleman to contradict her. She accepted his arm and strolled along in silence until they had indeed reached the rose garden. She wondered what he had found to say to the plain Miss Turner when they wandered here yesterday.

Westcott seemed at a loss as he glanced about him at the roses he had not intended to view when he ventured out.

Louisa took pity upon him, though goodness knew he did not deserve it. ''You wished to talk to me, doubtless about the scene with the children. You must admit it was a lovely warm day and they took no harm from the exposure to the water or the sun. They both eat well and sleep better after being in the fresh air. Not only will I refuse to say I am sorry I had them out by the stream, but I may take them there again. Those dear children have been very obedient and willing to learn. They are all any nanny or governess . . . or tutor could wish for!'' Her manner was her customary positive one, lighthearted and sunny. Her charming smile was pasted on for his benefit.

''You were highly improper.'' He felt his argument slipping away from under him like a sodden sandbank. Her words of approval plus her compliments on the children were not what he had expected to hear.

''I daresay you refer to my pulling my gown up above my knees. Pray tell me how I was to dangle my feet in the water unless I did so? It was excessively welcome on a lovely warm day, I can assure you, suh.'' She nodded her emphasis, the enchanting black curls dancing about her head with great charm.

Drew tore his gaze from the gentian depths of her eyes to look across the lawns. It was a far safer view.

''You make me feel like a stuffy old man. It is only my concern for you . . . and the children that prompts the words. If someone should have come upon you there . . .''

''On your land, so close to the house? I rather doubt it.'' She frowned a moment, then added, ''Although I recall my papa showed similar regard. He claimed one never knew when a vagrant might intrude on the property.''

''Was your farm so large? I confess I have no idea as to the size of American properties.'' Westcott decided it was hopeless to scold the young American. She took his arguments and turned them about so that he scarcely knew how they had begun.

''My father settled on a sizable piece of land, suh.'' She was inclined not to explain her precise standing to him. He had labored under the impression that she was poor. Now that she was soon to depart, it made no difference what he thought of her. Did it?

Pamela came dancing up to where Louisa stood next to Westcott, shyly beaming a smile at them. She carried the

French doll Louisa had purchased in Chester that fatal day she met Lord Westcott.

"I have named my doll, Miss Randolph. She is Molly. I can say that name, you see." Pamela held up the exquisite figure clothed in muslin and lace. "I do like her ever so much."

Toby came walking up behind his sister. "Miss Randolph, Pamela gets to take her doll out of the house, but I cannot play with my ark unless I am in the nursery. I think it vastly unfair."

"Perhaps your grandmama will permit you to bring it to the drawing room, come teatime, so that you may show her Noah and all the animals." Louisa glanced at his lordship, wondering if he would censure this action.

Lord Westcott sighed and turned toward the house. It seemed he was defeated for the moment. To have a private conversation with Miss Randolph was near impossible. Of course, he knew it was also a bit improper. But since she was a guest in his home and acting as an unofficial governess to the children, it behooved him to discuss certain things with her.

"We had best return for tea, in that case. I shall speak to your grandmama on your behalf, young Toby," said Westcott. With the pleased smiles from Miss Randolph and Pamela and a whoop of delight from Toby, Lord Westcott completely relinquished the scold he had intended to deliver, a scold that was to have been far more severe than the mild words exchanged.

The following afternoon they were gathered in the drawing room for the tea ritual when Newton announced Miss Belinda Selwick and her aunt, Miss Fanny Selwick.

Louisa glanced up from where she knelt beside Toby to see a delightful-appearing young woman followed by an elderly lady of sizable proportions. Her shawls cascaded over her gown to resemble a many-layered silk tent.

Lady Westcott rose to greet them with an effusive charm. "My dears, I am so pleased you could come for tea. It is too long since you have honored us with your presence."

Louisa thought that if the demure glances Miss Selwick was casting at Lord Westcott were any sign, the absence was not of her doing. Miss Selwick seated herself on a chair after fussing with the delicate primrose jaconet gown she wore, supposedly to prevent it from wrinkling. Louisa knew better, she thought. The lovely contours of Miss Selwick's body were nicely revealed by her motions. And nothing was missed by that elegant lord leaning against the Adam mantelpiece. Drat the man. He could have at least turned his head to look out the window.

Miss Fanny glared at Toby, absorbed in setting out the many animals that came with his ark. The cleverly made vessel had doves perched on the roof, while Noah and his family paraded about on the deck. Around the boat on the floor were camels and elephants, lions and tigers, exotic birds and others, all beautifully carved and painted creatures.

"I see we have come on a family day," Miss Fanny intoned in a rather pained manner.

"Oh, but, Aunt, see the dear little animals." Miss Selwick bobbed up from her chair to inspect the items she thought her host might have presented to the little boy. She did not care much for children, considering them a necessary evil. Mind you, she knew her duty and would fulfill it to the letter. When she got the chance. She glanced again at the attractive man who continued to prop up the mantelpiece.

She knelt opposite where Louisa now sat on the floor. Reaching out, she touched one of the striped horses, thus managing to knock over a large number of the figures that Toby had so painstakingly assembled.

"Oh, dear me!" she exclaimed. "My silly hand." She jumped up, oversetting the ark, to send Noah's family sailing across the floor. That none of them broke attested to their solid construction.

Further comment was forestalled by Newton when he entered bearing the massive tea tray. He was followed by a footman, who proceeded to hand round fragile porcelain cups of fragrant tea. The array of breads and biscuits, not to mention tiny sandwiches, was decidedly mouth-watering. Miss Selwick eyed the feast with delighted eyes, then helped herself to a generous selection, unmindful of the glare from her aunt.

Lord Westcott left his position by the mantel to join them, entering into the conversation with polite enthusiasm. He referred to a number of local events soon to take place in an effort to place the guests, especially Miss Selwick, at ease.

Louisa reflected that she was relegated to a different status, that of "someone who has been here awhile and no longer needs to be entertained."

It was evident to Louisa that Miss Selwick was torn between eating the tasty tidbits on her plate and conversing with the man she obviously found most desirable. She nibbled and nodded between murmuring agreement to whatever he said.

What a comfortable wife she would make, Louisa decided. But undoubtedly plump before too long, she amended as Miss Selwick helped herself to another plateful of treats. Belinda was undoubtedly slated to resemble her portly aunt.

Toby had at last replaced each of the animals and figures precisely as he wished them to be viewed by his grandmama and Miss Randolph. He patiently waited until one of those lulls entered the conversation.

"Would you look now, Grandmama? I think they are jolly good, all set up like this. Splendid, what, Miss Randolph?"

Miss Selwick shifted in her chair with results Louisa might have predicted, considering the precarious manner in which she handled everything. The exquisite cup and saucer, followed by the beautifully painted plate, crashed to the floor. China tea stained the fine Turkish rug. A salmon sandwich, lemon biscuit, and tiny white cake lay squashed down on the highly polished oak planking.

"You naughty boy! See what you have made me do." Miss Selwick jumped up, stepping on the salmon sandwich in her agitation.

Toby gave Louisa a bewildered look. This was one time he truly had had nothing to do with a disaster. Totally innocent, he opened his mouth to make a vigorous defense of himself, when Lady Westcott intervened.

"Newton will see to the damage, my dear. In the meanwhile, come with me. I perceive your lovely dress is quite damp from the spilled tea.'' Lady Westcott held out a comforting hand, much as she had two days before to the unfortunate Miss Turner. Miss Belinda Selwick gave her a watery smile, then joined her in the walk to the door, the heel of one slipper squelching ever so slightly from the remains of the salmon sandwich that still clung.

Belinda was sniffing most becomingly into her square of linen. From where she sat, Louisa could see her graceful carriage as she sought forgiveness from her hostess. The girl had recognized the pattern of the Wedgwood china she had just broken. It was a new, and vastly expensive, bespoke design.

Louisa could not stifle a gasp when Belinda flung out an arm as she expressed her distress. One of the elegant vases that had stood in the hall beside the door teetered perilously, eluded the frantic grasp of a footman, and crashed to the gray slate floor.

Silence reigned for a few moments. Then Miss Fanny abruptly set down her cup and with a deep sigh rose to hurry from the room without so much as a by-your-leave.

''Thank goodness,'' muttered Cecil. ''I feared there wouldn't be a piece of porcelain left in the house. I gather that there is one young woman who will be under a cloud for a day or two.'' He took one last sip of tea and relinquished his cup to the footman.

''Temporary disgrace?'' said Cosmo, tilting his head to lone side. ''Permanent, I should say. I wouldn't touch that chit with a pair of tongs. Imagine going through life having to order new dishes and decor every month. Could drive a fellow to the wall in no time.'' Cosmo threw up his hands in horror at the very thought.

''Must take things as one finds them,'' reminded his brother. ''She is a pretty slip of a girl.''

''Thought she could steal a march on the others, y'know,'' offered Cosmo with a wise nod, his wild hair a halo of wispy brown about his head.

The two men totally ignored the others in the room. Pamela edged close to where Miss Randolph sat, as though to become invisible by this means. Toby merely sat by his ark, quietly moving the figures about while listening in hopes of figuring out what was being said.

"True," replied Cecil, casting a narrow look on his nephew. "I have no desire to spike our sister Cordelia's guns. We shall leave be, I think."

Cosmo pouted. "I should like to see the sackcloth-and-ashes bit, if you do not mind."

"And what makes you believe she will suffer the pains and penalties due to her? Never." Cecil rose and walked around the room, pausing to look out the window. "I believe there will come another day, dear brother." He turned in the direction of the door.

"Really?" exclaimed Cosmo. "How very interesting. Who shall the next be, I wonder. Do you know?" He jumped up to follow Cecil from the room. Their voices faded into the distance as they walked up the stairs to their private sitting room.

With a perplexed frown on her brow, Louisa watched the twins leave. Although she understood the words, she certainly could not follow their conversation. She had the vague notion they somehow referred to Miss Selwick, but as to the remainder, that was yet a puzzle.

Toby claimed her attention. Tugging at her arm, he whispered loudly, "Is tea always this exciting, Miss Randolph?"

A chuckle from Lord Westcott caused Toby to whirl about. "You think it to be fascinating, young man? I fear it is more apt to bore than stimulate. Unless, of course, you are a young swain calling on a delightful young miss."

"Ugh," declared Toby inelegantly. He promptly picked up his animals, and with a footman—carrying the ark and Noah plus family—trailing behind him, left for the nursery. Pamela followed after planting a moist kiss on Louisa's cheek.

Louisa watched them go with an affectionate look in her eyes. They were really quite dear once you got past the reserve they had built up.

"You are good with the children." Westcott had remained

very quiet throughout the past scene, watching with a sort of detachment as pretty Miss Selwick made a hash out of teatime. "Pamela seems to have taken to you, at any rate. I suspect Toby is fond of you as well, in his own boyish way. Little lads are not prone to bestowing affection at his age."

"I expect he will change once he grows up. You did, I would wager." She gave him a daring grin, noting with pleasure his answering smile.

"Mother said you have plans for the morrow," he said, changing the subject to a less dangerous one. Not that he felt Miss Randolph was casting lures in his direction. She had been almost unflatteringly discreet in that respect.

"True," replied Louisa, taking note of his verbal retreat. "I believe she plans to teach me how to make slippers in the morning. She said it is the very latest craze in London. A shoemaker is to come to the house for an hour or two to explain the procedure to us, and then we hope to cut out several pairs from the fabric that you brought. 'Tis most elegant to have slippers that match a gown, I think."

She gave him a wistful smile, recalling all the many projects she had engaged in with her mother. They had made reticules and decorated bonnets with much laughing and silliness. How she missed her family, especially when surrounded by this group.

He was about to ask if slippers were so very expensive, then realized that if his mother—who certainly had no need to economize—went to this length to help her guest, it was most ungentlemanly of him to comment adversely. "That sounds quite admirable. And what of this evening? She said something about a treat in store for us."

Louisa pondered a moment, then shook her head. "I know not of anything, other than I promised to cut silhouettes of everyone who wishes it. I have done one of each of my family, and I treasure them dearly."

"Silhouettes? How very clever you are, Miss Randolph," exclaimed Miss Selwick from the door. Off to one side stood a footman, looking as though he intended to hover over the young woman until she was safely beyond the walls of the house.

"Oh, not so clever. 'Tis merely a way to pass the evenings in the winter," said a modest Louisa.

"To think you two may be cousins," offered Lord Westcott with the air of one about to set the cat among the pigeons.

"Cousins?" inquired a suddenly alarmed Miss Selwick.

"Lady Westcott believes I may be the granddaughter of the Duchess of Emmerton. She said you were also related to her. I have missed having a family," said Louisa. There was no melancholy about her words, but a touching simplicity of emotion, honest and true.

"A family! Well!" Miss Selwick wheeled about, her nose in the air. The footman grabbed at a ewer that stood on a cabinet behind the chair while the young woman marched to the door, where she greeted Miss Fanny with the announcement it was time to depart.

"I declare," said Louisa in the softest of voices, "I believe Miss Selwick was less than pleased. I wonder why."

9

"I shall most definitely require more paper and ink before long, Tabitha." Louisa sighed at the tidy pile of neatly written script. She was trying to remember all the tales she had told her sisters over the years, and it was distressing to discover how her memory of them had dimmed.

"Best ask the steward for them, miss. He is not quite so starched up as that Newton." Tabitha bowed her head before resuming her duties. She quietly hung up the light pelisse Louisa had worn while taking a walk with Pamela and Toby after breakfast. Toby had been anxious to show off his puppy's growth. Pepper was indeed a pampered pup, and Louisa had been appropriatcly impressed. The newly purchased pony was now stabled and reaping his share of estatic attention from Toby as well.

Louisa reflected that she knew nothing more of her abigail than on the day she had been hired. The girl was neat and clean, very eager to please, and quiet to the point of excess. Leaning forward to rest an elbow on the desk, Louisa inquired, "Are you happy here, Tabitha?"

The question clearly startled the maid. That she did not expect such was evident. "Happy, miss? Well, an' I suppose so. Never thought on it." A sudden frown crossed her brow. "You ain't displeased with me, are you, miss?"

"You are the perfect maid. I have no complaint on that score." The girl's relief made Louisa feel guilty that she had not offered a few more words of praise in the past days. "What I wished to know was . . . if everything was all right with you. Forgive me for probing, but you seem so withdrawn. I feared you might be unhappy."

That drew a small smile from the maid. "Not at all. I seeks to satisfy. I have no desire to lose my position and have to go home."

Gently Louisa asked, "And home was none too pleasant?"

"Me mum and da have nine of us living. 'Tis hard to feed so many mouths on a farmhand's wages. Da is a fearsome one as well, stern and none too careful where he swings his hand. I've no wish to return." Her face revealed nothing of her fears or the past aches and pains.

"And your brothers and sisters?"

"Two sisters are married, and one's a chambermaid. One brother's a cutler in Sheffield, another works with Da, and the rest be too young. Da talked of setting them to work in the factory. But Biddy wants to be a dairymaid. They do right well for themselves. She could, too, if Da will let her wait a bit." The terse words ended, Tabitha clutched her crisp white apron in her hands, revealing her anxiety by this small action.

Scarcely knowing what to say to this recital, Louisa rose to place a comforting hand on Tabitha's arm. "Perhaps I might be of help. It could be that Lady Westcott may be willing to take on Biddy, even if she is a mite young. An apprentice dairymaid, at it were."

Tabitha's gray eyes gleamed with hope. "I daren't ask such a thing, miss. Asides, they have full staff here."

Louisa surmised from those words that the maid had already nosed about the place to discover what she might.

"Nevertheless, I shall inquire in some manner."

"An' if it please you, I shall ask for more paper and ink." The abigail curtsied, a grateful smile in her eyes, then paused at the door leading to the hall. "You remember Lady Westcott said for you to be in the sitting room along about now, miss. Slippers, it was?"

"Gracious, yes. Thank you for reminding me, Tabitha." Louisa replaced the cover on her inkwell and, after wiping the nib of her pen, put it on the desk, making sure the quill pen would not roll off the stand. She retracted the knife of her little ivory quill-pen cutter and dropped it into the desk drawer. Tomorrow she would continue her writing. She knew she could trust Tabitha to keep her story-writing a secret, though the steward would believe Louisa either ruined a lot of paper with blots or else wrote a progidious number of letters.

She hurriedly left the pretty pink bedroom she had come to enjoy, whisking herself down the stairs and into the cream-and-blue sitting room. A neatly dressed gentleman stood politely beside the table, his tools spread out and a pile of fabric nearby. With a start of guilt, Louisa saw that her abigail had thought to bring down the pieces of silk and cotton from which Louisa hoped to make slippers.

It was amazing to see how easily the slippers were cut out and how simple the tools were to use. It was no time at all before Lady Westcott and Louisa had each cut a piece of fabric into the proper size and shape. Stitching the pieces together was not too difficult, and soon Louisa was tacking the lining of her first slipper into place. She was pleased with the sturdiness of the leather for the sole. Too often she had found a pair of slippers worn through after a few uses.

She held a small awl in her hand, when she sensed the presence of Lord Westcott in the room. Turning slightly, she saw him standing by the doorway.

"Good morning, suh," she said. Her soft accent seemed more pronounced when he was around. She dipped a very proper curtsy to him, admirably concealing the grin that longed to burst forth. Perhaps he would smile that wondrous smile once again. The one that nearly made her heart stop. The dear man looked so disapproving. One would think they were doing something sinful!

"I could not credit you actually intended to have a try at this business. I trust you pay the man well for taking his bread from his mouth." In spite of his stern words, Louisa thought she detected a twinkle in those brown eyes.

Lady Westcott drew herself up sharply. "We have ordered several pairs of the prettiest half-boots, and Louisa needed a new pair of riding boots. He shall not be sorry he came here. And we shall have the satisfaction of slippers to match our gowns, with the ability to replace them quite easily. I vow, I became most annoyed with how quickly my old ones wore out."

"That was because you walked in them, Mother." Lord

Westcott chuckled at the grimace his elegant mother made. As accustomed as he was to seeing her with needle in hand, it was a surprise to discover she actually meant to make slippers for herself. And Miss Randolph? She had ordered several pairs of half-boots and he had no doubt the riding boots were expensive, if he knew his mother's urgings. He wondered if she truly could afford the cost. He found it really didn't matter to him, for his wished to see those dainty feet well-shod.

He watched Miss Randolph punch the awl through the pieces of blue silk, then prepare to bind the holes with black satin. There was a neat bow at the front of the heelless slipper. Drew wondered if he would get to see the dainty slipper when worn. He had to confess it was a pretty little thing.

"How do you plan to keep it on?" he wondered aloud, standing so close to Louisa she nearly stabbed her hand with the awl in her nervousness. How odd that Mr. Moss had not affected her in any like manner.

"There will be silk loops to hold the ties that go around my ankles." Louisa was grateful when Pamela entered the room, Molly carefully carried in his arms.

"I would like to make my doll a pair of slippers, if you please," she said. "She is a very good girl."

Westcott's reserve seemed to melt a bit as he swung his niece up to sit on the table where she could observe the procedures. Lady Westcott paused, needle in hand. "I imagine it might be arranged. What think you, Louisa?"

Lord Westcott took note of his mother's use of Miss Randolph's first name. Surely that was overly familiar?

"But of course." Louisa set aside her own slipper to probe in the stack of fabrics. Shortly she located a scrap of black satin that was just right to make a pair of doll slippers. "And I believe we can make her a reticule as well, if I cut carefully." Louisa bent her head over the task, thus able to block out the slightly intimidating man so close by.

Deciding the ladies did not need his presence, Drew prepared to leave the room. He paused at the doorway as his mother spoke.

"I thought to have a small party tomorrow. Just a few friends, if that meets with your approval?"

"I see no reason why not. Who is invited? I trust not Miss Selwick. Else I should have all the vases and breakables removed."

Louisa glanced up to catch sight of a decidedly twinkling pair of eyes. How good it was to see him smile. Of course, it was at his mother. Louisa was surprised a man would let a small thing like awkwardness stop him if he was truly interested in the lovely young Miss Selwick. Perhaps it was as Lady Westcott's brother had said, that a man has to think of the future. It could become costly to have Miss Selwick around very long. Poor girl.

With Lord Westcott gone, it took very little time to complete the slippers for the doll. Louisa cut and sewed a dainty reticule to match, to finish in time for their nuncheon. She swung Pamela to the floor, then handed her the doll, the new slippers, and the reticule. "Take care of her now, and mind you eat well. I promised Toby we would ride this afternoon, and you shall go with us. I declare, you are such a good little girl, I could never leave you at home."

Pamela floated blissfully from the room, the praise from her friend ringing most pleasantly in her ears. Her previous nanny, a crabby old stick who had made her eat cold porridge, had had never a kind word to say, no matter how Pamela tried to please her.

"You do so well with the children," observed Lady Westcott, taking a final stitch in her second slipper. " 'Tis a pity they could not really have you for their governess."

"You know I have no financial need for such a position. But if I did, I would hope to have children as dear as they." Louisa's soft smile met an approving one from the countess.

Following her early-afternoon nuncheon, Louisa donned a dark blue anglo-merino riding habit. She liked the lightness of the fabric, which, in spite of being wool, weighed no more than her muslin. She set her little blue hat at a jaunty angle, then gathered up her York tan gloves. There was little point in bothering with a whip. When riding a donkey, one needed only carrots and patience.

The donkeys stood with their usual placidity. Toby was proudly mounted upon his new pony and waited with great impatience as Louisa first saw that Pamela was settled on her animal.

"We shall ride out to the stream today, I believe. Does that meet with your approval, Master Toby?" Louisa beamed a smile at him, knowing full well that he was happy to go anyplace, as long as it was astride his beloved pony, Jack. The pony was a sturdy little fellow, about twelve hands in height and a pretty brown in color.

Grimacing at her balky steed, Louisa urged him down the lane, keeping a watchful eye on Pamela. Toby had acquired the services of a groom for when he rode. Louisa was quite approving. He needed to be taught proper riding techniques, which he certainly would not get from her.

It was a lovely day, though a bit on the cool side. The sun played games, peeping from behind clouds like a naughty child who is hiding from his mother. Pretty blue blossoms of meadow cranesbill bloomed amid the hedges that grew along the path they rode. Here and there, prickly wild roses made pink patches among the grassy banks.

No word had come from the solicitor in Chester. Louisa devoutly hoped that Lady Bellew would have some knowledge of the family Louisa sought so earnestly. How many days would it be before a reply might come? Oh, let it come soon, she prayed. Lord Westcott had far more effect upon her senses than was wise to permit. Of course, he could not help that he affected her so strongly.

"Look, Miss Randolph, how lovely the stream is today. Hardly a ripple." Toby gave her a look of appeal as they rode over the slight rise and down the incline to the water's edge.

Recent rains had raised the stream level. Louisa paused to gaze upon the tranquil water. How inviting it was. She glanced at Toby to note that he seemed hot, in spite of the fact she had managed to sneak him from the house wearing a nankeen skeleton suit with a brown spencer jacket. As long as Lord Westcott had been away, there had been no problem in that regard. Now she took caution. Pamela wore a sensible riding dress, plain blue poplin with military-style trim. But she, too, looked to be warm. Louisa longed to cool her feet in the stream. Why not? The groom would never say a word, especially if she let him watch the animals on the other side of the rise while she and the children walked along the bank. And if they paused to sit awhile, who could be the wiser?

No sooner had the thought occurred than she was off her stubborn beast and helping Pamela down. The groom nodded at her request, not seeming to think it odd in the least. If he intended to relax in the shade, who should care?

"Is it not lovely, Miss Randolph?" exclaimed Pamela. She knelt to run her hand along in the water.

"I believe I should like to dangle my feet today," announced Louisa, halting so they might all sit down.

"And tell us a story," insisted Toby, hoping to hear another installment of his favorite dragon-and-Robert adventure.

It was nearly an hour later when they heard footsteps behind them. Louisa anxiously checked her lapel watch to note with dismay how much time had elapsed. "Hurry, children. The groom must think we have fallen in the stream and washed clear to the ocean."

Pamela giggled at this patent nonsense. Toby jumped up, reluctant to leave, yet happy to ride once again.

"So this is how you spend the afternoon. I was told you were going for a ride." Lord Westcott stood glowering down at Toby. The boy respectfully nodded his head, then remained quiet while Louisa brought Pamela forward after hastily pulling on her stockings and boots. Toby had managed his own.

Louisa was still barefoot. It couldn't be helped. There had not been time to dress Pamela and herself as well. She was horridly conscious of her disheveled appearance. She hoped the long grass plus her habit would cover her deficiency. "Good day, suh." Her musical voice was soft and low, yet a touch defiant for all that.

"You may not have noticed, for you seemed to be strangely absorbed in something, but the clouds have gathered and I believe we may be in for a rainstorm. Allow me to assist." He tossed Pamela up on her donkey while the groom saw to Toby.

Louisa backed away as he neared her. The grass tickled her feet. She longed to giggle, with nervousness most likely. "I will follow in a few moments. If you would be so kind as to ride on with the children?"

Curiosity quite evident on his face, he shook his head. "I trust he can manage them both. I shall stay and see you back." He looped his reins over a low-hanging branch and began walking toward her.

Louisa backed away again, unfortunately in the direction of the stream. At least she might find her stockings and boots in a moment, after surreptitiously searching with a hesitant foot. If she could figure out some way to distract his attention, she might cope with the entire scene and not disgrace herself. A true optimist, she supposed.

"Trouble, Miss Randolph?"

"Oh, no, not in the least, suh," she sunnily assured him. "It was a lovely afternoon. The children enjoy watching the stream and the birds." She uneasily felt about with a cautious foot, wincing when it came rather forcefully in contact with a stick.

"I believe you *do* have a problem. Could it be these?" The odious man bent over and triumphantly held up a pair of glossy black riding boots in one hand. From the other hand a pair of pink silk stockings fluttered in the rising breeze.

She stared at him, unwilling to admit how utterly embarrassed she was, or how she wished him to Jericho. "Why, there they are!" she exclaimed as though she hadn't been frantically hunting for them with her bare feet all the while.

Then she did what any well-bred Virginia lady would do. She performed an exquisite curtsy, smiling graciously up at his confused face. "What a thoughtful gentleman you are, suh." Seating herself on the grassy bank, she gave him a demure look. "Now, if you will be so kind as to turn aside while I restore my appearance, I shall be ever so grateful.''

Drew dropped the boots to the ground, then tossed the pink silk stockings into her lap. Feeling definitely thwarted, he stalked off along the stream. How the devil had she managed that scene back there? he puzzled.

It was peaceful by the water. The tranquillity seeped into him, and he felt the tension in his shoulders ease as he strolled.

She had done it again. He had stormed down here fully intending to give her a royal scold, and she had disarmed him with that sunny smile and graceful manner. He had intended to remind her that she still knew nothing of her relatives, but found he no longer had the heart. That cheerful romantic he saw by the stream did not need to be brought down from the clouds. Thoughtful gentleman, indeed. She had looked the picture of guilt, or something close to it, when he rode up to where she and the children sat so cozily on the bank. Toby and Pamela had snuggled up against her so trustingly, their little faces intent on whatever story . . .

He halted in his tracks. His steward had mentioned in passing about the request for ink and paper. Drew thought he knew what she intended to do with the materials. And he did not believe for one moment that it was to write children's fairy tales!

He turned around and marched back to where she now waited. Her hat sat at a jaunty angle on her curls. The blue habit was neatly straightened, and he could observe the tips of her black boots peeping from beneath the skirt of the habit. Then he sighed. He must be getting soft in the brain. There was no way he was going to bring up the subject of the writing and the letters in this pastoral setting. Especially with her smiling at him so cheerfully, as though he was her gallant rescuer instead of one come to read a scold.

He sighed, defeated, but only for now, mind you. He would still talk with her. ''I shall escort you back to the house, Miss Randolph. No doubt my mother, Pamela, and Toby, not to mention my uncles, all believe I have eaten you alive, much as that dragon might that Toby told me about.''

Louisa stifled the grin that insisted it wanted to settle on her mouth. She extended an amiable hand to him as he made to assist her onto her beast. She couldn't hide the grimace as the animal proceeded to trot in the direction of home, refusing to so much as permit her guidance.

"I should never have to worry while riding this donkey. I believe he has discovered that the carrots went with the groom and intends to seek them out." She gave an infectious little giggle that brought a circumspect smile to Drew's face.

Cosmo and Cecil were on the front steps when Lord Westcott rode up with Louisa trailing behind him.

"I say, the sight of you two beggars description, it does," commented Cosmo, compressing his lips as he watched a somewhat grim nephew assist Louisa from a most recalcitrant animal.

"Donkeys," added Cecil. "They get you where you wish to go by hook or by crook."

"And blow hot and cold," said Cosmo, not bothering to hide his grin anymore.

"Miss Randolph must feel as though she is between the devil and the deep blue sea," Cecil said in an aside that was loud enough to be heard by Louisa.

She glanced up with a worried expression on her face. Those two were beginning to make sense to her.

"Drew is a chip off the old block, m'dear. Have no fear. Rest easy. As I tell Cordelia ever and anon, one merely needs to hold one's own."

With that last remark, the two glanced up to note the lowering clouds and rising wind before hastily returning to the interior of the house.

Louisa hurried up the broad steps to the entry level of the house, only to find a restraining hand on her arm. She looked up at Lord Westcott, a question in her lovely eyes. "Yes?"

"I still wish to speak with you. Let us meet in the library in half an hour. I trust you can manage that without getting lost." His eyes held a glint she hadn't seen since Chester, and her hopeful heart took rise.

She nodded, then said, "I plan to gather my paper and scissors so I may cut silhouettes later. The children wish one for their parents as something special for them. I should not be above a few minutes after I effect a change of clothes.'' She edged toward the door.

''Mother said you will play the pianoforte for us this evening. Apparently, if the rain does not materialize, we are to have a few neighbors dropping in for a visit. There seems to be no end to your talent.'' He ushered her to the front door, which again was silently opened for them by the ever-present Newton.

She gave Lord Westcott a strained smile. ''Oh, I assure you that there is.'' Without explaining what her shortcomings might be, she hurried away from where he stood. Whisking herself around the corner, she flew up the stairs to her room. Tabitha had a pretty dark rose muslin round gown laid on the bed. Lousia was out of her riding habit and into the gown in record time. Gathering up the black paper and scissors, she sedately walked down the stairs to the door of the library.

Here she paused. Taking a deep breath, she bravely knocked on the broad panel of dark oak with a trembling hand. She had few illusions as to what this talk was to be about. Lord Westcott was displeased that she had taken the children down to the stream and allowed them to dangle their feet in the water. Well, she would stand her ground.

''Enter.'' Lord Westcott stood behind a beautiful desk of enormous proportions. As Louisa came closer, she noticed there were lovely designs inlaid in the wood, symbols of art and music. Glancing nervously about her, she dimly perceived walls lined with white-painted bookcases and a cheerful fire burning in the grate of the fireplace at the end of the room. She looked longingly at that, wishing she might draw one of the pretty ornamental chairs up to the blaze to take away her sudden chill.

''I have been told you have requested more paper and ink.'' His voice was cool and those beautiful eyes held not a speck of warmth in them.

''True.'' This was not what she had expected to hear from him. She gave him a puzzled look.

''I was under the impression that you have promised not to write anything about my father and . . . ah . . . your mother.'' Westcott was finding this more difficult than anticipated. She stood there before him looking as innocent and fresh as a just-picked wildflower. If only he did not find her so appealing. He knew very well what was due his name, and in spite of his mother's fondness for Miss Randolph, he doubted it would extend to anything as permanent as marriage. He mentally shook himself and tried to concentrate on what must be said.

"You believe I am writing about your father?" Louisa could not credit what she had heard. He was not upset about the children. He thought she was concocting some fabrication about his parent. It was not to be borne. Her anger grew as she considered the matter.

"And . . . your mother. I must say, it is a fine way in which to repay our hospitality." This was becoming awkward, to say the least. The chit was looking at him as though he had lost his mind, and he was starting to have his own doubts.

"You do not accept that I intend to write stories for the children?" She spoke slowly, carefully, as though to someone who was not quite bright.

"Not really," he said firmly, while trying to convince himself that this flower of a woman could be so deceiving.

"Well, I am!" She pounded her fist on the desk, satisfied to see him jump a trifle. Whirling about, she stalked from the room on silent slippers before he could protest.

"Really," Louisa exclaimed to the Grecian statue in the hall, "that man!" Outside could be heard a rumble of thunder.

"I have been saying that for years. I am so pleased to see someone agrees with me," said the countess in her gentle, reserved voice.

Louisa blushed a fiery pink. "Oh, do forgive me, dear ma'am. I ought not have said such a thing." Then she paused and stared at the countess. "And how did you know I meant your son?"

"I am certain no one else could bring such a reaction. Cosmo and Cecil might confuse, but never anger." She placed an arm about Louisa, guiding her along to the sitting room.

Momentarily diverted, Louisa glanced at the countess. "Then you sometimes . . . ?"

"Oh, yes. But they are dear souls, nonetheless. Now, tell me, what did my son say to upset you so, eh?"

As they crossed the lovely cream-and-blue sitting room, Louisa explained what had transpired during the brief confrontation. The telling brought sparks to her eyes, and color flared in her cheeks once again.

"As though I would do such a reprehensible thing. I ought to have told him I gave you the letters weeks ago, but I was so angry, I simply marched from the room lest I say something terrible."

"No," said the countess, a considering look on her face as she motioned Louisa to a comfortable chair. She took the companion seat and studied her hands a moment before shaking her head. "I cannot tell you what I plan, for that might spoil it. But something must be done, my dear."

A crash of thunder was followed by an ominous silence.

10

"I am not without influence," declared Lady Westcott. "Merely because I chose to remain in the country, rather than suffer the journey to town, does not mean I have no connections. Eudora knows everyone. If your little stories are good, I shall see to it they are published. It is really too bad of that son of mine to behave so." The countess gave a satisfied smile as she contemplated the idea of publishing Louisa's children's tales.

Lousia moved to protest, and the countess shook her head. "As I said, he needs to learn a lesson. I shall think of something." She considered the matter for a moment, then changed the subject, much to Louisa's relief. "Now, do one of those charming silhouettes of me. For I have a notion to be preserved as I am today."

Shrugging her shoulders in amusement, Louisa placed her black paper and scissors on a table, then positioned the countess so that bright light was behind her. "It makes it much easier to get a true outline if I do not see your face."

She was snipping away with the tiny scissors she preferred when Cosmo and Cecil entered the room.

"What ho?" asked Cosmo, ever ready for something new and interesting.

"I perceive Cordelia is having her likeness done. I would that you do me as well," insisted Cecil in his affable manner. He nicely refrained from looking over Louisa's shoulder, something she utterly detested.

"I shall be happy to oblige after dinner, gentleman. I fear that when I finish doing Lady Westcott, it will be time to dress." Louisa tossed them an affectionate look. The strange uncles were becoming quite dear to her.

"Nonsense. You changed when you came home from riding, and you look just right as you are at this moment."

"Cosmo," chided the countess, "do let the girl be. If she wishes to make herself even prettier than she is now, it is only to your ultimate benefit. Hush."

Cosmo chuckled and agreed. "It is pleasant to see you so relaxed, Cordelia. I quite like the new you." He smiled mischievously at her before continuing. "The rain is dwindling to a mist. Will the neighbors came this evening?"

"Camilla Swinburne would never permit a minor matter like a bit of damp weather to stop her from doing anything she wished to do. I should safely say she and her parents will be here. I do wish Louisa to become acquainted with a few of the neighbors, as I may have mentioned before." She fixed her gaze on her brother without moving her head one whit. He was silenced.

Louisa gave Cosmo a perturbed look, then concentrated on the countess so the silhouette might be completed before the first dinner gong was heard. Something was going on. She could sense undercurrents in the room, and she was in the dark as to what they were. Was Lady Westcott bringing another young lady over for Lord Westcott to inspect? It was nice, but hardly necessary, for Louisa to get to know the younger women on the neighborhood.

"She still in first looks?" queried Cecil. He strolled about, casting curious glances at the black paper that Louisa held in her hands. A remarkably good likeness of his sister was emerging from those talented fingers.

"I saw her last in church. She seemed remarkably attractive then," replied the countess.

"I detect a note of reserve in your voice. However, I shall not tease you about the matter. See how good I am becoming? I believe it is Miss Randolph's influence." Cosmo's air of righteousness was ruined when his brother gave a bark of laughter.

The first gong rang in the distance and Louisa sighed as she put down her scissors. She placed the completed silhouette against a sheet of stiff white paper to show it off at its best. Lady Westcott was the first to view the finished likeness.

"Why, Louisa, dear girl, you have made me quite nice.

I am most pleased with the result. I shall order a frame at once.'' Lady Westcott so thawed as to give Lousia a swift hug, something that would have amazed her daughter. There had been little contact between those two while Felice was growing up. And now it was undoubtedly a bit late.

Cosmo and Cecil crowded about to admire the artistic piece, both demanding their heads to be done immediately after dinner.

''Pamela and Toby are to be first. I promised, gentlemen.'' Louisa gave the Tewksbury twins an admonishing look and was pleased to see them nod in return.

''Mustn't disappoint the little shavers,'' said Cosmo.

Hurrying from the room, Louisa began to run up the stairs to change for dinner—and the arrival of Miss Swinburne—when she almost careened into Lord Westcott. He steadied her by placing his hands on her shoulders. Louisa desired to look anywhere but at his face. She was afraid what she might see there.

''Off to do battle, Miss Randolph? I had no idea I had invited such a termagant into the house.''

There was no clue to his inner feelings in his voice, Louisa decided. Quite stiffly she replied, ''Hardly, suh. I must apologize for my abrupt words while in the library.''

''No, no, don't do that, it would spoil the entire effect.''

Startled, Louisa glanced up to see what might be detected in those rich brown eyes of his. The oil lamps hanging in the stairwell had been lit, and cast excellent light on his face. She drew a cautious breath, for he did not seem angry, merely amused. Or watchful?

''You made me angry, Lord Westcott. I am not accustomed to having my word questioned.'' She held her ground, determined that this odious—though undeniably handsome—man would not provoke her to unladylike behavior once again. She desired to remain here for the nonce; Lady Westcott offered help on every score—her stories *and* family.

''I would say it is about time. I gather you intend to put Toby back into that outlandish garment again?'' At her slow nod of confession, he went on. ''I suspected as much. And you are writing stories?''

"I told you before that I am writing *stories*." Louisa was most indignant. Really, the man was so annoying.

"I should like to see them when you are finished, Miss Randolph." The silky note in his voice did not fail to register on Louisa. He released her, continuing on down the stairs in his dignified manner.

She stood a moment before collecting herself and rushing up the stairs to her room. Firmly shutting the door behind her, she hurriedly began to untie the tapes of her rose muslin with fumbling fingers.

"An' it please you, miss, permit me to help you," murmured Tabitha. She efficiently managed the awkward tapes and pins so Louisa could step from the muslin.

"The blue twilled silk for this evening, I believe, Tabitha." Louisa stepped into the gown, then obediently stood still to allow it to slip up over her petticoat and stays. She poked her arms through the dainty sleeves while wondering what Camilla Swinburne would be wearing.

"It be nice you got all those clothes from Lunnon, miss." Tabitha hurriedly did up the closings on the blue silk, tying a tiny bow beneath the bust as a finishing touch.

"It was kind of his lordship to see to the order. I am quite certain it received faster attention from his direction than had I sent a letter." Louisa sat down at her pink-skirted dressing table to hunt for her pearls. While Tabitha arranged her curls in a becoming design, Louisa inserted the pearl studs into her earlobes, then fastened the single strand about her neck.

She glanced at the finished effect before leaving her room. Gentian-blue gown, demure pearls, and a black cap of hair for contrast. Hardly the proper little unmarried miss in a white dress. Her gown was of the latest cut, having a low neckline, with tiny puffed sleeves and a simple skirt with a worked border. She considered it prodigious elegant, believing she had never had one quite so pretty before.

"Oh, the second gong. I had best be on my way. I've not had a chance to speak to Lady Westcott about Biddy as yet, but I shall, never fear." Giving Tabitha a pat on her arm, Louisa gracefully exited the room, then floated down the stairs, assured she was in "first looks."

Cecil and Cosmo both insisted on squiring her to the table. They fussed nicely and Louisa felt much in charity with them.

She listened to the twins' conversation all through the *haricot* of mutton and roast goose, nearly choking on apple sauce at a quip from Cecil.

Roast veal and boiled haddock with broccoli followed, while she waited in vain for Lord Westcott to say something. Anything. When the scalloped oysters, mushroom fritters, boiled beef, and greens, along with apple pie, were brought in, she wondered what was going on in his head.

At last, while stewed celery, jugged hare, custard pudding, potatoes, pickles, and tarts were set before her, she ventured a comment. "I trust you had a pleasant day, Lord Westcott?"

"Hmm?" He was clearly abstracted.

Louisa repeated her question, and waited politely.

"On the whole," came the reply, while his eyes gleamed with some nameless emotion. "I spent most of it with my steward, then rode out after you three. I trust Toby and Pamela came to no harm?"

"Indeed not," she answered, with a peculiar knot forming in her chest.

"And you?"

This time Louisa definitely saw something in those eyes. His gaze seared her, causing her appetite to fly away and her mouth to feel like the desert of Araby. She replaced the spoon holding a portion of berry tart on her plate. She wanted to drop her lids over her eyes, to hide from him, for he seemed to see far too much. But it was only dinner. What could he do to her here?

"I feel just fine," she managed to get out. Could he have murmured something that sounded suspiciously like "I know?"

"I ain't going to sit with port tonight, nevvy. Miss Randolph has agreed to cut my silhouette," announced Cosmo to a suddenly frowning nephew.

"The children first, remember?" added Louisa, giving Mr. Tewksbury a fond look.

"I believe you are finished. Cordelia?" Cecil cast a concerned look at Louisa's plate. The third course had scarcely been touched. And those berry tarts had been particularly delicious. He shot a glance at his nephew, wondering what unspoken threat he had given dear little Miss Randolph to cause her to react so.

Lady Westcott rose from the table, leading Louisa and the uncles from the dining room. Lord Westcott remained in stately splendor. All alone. Save for two footmen and the butler, who were unobtrusively clearing the sideboard and would be gone in moments.

Blast the chit. Why did he have to feel pulled twenty ways when she came near him? He sipped his port in a most pensive manner, waving away the attentions of Newton when he hovered nearby.

He was suspicious, distrustful. He doubted her word. Yet another voice within him insisted that she was merely a romantic daydreamer, a weaver of tales. She certainly had enthralled the children. The vision of the three of them reposing on the grassy stream bank returned. Pamela had nestled against Miss Randolph's breast in a most confiding way. Even Toby had leaned against her arm, gazing up at her with an adoring look.

Damn and blast!

Drew rose from the table to slowly amble down the length of the room to where a small fire remained in the grate of the fireplace. He glanced out the window. Though usually still light at this hour, a gloom had settled about. A low mist was creeping over the grounds, an ethereal sort of thing that made the shrubs and statues seemed to float in midair.

She had asked for more ink and paper. She admitted she was writing. A slow smile, a rather nastily cynical smile, crept across his face. He raised one rather nice brow and nodded. He would see for himself. He had keys to everything in the house . . . somewhere. He would wait until she had gone off with the children, send her maid on an errand, and then investigate for himself.

His sigh was self-congratulatory. After all, he was only doing this for his mother. It wasn't as though he made a practice of invading the privacy of others. Heavens, he was the most proper of Englishmen!

"Are you going to come now, Uncle?" inquired a small feminine voice from the door. Braving the admonition not to disturb her uncle while at his after-dinner port, Pamela stood hesitantly just inside the broad oak panel, looking as though she might flee at the wink of an eye.

Drew turned his head, then smiled at his little niece. Feeling quite pleased with himself, he nodded, downed the last of his port, then joined her. "I believe I shall. Are you enjoying yourself, poppet?"

Delighted at this rare sign of affection from a very handsome uncle, Pamela smiled shyly. "Oh, I believe this is the best visit I have ever had."

Considering she was all of five years of age, Drew accepted this encomium with a dash of salt.

A peculiar sight met his eyes when they entered the drawing room. Cecil sat stiffly at attention, smiling faintly as Louisa stared at him while cutting away at a large piece of black paper. A candle had been set directly behind Cecil so as to place his figure in sharp relief and cast his face into shadow.

"Come and see, Uncle Drew," insisted Pamela in her high soft voice. She took his hand to lead him to the table, where three silhouettes were displayed against white paper.

"Very good," he offered with some surprise. There seemed to be no limit to Miss Randolph's talents. No, she had corrected him on that score. Said something about it being far from the truth, didn't she?

"I would that you permit Louisa to do you as well. I have no recent portrait of you and I should like this very much," Lady Westcott said in a soft, yet clear voice.

Drew felt there was no way he could gracefully demur without hurting Miss Randolph's feelings. He confessed—only to himself, mind you—that he would like to see just how she perceived him. "Very well," he agreed, strolling across the room to lean against the mantel of the fireplace, gazing at Louisa with disconcerting directness.

Cecil's portrait completed, Louisa commenced doing Cosmo. He had insisted on all the others going first, for he wanted her sight to be keen when she got to him, he explained.

Louisa concentrated hard on Cosmo's outline. She had to, or she would find herself all thumbs. Why in the world had Lord Westcott consented to having her cut a silhouette of him? It was the last thing she wished to do. To calmly sit in front of the entire family and study that distinguished profile, a face a sculptor would find totally absorbing, daunted her.

The last snippet of black paper fell to the floor and Cosmo was "finished." She placed this piece on another sheet of white paper, thankful it had turned out so well.

"Delightful! Delightful!" exclaimed Cosmo. "I should like to see Miss Swinburne compete with that," he whispered in an aside to Cecil.

Cecil merely returned a knowing look.

Drew walked the length of the drawing room, sitting down where Cosmo had posed. "Are you ready, Miss Randolph? How do you want my head?"

Louisa stifled the desire to tell him "on a platter" and simply said, "Look at the painting of that lovely woman, the one next to the door at the far end of the room. That seems to work out well as a point."

Dispassionate. That was what she must be.

"My grandmother? Very well. I am pleased you find her so well-looking. She was considered a very handsome woman in her day." Drew shot a darting glance at the discomposed Miss Randolph. It was fun to tease her, he discovered.

"I am certain. Your mother is very lovely as well. She has such delicacy of features, and a truly lovely nose. You must take after your father," Louisa said with a deliberate charm.

Cosmo laughed, then took his brother's arm to stroll down the room. Toby sat quietly near the fireplace, playing with the ark and animals, while Pamela put the new slippers on her doll. Lady Westcott busied herself with a new piece of embroidery, a pretty design of flowers for a chair cover.

It is merely a head, Louisa told herself. A rather long nose and very noble forehead. A firm chin showing good bone structure. A marvelous shock of brown hair. It seemed to have a life of its own as it waved and curled atop his head.

What thoughts went through his mind as he sat while she studied him? She knew very well how she felt about the dignified Lord Westcott. She longed to see him wading in the stream, walking in the rain, relaxed at play. Underneath that controlled exterior was a different man, a warm, caring person. She felt strongly it was so. And she cared far too much about him. Unhappily, she suspected it to be a futile cause. How could a little colonial, as he liked to call her, cut through that modest assurance and calm confidence he possessed? That faintly cynical distrust would never permit it.

It was undoubtedly the most difficult silhouette she had ever cut. Had she had any idea where this would lead, she would never have admitted to the ability. It fair tore her heart into bits and pieces to memorize his profile, knowing he was beyond her.

The last snippet of paper dropped to the floor as Newton entered the room to announce the Swinburnes.

Amid the business of greeting the guests, Louisa gathered up the scraps of paper, forgetting she could have called the footman to do the job. After one short glimpse of Miss Swinburne, she needed time to compose herself.

Had Louisa thought the ladies of England plain, she was disabused of the notion now. Miss Swinburne was breathtaking. Blond curls and baby-blue eyes with rose-tinted cheeks and bud-shaped lips were bad enough. But to be as lithe and graceful as the young woman appeared was quite sufficient to make Louisa gnash her teeth.

"Camilla," said Lord Westcott, imbuing the simple name with all sorts of meaning.

Sourly Louisa reflected that for all the time she had been in this house, she was certain he didn't even *know* what her first name was. Of course, he may have been acquainted with this young woman for donkey's years. She told herself to behave, and after sweeping the silhouettes together in a pile with her hand, she turned to face the assembled group.

Lady Westcott made the introductions with easy charm. Her hauteur was in place this evening. Louisa wondered at that, until she figured out that Lord Swinburne was only a baron, and that didn't rate the same condescension—unless one had pots and pots of money.

Miss Swinburne chatted pleasantly with the children, admiring the doll and the ark with no disaster befailing her or the toys. She conversed readily with the uncles. Louisa was about to admit the girl to be utter perfection when Lady Westcott insisted Louisa play for them.

Louisa complied, choosing a simple Bach air much loved by her papa. She finished, and rose to leave the pianoforte, but Lady Westcott politely requested, "Do remain and accompany dear Camilla. Such a unique voice quality."

Louisa subsided onto the little gold-upholstered stool. "What will you sing, Miss Swinburne?"

" 'The Lark,' " replied the exquisite girl, her rose gauze gown echoing her cheeks perfectly. She walked to stand by the instrument, as graceful and polished as a concert musician, Louisa thought.

Now, Louisa had played this piece before. It was a lilting song, well-suited for small, slightly trained voices. At her first note, Louisa's fingers nearly stumbled on the keys. The girl was not only off-key, she paid no attention to Louisa's meter. She sang the words to suit herself, evidently figuring Louisa would implicitly know when to speed and when to slow. Wincing at a particularly sour high note, Louisa thankfully played the final bars of the song. She rose to flee, then sank down again. They wanted more.

Lord and Lady Swinburne smiled fondly at their perfect daughter. Cecil and Cosmo looked as though they wished to edge from the room, but sat politely. Lady Westcott gave evidence she was transported. Louisa wondered where, and wished she might join her. Only Lord Westcott sat with a most noncommittal expression on his face. It was impossible to tell what he was thinking.

"I shall sing 'Love's Sweet Melody,' " Miss Swinburne announced with demure assurance.

Louisa wondered that the girl couldn't tell she was off-key. Well, maybe not. Perhaps if one sang loud enough, it was impossible to detect. But surely she could notice that Louisa found it difficult to follow where she led? Then Louisa acknowledged that if "dear Camilla" wished to make her accompanist look bad, she would sing at her own tempo.

A strong desire to play the correct three-quarter time possessed Louisa, and only her fondness for the countess forced her to fumble along until the torturous conclusion. This time Louisa smiled and shook her head at the request for another song. Lord Westcott was welcome to play for "dear Camilla" if he wished. Louisa had had enough!

Newton entered bearing a magnificent tea tray with an assortment of the tarts Louisa had forgone at dinner, plus a number of other delights. Pamela and Toby had silently crept away at the first notes from the incomparable Miss Swinburne. Louisa resolved to sneak some treats to them.

Lady Swinburne bore down upon Louisa where she had sought a quiet corner. "My dear Miss Randolph, how well you play. Of course, you had a little trouble keeping proper meter," Lady Swinburne playfully admonished. "However, I have observed most pianists are so stunned by my Camilla's voice that they have similar difficulty."

"Yes," Louisa said with heartfelt agreement. She could easily believe that to be true. "I must concur that Miss Swinburne's voice is most stunning." Louisa decided that she could not have found a more accurate description had she searched for an hour.

Across the room Lord Westcott seemed to find the tone-deaf qualitites of "dear Camilla" not in the least upsetting. He hovered over her, fetching her a second cup of tea and a berry tart to restore her energies after so arduous an effort.

Well, Louisa thought wryly, clinging to those awful notes must have exacted a toll. Then she chided herself on her jealousy. For that was the cause of her uncharitable reaction to the beauteous Miss Swinburne. Louisa was in love with that odious Lord Westcott, and it was painful to see him court a lovely and obviously suitable young woman. After all, he could store the pianoforte or even sell it. And they could avoid musical evenings for the rest of their lives. Unless Lord

Westcott was tone-deaf as well? Louisa had a vision of long winter soirees featuring the incredible voice of the young Lady Westcott and giggled.

"You fine it amusing?" whispered Cosmo. "I find it horrendous."

"Why, Mr. Tewksbury, I thought you liked berry tarts." Louisa grinned at him, mischief sparkling in her lovely eyes.

He shook his head at her. "I hope Cordelia knows what she is doing. Funny, I had not thought she intended *those* two to live happily ever after. But then"—he smiled at another thought—"there's many a slip between the cup and the lip."

Louisa wondered if he lay awake at night to recall all of those little sayings, or if they were merely a part of him. He must know hundreds of them.

"Oh, what a noble profile, Lord Westcott," caroled Miss Swinburne. "I vow it is very true to life." Turning to where Louisa edged forward, firmly propelled by a determined Cosmo, she continued. "What talent you possess, Miss Randolph. You can make a creditable living doing portraits, I imagine, should you need to support yourself. Dear Lady Westcott has told us your sad plight. Fancy coming so far to search for relatives one does not know for sure exist. I fear I could not force myself to do anything so daring or improper." Camilla gave a shake of her beautiful blond head. "La, I am a peagoose, I expect. I could not venture so far without the protection of a strong man." She fluttered her long, and slightly darkened, lashes at Lord Westcott as she bestowed a ravishing smile upon him.

Behind Louisa Cosmo muttered something that sounded like "Gadzooks."

At that moment Lady Swinburne joined them to remind dear Camilla that it was time and enough they depart for home. Within moments the group was shepherded out through the hall and across the well-lit portico to where their coach awaited. Camilla drifted down the final steps, a cloud of rose gauze with the ermine of her mantelet nestled about her throat.

Louisa had not gone with Lord and Lady Westcott to bid the guests good night. Instead, she gathered the profiles, picked up her black paper and scissors, then began to walk toward the stairs after saying her good-nights to the twins.

Her footsteps were silent as she passed the front door. She would have vowed Lord Westcott had not seen her, until she sensed his presence at her side.

"Good evening, suh. I shall no doubt see you in the morning." Louisa slowed her walk, but refused to look him in the face.

"Thank you for the very fine portraits. Allow me to take them for you. I shall be pleased to have them framed."

Still not meeting his gaze, Louisa nodded, accepting his thanks with a murmured " 'Tis nothing, I assure you."

"I am becoming used to the little suit on Toby. He looked happy this evening in that blue velvet. And you chose well with the ark. Pamela seems delighted with her doll. It appears I have much to learn about children and their likes." He slanted a glance at the stiff figure near him. She was prickly tonight and it was probably his fault.

"They are very direct. Children senses things, you know. And they do not pretend," she added, recalling how the youngsters had slipped from the room when dear Camilla commenced to sing, rather than partake of an entertainment they disliked.

"They left without thanking you this evening." He leaned against the stair rail, holding the profiles in careful hands.

"Oh, I was given whispered appreciation, I assure you. They are a bit shy, especially when you are near. You do tend to intimidate people." Except Miss Swinburne, she added mentally. Nothing would daunt her.

"But not you, I think. Why is that, Miss Randolph? Is it acquired as part of your colonial upbringing? Or is it merely a part of your nature to be independent? And always the hopeful dreamer?" Was there a faint sneer in his voice?

She did not care for the implication that her independence was somehow improper. She bristled with whipped-up indignation. "I imagine it is the romantic in me. And I believe in being positive. As far as yearning for the best, you . . . you, Lord Westcott, would carry an umbrella on a sunny day!'' With that final shot, she slipped past him and ran up the stairs to her room, slamming the door with satisfying force.

11

"Might you have need of an assistant to the dairymaid, Lady Westcott?" Louisa inquired in a soft voice the next morning as the two enjoyed a cup of chocolate in the sitting room. They each worked on another pair of slippers. As Lady Westcott pointed out, if they did not practice their new skills, they might forget them. After all, if the Princess Charlotte made her own shoes, surely they could.

Casting an astute glance at Louisa, Lady Westcott nodded slowly. "It is distinctly possible. I imagine you do not ask without a reason."

"My abigail has a younger sister who is being pressed to enter a factory. Tabitha wishes a better life for her. Biddy longs to be a dairymaid, so I wondered . . ."

"I shall tell the steward and you may inform your abigail that she can send for her young sister." Lady Westcott discovered she desired to please Louisa. The dear girl had withstood the rigors of the fruitless search for her family, not to mention Agnes, Belinda, and the lovely Camilla, very nicely. It was to be hoped that her forthcoming guest, Davina, might bring desired results. Really, she mused, if only she could rap some sense into her son's head.

"I intend to go for a drive this morning before nuncheon. Do join me, will you? I have not forgotten my promise to the Dunstable ladies."

"Of course," answered Louisa, feeling that anything she might do to assist her hostess was little enough to repay her for her gracious hospitality.

Gathering a completed pair of black silk slippers, Louisa removed them to her room. "Tabitha?" The maid came out of the small dressing room, a question in her eyes. "I have spoken with Lady Westcott regarding your sister, and she said you may send for Biddy immediately."

At first there seemed no reaction as Tabitha gazed at Louisa with guarded eyes. Then she sniffed back a tear and bobbed a curtsy. "Thank you ever so, miss. Biddy will be that grateful, I'm sure. I'll send a message now." There was an embarrassed pause; then she admitted, "I do not write very well, nor can Biddy read all of her letters. But the vicar would. Could you make up a little note, miss?"

There was no way Louisa might have denied that request. One look in those beseeching eyes was sufficient. She quickly dipped a pen in her ink bottle and wrote a plain request for Biddy to make the journey, then folded the letter. She would send enough money for the girl to travel by stage. "I shall take this to the steward for mailing. Do you get along well here?" Louisa was curious to discover if Lord Westcott's animosity extended to the servants. Tabitha would be the first to feel it.

"Oh, yes, miss. Everyone be ever so kind. The cook be pleased Miss Pamela is eating better, and Annie, the nursery maid, thinks you an angel for entertaining the young'uns so nice."

Louisa nodded, tying her chip straw bonnet on her head and picking up her gloves and reticule before leaving the room, letter in hand and a wry twist to her mouth. Angel indeed. More like an imp of the devil, if Lord Westcott could have his say.

The air was fresh and most pleasant that morning. The countess instructed the groom to stop at each of the cottages on the country lane that wound through the estate. Louisa was impressed with the affection, reserved though it might be, that could be seen in the people at each neat little home. The roofs were well-thatched, the house walls whitewashed, with a few flowers blooming on both sides of the doors. Most of the cottages had small garden patches in either front or back, with evidence of healthy plants to be seen.

Lady Westcott chatted briefly at each dwelling, and left pots of calf's-foot jelly and other remedies for ailments with those who suffered one way or another. She commented to Louisa as they drove back to the house, "You noticed I omitted the Psalm reading? I find it sensible to obey my son's injunctions, except when matters dictate otherwise. It does not do to upset the dear creature.'' The arched brow and knowing look said volumes.

So the preaching was left to the vicar, a pleasant young man of hearty voice and disposition, who also had the good sense to bring any serious problem to the steward's attention.

Following nuncheon, Louisa took Toby, dressed in a simple skeleton suit and spencer, along with Pamela in her usual frilly dress with pantalets, out to play on the south lawn. Louisa rather pitied the children, with only themselves for company. She had been blessed with a brother and sisters, and it had made growing up a deal more fun.

''I wish that we could play a game,'' said Toby with determination.

''Perhaps we might play hide-and-find?'' suggested Louisa.

''Oh, jolly good,'' answered a delighted Toby. ''I shall be first. But we ought to have more people.''

Louisa recruited Annie and a very young groom to participate. Together they made a very odd assortment, which bothered young Toby not one whit. He instructed them all to hide while he buried his face in his hands and slowly counted to a hundred. If his counting was a bit creative, no one complained.

''The cock doth crow, the wind doth blow, I don't care whether you are hidden or no, I'm coming,'' shouted Toby before he began his search.

All but Louisa were readily found; then she, too, was uncovered. They continued the game until it was Louisa's turn to be ''it.''

She carefully counted while smoothing her hair away from her face. She must look a fright, hair mussed, her blue muslin round gown snagged on a hedge. She had persuaded Pamela to leave her bonnet on a bench, then been obliged to leave hers there as well when Pamela declared it not quite the thing to play in a bonnet.

''I hold my little finger, I thought it was my thumb, I give you all a warning, and here I come,'' called Louisa gaily.

She dropped her hands and spun around to begin her

search, only to come face-to-face with Lord Westcott and a very elegant young woman as polished as a Grecian vase. Her hair was sculptured about her face in perfect curls. The gown she wore fell in utterly gorgeous folds, the effect quite superior. She made Louisa feel the veriest frump.

"I gather we have caught you out, Miss Randolph," said Lord Westcott in the driest of tones. "I should like to make you known to Lady Davina Riddel. Miss Louisa Randolph, lately of Virginia in America. Miss Randolph seeks to locate her family in England." Drew studied the flushed cheeks of the young woman who had captured the hearts of his niece and nephew. Crumpled she might be, but she was very alive, and quite desirable with those bright eyes shining defiantly up at him and her enticing figure delightfully revealed in her windblown gown.

"I declare, I had no notion you were expecting company. I'm right pleased to meet you," said Louisa, her soft accents thicker than usual in her dismay. Only by strong will did she prevent her hands from flying up to smooth her runaway curls or catch up her bonnet from the bench not too far away. The brilliant sparkle in her eyes would have been a clue to her emotions to anyone who knew her well. The flash from them could easily have started a blaze.

"I confess I am confused," said the cool Miss Riddel. "Westcott indicated you are a guest, yet we find you playing with the children like a governess." The word "playing" was made to sound like something particularly nasty and preferably to be buried deep. Cool gray eyes that matched her gray silk gown swept Louisa in an appraising look.

Louisa took umbrage at the implied insult. "It is my pleasure to join the children in the afternoons. Do you not ever long to return to the days of your childhood once in a while to recall the simple joys of games and such? But of course, I realize that it cannot appeal to all." Louisa swept the other woman with a composed glance before calling the children to her side. She curtsied, as did Pamela, and the three stalked off to the house, unmindful that they had neglected to beg Lord Westcott's pardon or excuse themselves. The nursery maid and the groom had vanished as though by magic.

The march to the nursery was halted when Louisa realized she had permitted that ice maiden to so bother her that she had quite forgotten who and where she was. "I believe we shall walk to the stream, children."

Two little faces cheered immeasurably. They skipped along, chanting silly nursery rhymes until Louisa smiled at their obvious attempts to restore her good humor. They happily settled at her side while she wove another of the fanciful tales they loved to hear. Louisa resolved to write it down this evening while it was still fresh in her mind.

Later Louisa slipped up to her room to discover from Tabitha that Lady Riddel was a guest for tea. She and her mother were well-known to the countess. They had jaunted over at Lady Westcott's request from where they were visiting the Dunstables. Lady Dunstable had begged off due to the sniffles. Miss Dunstable tended her mother.

Dismayed beyond all proportion, Louisa urged Tabitha to fuss with her hair after searching the wardrobe to examine every gown she possessed to find precisely the right one.

Once dressed and hair exquisitely done up *à la greque*, Louisa felt ready to do battle. She had recognized all the little signs of a female on the hunt. Although the woman was perfection itself, Louisa wondered how a man could care for one such as Lady Davina. Unless, of course, one was apt to prefer cold lemon tea to strong hot coffee.

Glancing at her own toilette before leaving her pink-taffeta sanctuary, Louisa was pleased with what she saw in her looking glass. It was an unexceptionable view of a young woman with black curls, pink cheeks, and blue eyes dark with emotion. Her gown of blue sprigged muslin was artfully draped on her slender frame. A delicate ribbon hung from the pretty ruff at the neck of the gown. Louisa tugged on her second glove before glancing to Tabitha. "Will I do?"

"More than enough," replied the abigail with a fond expression in her eyes.

In the drawing room, Louisa found the others already

assembled. Not one whit discomfited that she should be a bit late, Louisa curtsied to the countess with perfect manners.

Tea that day was an event Louisa would not have missed for all the world. The profusion of cakes and biscuits rivaled anything she could imagine. The tea was the most fragrant she had ever tasted, and the china a pattern not seen before. When it was remarked upon, the countess, pleased as a child with a new toy, replied, "It is a new set from London. Westcott ordered it for me while he was there recently. He stopped in at the Wedgwood showroom and thought I might enjoy this."

The china displayed on the tray was delicate blue jasper with white relief. Louisa considered it most charming and felt more in charity with Lord Westcott for thinking of his mother while far away in Town.

"What a dear, thoughtful son you have. He will make some fortunate miss a very good husband," remarked Lady Riddel with good humor.

"I feel sure he will," murmured Lady Westcott, glancing at her son, who was quietly conversing with Lady Davina not too far away.

Louisa sat very still at those words. Was the countess implying that she approved a connection between Lady Davina and Westcott? From what Louisa had observed to this point, the correct young woman, though lovely, was a cold stick. What a pity. A chilled lump formed at the pit of Louisa's stomach at the very notion.

Cosmo and Cecil sat silently on one of the sofas, observing the group, occasionally exchanging glances. They enjoyed an excellent tea all the while.

"Would you care to stroll in the gallery, Lady Davina? In addition to the family portraits and some rather nice landscapes, I have installed a billiards table." Lord Westcott spoke just loud enough for Louisa to hear him. He had never offered to show *her* the gallery and new table.

At those words, Lady Davina's face became almost animated. "Oh, I should like that excessively." She rose from her chair in one lithe movement, placed one languid hand upon Westcott's most properly extended arm, and commenced to walk toward the door, then paused. "You will come with us, Miss Randolph?" making it sound like a command rather than a polite invitation.

"I declare, I believe I should like that." Excessively. Louisa took a deep breath, glanced at Lady Westcott, then followed the others to the rear of the house, where the lovely gallery ran the length of the building.

The one-hundred-and-thirty-foot gallery would be overwhelming in other homes, Louisa supposed. However, the countess, with her customary good taste, had created a charming atmosphere. Louisa could not fail to note that Lady Davina appeared most appropriate in Adam's Grecian decor. Although in here the accumulation of furniture about the room made it cheerful, rather than austere, as the entry hall appeared.

Lady Davina aimed, in a desultory manner, directly toward the billiards table. Surprised that the lady fully intended to take cue in hand, Louisa continued to follow.

"Shall we hazard a game?" challenged the elegant lady.

"By all means," chimed in Louisa before Westcott could voice his opinion, "although we lack a fourth." She gathered that Westcott was not averse or he would never have mentioned it in the first place.

Louisa had played billiards with her brother infrequently before his death, but she doubted that even with a good deal of practice could she begin to match the skill possessed by Lady Davina. Her motions were perfection. Every stroke of the cue was calculated to strike the ball at the precise point to achieve her goal.

Before long it was evident she outclassed Lord Westcott to a painful degree. Louisa cast him a commiserating look. She herself was being defeated badly, but one expected a man to do rather well at this sort of thing. But although he was adequate, he could not compare to the perfect Lady Davina. She put him quite in the shade.

Louisa replaced her cue at the conclusion of the game, feeling not too badly, as Westcott had also been defeated.

"Well, well, what have we here?" said Cosmo in a hearty

voice as he strolled into the room, apparently having satisfied himself on Cook's biscuits and cakes.

"A little game," exclaimed Cecil, rubbing his hands together with obvious delight. "May we join you?" Not waiting for his nephew to agree, he picked up a cue, preparing to enter the fun.

"What say a small wager to make it interesting?" said Cosmo with an impish twinkle in his eyes.

Ignoring the gentleman at her side, Lady Davina leaned against the table, her eyes assuming an animation heretofore not seen. Still correct and perfect in her carriage, she nodded. "Four guineas?"

Louisa was accustomed to being around money, but four guineas would be the equivalent of the amount they had paid the dancing master for an entire year of lessons for the girls. And that had included deportment!

A silence of the sort that descends over a gambling table where the stakes are high soon settled on the four at play. Louisa was relieved she might watch from off to one side.

It shortly became evident to Louisa that Lady Davina was not only an outstanding billiards player but also somewhat addicted to gaming. Bets were placed from a seemingly bottomless reticule. At last the lady touched the exquisite string of pearls at her throat. "Add these," she said as she sought to double her gain.

Louisa gasped. She well knew the value of such pearls, having prudently had her mother's jewelry appraised before the journey to England. From the delicate luster and sapphire-studded clasp, these were not the sort of thing you so nonchalantly threw on green baize, never mind that you were expert at the game.

Cosmo turned his head to meet a silent stare from his brother. It seemed to Louisa that some communication traveled between the two. Cosmo nodded, then smiled at Lady Davina. He named the amount of gold coins he would bet, then waited for the lady to play first.

Lord Westcott said nothing, merely watching the actions of the others with a shrewd gaze.

Lady Davina appeared amazing to Louisa's eyes. The ball

she played went precisely where it ought. She did not lay her ball safe, as one might do with a first play. She had a winning hazard on her initial stroke.

Cosmo scored a cannon, then a red hazard, thus bringing his score higher than Davina's. His face was devoid of any emotion, and Louisa wondered what was going on behind those shuttered eyes.

A foul stroke cost Lady Davina points during her next turn. Louisa observed the cool woman actually bite her lip in vexation. It seemed the game was not going as planned.

Then the game fell apart with great rapidity. Lady Davina first pushed her ball, thus losing the points she might have made. Then she erred in playing the wrong ball, something Louisa could not credit, given the icy calm of the lady as she played, as well as her expertise.

There seemed a reckless glitter in Davina's eyes. She grew careless. Louisa winced at another bad stroke of the ball.

Then all was over.

"One hundred," announced Cecil with a detached calm. "You win, Cosmo."

Cosmo scooped up the pile of coins that Davina showered onto the table. He watched as she calmly removed the string of pearls from her neck, casually tossing them onto the green baize as though they were not priceless. Cosmo gingerly gathered the beautiful necklace in one hand, casting a questioning look at Davina first, then at Westcott. His nephew gave a faint nod. A gambler always honored his wagers. Lady Davina stood stiffly by the end of the table, not a trace of emotion on her face at losing such an exquisite piece of jewelry.

The thread of tension broke as Cosmo declared, "I cannot find it in my heart to accept the necklace, dear lady."

A dry, tired voice from behind them said, "It is not the first time she has wagered such. She did not plan to lose, you see. It is time and enough she understands that while she may be good, there are others who are better." Lady Riddel walked into the room with a measured tread. "I believe it is time we start for the Dunstables', my dear."

Lady Davina followed her mother without demur, nor a

backward glance at Lord Westcott. Only the necklace still dangling from Cosmo's hand earned a look from those expressionless gray eyes.

There was total silence for several moments following the departure of the Riddel ladies. At last Cecil coughed before he said, "Not quite the thing, you know, to win a necklace like that from the gel. She had no notion you are such an expert at the game, brother."

Cosmo shook his head. "I intend to convey it to her mother before long. I recall there is a younger sister who may place a higher value on it. But Lady Riddel was correct. Lady Davina was in need of a lesson. Pity the poor chap who succumbs to that bit of ice, what? Pretty is as pretty does, so I have seen. Alas, gaming fever can wipe out the pocket."

"As you well know," Cecil replied as he replaced the cues and guided his brother from the room.

Louisa sought to leave as well before anything else might be said. She had no idea whether Lord Westcott had been enamored of Lady Davina or not. Certainly the woman was beautiful in a cool, sculptured way.

"You appeared not to care for gaming." Westcott walked away from the billiard table to saunter along the room toward where Louisa now stood surveying the view out the window facing north. She toyed with the ribbon on her gown.

"I fear I am not a sufficiently good player to wager any sum upon my efforts, and certainly not the amount bet by Lady Davina." She edged away from him. He seemed in a peculiar mood, abstracted, a true brown study. In her nervousness, she began to hum the little tune about the lark that Camilla had sung. Her voice was true, but quite small. She had never considered herself a songstress.

"You are not a singer either," he observed in a rather distant manner, as though summing up her assets.

Annoyed, Louisa retorted, "But at least I know it." Then she spun about and marched from the room on her soft little slippers, leaving behind her a man wearing a highly amused expression on his face.

In her room she sent Tabitha off to have a cup of tea. Louisa desired peace and privacy. Turning to her writing, she penned the little story she had told the children early that afternoon. Once finished, she sifted through the growing pile of stories, quite satisfied with the result of her efforts. All the Robert-and-the-dragon tales were gathered to place in a folder of pretty pink marbled paperboard. Then she took the others and tucked them into a second folder, stowing them all in her desk drawer.

First locking the drawer, she then dropped the key in her reticule as usual. Although she doubted anyone would seek her writing, she felt more secure once that was done.

The first gong for dinner brought the return of Tabitha, who had well understood why Louisa had wished to be alone. The maid was only too pleased for a few moments to herself. The second footman was becoming more friendly, and she enjoyed a bit of flirtation on the back stairs. She was shyly happy when her mistress informed her that she could spend more time downstairs, rather than work while Louisa was at dinner.

Louisa slipped down to the drawing room, not quite certain what to expect. Cecil and Cosmo were there, dressed in royal-blue velvet with silver lacings. If they were a mite behind the current mode, they were elegant and very charming.

"Ah, the timid soul. You did not join in the wagers."

Giving him a knowing look, Louisa replied, "My papa taught me not to enter into such when it is a foregone conclusion that I would lose."

"Wise papa. Would that ours had done as well." He stared out the windows while seeming to reflect on this a moment before looking at her again.

"Forgive me, but I had the feeling that you knew Lady Davina enjoys a flutter at gambling," she said with a bit of daring. Louisa walked closer to where they stood by the fireplace, peering up into Cosmo's face with wary eyes.

"Yes, well, and so we did," he confessed. "Lady Davina is not in her first Season, you see. When she was in Town it was bruited about that she played well, but a trifle deep. It is best for a person to learn lessons at a young age," he said with a sage nod.

"The younger, the better," added Cecil.

"I had not thought to bring her to her knees, however." He glanced at his brother, then turned back to Louisa. "How goes the scribbling?"

"Well," said Louisa a trifle guardedly, "I have put together a selection of stories that please Pamela. And then there is the series of tales for Toby about Robert and the dragon."

"Fine, fine." He bestowed a benign smile on her, then glanced at the door. "Wonder where Westcott is. He isn't usually late for dinner." Cecil glanced over to see Lady Westcott enter the room.

"You are naughty boys," the countess scolded. She drifted toward them on her slippered feet, her smile belying any thought of anger. "However, it was well-done."

Louisa wondered what was meant by that oblique remark and decided she would rather not know.

Upstairs, Lord Westcott strolled down the hall while watching the departing figure of Miss Randolph's abigail. Earlier he had caught a glimpse of Miss Randolph as she left her room to go down for dinner. Now. The time was ripe. He did not feel in the least comfortable about poking around in another's room, especially a place as personal as a bedroom.

The door was unlocked and he was inside in a moment, closing it behind him with a gentle hand. Swiftly he crossed to the most likely place for letters and papers. Her desk. The locked drawer did not stop him for long. A key on his chain opened it in a trice. He found the pink folder and opened it, feeling like some sort of voyeur.

Nothing lay within but short stories of the sort to appeal to Toby. Were these the ones she told on those jaunts to the stream that kept Toby so enthralled? He set it aside to pick up a second folder, and found more stories inside.

It was a remarkable way to hide her true work. Westcott began to sift through the remainder of the contents. Not only was there no sign of any writing about his father, he could not discover the letters of which she had spoken. Where were they? What had she done with them? Did they truly exist?

Replacing everything as he had found it, he closed the little drawer. Deep in thought, he walked to the door. He peered around the hallway, then, seeing no one about, left the room.

Dinner was pleasant. The various dishes were sampled and pronounced delicious by Cosmo, who looked to be gaining a little weight since his arrival.

The guests for the evening were not due to arrive until shortly after dinner, the countess had explained. Louisa wondered at them. What would Miss Ernestine Blythe be like? She had overheard Lady Westcott mention the name to Cosmo, who had merely said, "Quite so."

Following dinner, during the exodus by the ladies, Louisa recalled that she had promised to show the folder of stories told for Pamela to Lady Westcott. She excused herself and swiftly walked from the eating room across the expanse of the hall to the staircase. She walked up the elegant steps, casting a quick look at the figures cavorting on the ceiling above her, then rounded the pillars at the landing to hurry to her room.

She preferred to be settled in an unobtrusive corner when the visitors arrived, rather than draw attention by arriving later. Peeping from her window, she thought she could see a horse and carriage coming up the long drive to the house.

Crossing to her desk, she bent to open the drawer. It was unlocked. Opened while she was downstairs. And she knew she had locked it. Who could have done such a thing? And why?

Then a chill washed over her as she knew the answer. Lord Westcott. Anger replaced her first reaction. How dare he pry like this! But, she reflected, if he had intended to expose her writing about his father, he had failed miserably. Even the letters were no longer in her room. She didn't know whether to be glad she had given them to the countess or not. Had he read them, he would know the truth.

As it was, he would have to find out from his mother. And would he ask her? Louisa thought not, and wondered how to deal with her problems—the greatest of which was Lord Westcott!

12

*M*iss Ernestine Blythe was the prettiest little thing Louisa could recall seeing in some time. Short bouncy curls of honey brown peeped from beneath a clever little evening hat with pale pink roses decorating it. From where Louisa stood in the shadows of the hall, she could see cheeks dimpled with pleasure as the girl greeted Lord Westcott. Why not? His lordship was as eligible a catch as she might find outside of a London ball. Then Louisa scolded herself for becoming as cynical as Westcott.

Drawing closer, Louisa noted blue eyes brimming with joy, and plump arms—not too plump, mind you—below her puffed sleeves. Above her pale pink gown Miss Blythe revealed a delightfully full bosom, a bosom that Louisa privately considered excessive. She much feared Miss Blythe would run to fat as she grew older. But for now there was an enchanting smile on her heart-shaped face.

Depressed beyond all measure, her skirts whispering about her as she walked, Louisa crossed the hall, intending to get the introductions over with as quickly as possible. This was done with gratifying speed.

"Ernestine, we should like to make you known to our guest. Her parents were dear friends of my husband while he was in America. She has done us the favor of a visit." Lady Westcott graciously placed a gentle arm about Louisa, drawing her slightly closer to emphasize the connection.

Louisa thought she had never seen such a charming curtsy. Miss Blythe fluttered a pink silk fan painted with full-blown roses and bubbled a reply. "I am delighted to meet you, ma'am." She made Louisa feel at least one hundred years old with her fresh, naive beauty. Watching her flirt with Lord Westcott while waving that exquisite fan about in the air was enough to set one's stomach on edge.

Walking to one side of the entry hall with Cosmo and Cecil, Louisa observed Westcott stroll into the long gallery with Miss Blythe clinging to his arm, her parents following behind with Lady Westcott. Louisa was surprised to discover a number of guests in the room. Among those milling about in the gallery were Camilla and her parents plus Lady Davina Riddel and her mother—quite removed from the green baize of the billiards table. Said article had been placed as far down the room as possible for the evening.

Agnes Turner chattered with Camilla while her parents stood stiffly conversing with the vicar beside the fireplace at the far end of the room.

Louisa was most astonished. Had she been upstairs so long after the shock of finding her room had been entered and explored? Near the billiards table a group of three musicians sat tuning up. Apparently Lady Westcott intended more than a simple gathering of neighbors as mentioned to her son.

Old friends greeted one another and circulated about the room, except for the Turners. Even the pretty Miss Selwick was there. Glancing about, Louisa observed that all delicate breakables had been removed from the gallery.

"Miss Randolph, are you still here?" said a curious and faintly hostile Miss Turner. "La, I thought you would have been gone before now. In fact, I had just commented to Miss Swinburne that Lady Westcott has been extremely generous to care for you so long."

Louisa wondered how to reply to this breach of good manners, when Cosmo popped up at her elbow. "They are going to play a tune, my dear. I beg your second dance, but Westcott claims the first, since you are our honored guest."

Whirling about, Louisa saw Lord Westcott walking toward her from the end of the room where the musicians waited in readiness. She could not begin to interpret the expression on his face. Piqued? Perturbed? Or merely pleasant?

She brushed nervous fingers across the silver tissue over the deep lavender slip of her low-necked gown. While she didn't display the amount of bosom that Miss Blythe offered, she thought her figure seemed acceptable.

He bowed before her, then offered his hand, which she

took with hesitancy. Suspecting what she did about him, how could she pretend not to be angry with him? Hence her curtsy was stiff, not fluid, as was her wont.

"Lord Westcott, I confess I am more than a little amazed at the gathering this evening," she said softly as they joined Lady Riddel and her partner, the local squire's handsome son.

"Mother will be pleased. She sought to surprise you with this little party. I am delighted she succeeded so well." Westcott studied the demure and very charming face so close to him at this moment. She was such a happy balance. Lady Riddel was too reserved—not to mention a shocking gamester—and Miss Blythe was more than a trifle fatiguing with her fan. "I trust you will enjoy the evening." Then he relaxed, determined to set aside the disturbing letter-writing affair, and concentrate on a beautiful young woman.

Bah! He said those words as though pronouncing a *fait accompli*, thought Louisa, while she smiled at him as if she did not wish to stomp on his foot or do something more satisfying violent.

"I shan't dream of disappointing your mother," said Louisa sweetly. She spun about, then clasped the hand of the squire's son in the next movement of the country dance.

When she returned to Westcott, they went down the middle of the dancers, Louisa avoiding his eyes most assiduously. Her silver-tissue overskirt was poufed about the hem, and now it floated about her in what she considered a rather nice way. Although the sleeves of her gown were not as bouffant as Miss Blythe's, they had traceries of embroidery on them that continued across the bodice most elegantly. But then, she admitted, she was trying to bolster her self-esteem. It was difficult to partner the most handsome and distinguished man in the room while fighting the realization that she had fallen hopelessly in love with him.

Impossible man. What thoughts were crawling about in his brain? What little scheme was he hatching to undo her? And when? Louisa smiled serenely and took his gloved hand as they whirled about in the dance. How thankful she was her hands were well-gloved too. To touch his bare flesh would be intolerable.

They joined the couples promenading, hands crossed in front, then performed a whole poussette, dancing round each other twice to finish in a new place. Louisa suffered him to hold her hands again as the figure of the movement required, then curtsied as the dance concluded.

Somewhat breathless, she glanced at him, cheeks flushed, eyes sparkling. "Thank you, sir. 'Twas delightful to dance once again. It has been some time, and these steps are slightly different from those I have danced before."

"One would never know it, for you seemed to make all the correct moves. And very lightly, I might add." He walked with her to where his mother sat with several of the older women, bowed most properly, then sauntered off to where Miss Blythe awaited him, fan madly batting the air.

"Waiting" was how it appeared to Louisa's envious eyes, for the young woman seemed very sure of herself. Ernestine Blythe had curtsied to her previous partner, then stood by her mother while casting flirtatious glances over her fan at Lord Westcott. How lovely to be able to summon the man with a pair of fluttery lashes and a peep above those painted roses.

"I have come to make my claim." Cosmo offered his arm and Louisa thankfully placed her hand on the blue velvet.

Cecil appeared on the other side. At her questioning look he said, "This is a Scotch threesome, a reel of sorts. Rather than each of us cope with two ladies, Cosmo and I decided to share you." He said the words with the air of one who had performed a rather good trick.

Louisa had to rely on their softly voiced instructions, for the dance was far too sprightly for her to watch the other performers for clues. She began by passing left shoulders, then the right, then followed those moves with more complicated repeats, using curving sweeps that left her gasping, especially when she found she was required to execute a hop as she back-stepped. The two elderly gentlemen were anything but stodgy.

"You do well, Miss Randolph," puffed Cosmo, perhaps a bit sorry he had put on those extra pounds.

"Indeed, very well," added Cecil as he back-stepped with wonderous agility. He hopped about as she caught sight of others doing; then she did the same to complete the movement. It was amazing how warm one could get. Louisa longed for the fan that dangled on Miss Blythe's arm.

At the conclusion of the dance, Louisa sought the eating room, which opened off the gallery. She suspected that refreshments might be found there, and she desperately desired a glass of lemonade. With any luck, the countess would have ordered up some of the ice stored for summer amusements.

"Did my uncles desert you, Miss Randolph?" Drew wondered if he dared to use her first name, as his mother did. After all, she had been a guest in his home for some time. He accepted that he had wanted to maintain a distance between them, not trusting this sensation that stirred within him whenever she was close.

Yet tonight he wanted nothing more than to forget what he had not found in her room. He gazed down into those gentian eyes to wonder what it might be like to hold her. Or more. She had been tantalizing him all these weeks. He had hared off to town to escape her, and she had followed in his thoughts, haunting him at all hours of the day . . . and night. And now she was standing close to him in the quiet of this room with no one other than two footmen around.

He admired the way she was dressed; the silver-and-deep-lavender gown she wore brought lovely depths to her eyes. But she seemed more surprised than delighted to be in here with him. Alone. Or as nearly so as to make no difference. With customary artistocratic disdain, Westcott rarely paid any attention to those who attended him, other than to give polite thanks for service rendered. He was neither haughty nor familiar.

"I wished some refreshment and noted that your uncles looked with longing at the billiards table," she replied carefully, conscious of his searching gaze. "I took pity on them." She attempted a laugh and found it possible. "They are very dear gentlemen. You must be fond of them."

"In a way. Their sense of humor can be a trifle wearing at times, you know. Do you ever understand them?"

"I am beginning to . . ." She did not conclude her thought.

"And it worries you not a little?" He laughed at her chagrined expression. Deciding he had had quite enough of not only Ernestine and her blasted flirting but also the others, he offered Louisa a glass of iced lemonade, accepted a drink for himself, then guided Louisa to the entry and out to the courtyard. "Have you seen the Doric Temple? Mother's rather found of it during the warm summer days." His voice was disturbingly close as they sauntered down the front steps onto the gravel drive.

Louisa shook her head, while wondering precisely what was going on. She knew he had searched her desk. Had the fact that nothing was found exonerated her in his eyes? Her heart gave a leap of hope. How wonderful it would be if he at last believed her to be innocent of his charges.

They strolled across the moonlit grounds, her hand firmly clasped in his. Fairy lanterns had been lit here and there, lending a festivity to the scene. Music floated from the open windows of the gallery, where the brilliant light of candles reflected in many mirrors could be admired.

In the tiny temple, two lamps were lit, revealing potted lemon trees standing against the walls like little soldiers. There was a mahogany table with several chairs. Pale green walls were decorated with the white reliefs Adam favored. She found her glass of lemonade removed from her hand and placed on the table. Inhaling deeply the scent of lemon, she turned to face him.

"Charming," Louisa said softly. "But I think we had best return to the house." She wasn't precisely uneasy with him out here. Alone. However, she had no desire to trap him into a marriage via the means of compromise. She moved to leave the little building.

"Louisa?" He stopped near the door to touch her chin,

raising it so he might see her expression in the dim light.

"Yes?" She hardly knew what to say. Perhaps it was wisest to keep silent. Then he smiled at her with that totally disarming and utterly charming smile. She hadn't observed it for such a long time. Not even in the company of the other young women who seemed to flock to him like lambs to a shepherd. And now that smile was hers.

No words of explanation were forthcoming. Rather, he bent his head to capture her lips in the kiss that he had wished for ever since that day she had tumbled into his arms. His hands slid about her to clasp her tightly against him. How well he recalled the feel of this delightful form; not too thin, not too plump, but marvelously right.

Louisa discovered she had lost her desire to return to the others. Her arms crept up to embrace him, and she forgot that she was most angry with this man. He had changed, she persuaded herself.

His kiss was all that she had dreamed it might be. A warmth stole over her. She felt on fire with longing, a strange longing such as she had never known before.

Drew released her to hold her loosely against him, his hands lingering on her body, enjoying the touch of her, and that delightful scent of honeysuckle that clung to her with nice delicacy.

"My dear," he said, his voice husky with emotion, "how glad I am that you came into my life. I really do not mind anymore that your mother had an affair with my father. If she resembled you, I can see where he would easily succumb to her charms. Let me have his letters and we shall put them in a safe place, or better still, burn them."

Louisa drew away from him, standing carefully erect as she tried to interpret what she saw in his face. Clutching her hands tightly together, she said, "As nothing of the sort happened, there is nothing to burn."

Forcing back the sob that threatened, she swallowed, then added, "Next time you have questions, it might be better to ask, rather than intrude into my room to prowl about. I could have told you what you wished to know long ago, had you simply asked. As a matter of point, I *have* tried to explain." She took another step away from him, then declared, "I believe I shall return. My lemonade is gone." With that, she picked up the forgotten glass from the table where he had placed it. She slowly, deliberately, poured the contents on one of the lemon trees, and left the room, skimming across the lawn to the house. He had succeeded. She was completely undone.

She dashed up the front steps, through the portico, then into the hall. She was about to flee to her room when she heard Cosmo call her name.

"Miss Randolph, Louisa . . . is anything the matter? You have a queer look on your face."

"No . . . no, nothing at all. I merely stepped out for a breath of air." Louisa wished she could run to her room, but that now appeared impossible, what with Cosmo at her side and Cecil walking toward them.

Cecil carried a tall glass with shaved ice and lemonade in it. He took the empty glass from her hand, then replaced it with the one he had brought. "You are a very fine dancer, my dear."

"How kind of you, Mr. Tewksbury. I try." She found herself tucked between the two gentlemen and walked through the hall into the center portion of the gallery. All appeared as it had before. Camilla danced with the squire's son again. Agnes had found a thin young man, possibly the new curate, and seemed at ease. Across from Louisa stood Lord Westcott, an incomprehensible expression on his face.

All her silly dreams had been dashed to the ground. He might be mildly interested in her. As a flirt, perhaps? A mere dalliance? He believed her to be rather impoverished, she had gathered from various remarks, though how a poor woman might pay for all of what Cosmo called fal-lal finery was more than she could see. Anything more serious, Louisa could not credit. No, but he was attracted to her. That she had sensed in his kiss.

The kiss. Such a simple word with an incredible depth of meaning. She would be forever touched by that kiss.

She *must* find her relatives. She had to, or else leave here as soon as possible. She was in an untenable position, desired and totally disbelieved.

Cosmo bowed. "Will you do me the honor of this dance? I see my nephew coming this way with the fair Lady Davina. I suspect dancing is better than billiards tonight, what?" He escorted Louisa to where the new set was forming. She found herself standing next to Lord Westcott as they made a square to commence a country dance.

"How flushed you look," offered Lady Davina quietly, apparently having some shred of sympathy for Louisa. "Are you feeling well?"

"Quite well, thank you. I felt an irritation earlier, but it has totally left me," Louisa replied politely. She turned her head to catch a dark look fleetingly crossing Lord Westcott's handsome face.

Considering that she had little interest in performing the dance and it was a strange variation at that, she did well enough at it. Cosmo led her very kindly, whispering little helpful asides from time to time.

She was grateful when the music ended and she was able to turn aside from Westcott and Lady Davina. Since Louisa was quite certain that young woman had little desire to chat with her or Uncle Cosmo, she felt no loss. Or almost none.

The hour grew late and people began to drift toward the door. Countess Westcott positioned herself near the entry, bidding farewell to those who had come. Lord Westcott joined in the adieus, standing with that well-mannered grace that was such a part of him.

Louisa found Cecil and Cosmo including her in the cluster by the door and offered her own good-byes to those she had met. They had all been kind, more or less, yet she knew she would not greatly miss them should she not see them again. Was it because she intended to depart from here, never to return? Did she deliberately withhold closeness? Or was it rather that the young women foolishly considered her a rival? If they but knew.

Louisa remained until the last guest departed, trying to conceal her yawns as best she could. Tomorrow would not be an early day. She could only pray that Pamela did not take it into her head to come tiptoeing into the bedroom at an early hour as she sometimes did.

"Thank you for the lovely evening, ma'am. I found the dancing quite delightful. Your brothers took excellent care of this colonial, teaching me a few intricacies of dances new to me. I should have been quite on the shelf had they not taken pity on me." She bestowed fond looks on the Tewksbury twins. "I will confess the affair was the greatest surprise. I had not a clue that such was in the offing. How very kind of you, dear lady."

It was Lord Westcott who replied, his customary confidence seeming slightly tattered about the edges. "As our guest, you do us great credit, Miss Randolph." His bow was as precise as an automaton doll Louisa had seen at the toy shop.

She curtsied gracefully. "You are kindness itself, milord." She deliberately chose the form of address used by the servants when speaking to him. Then, turning, she kissed both Cosmo and Cecil on powdered cheeks. "Good night, and thank you for your many kindnesses."

Skirts whispering about her, Louisa hurriedly skimmed across the large entry hall. As she turned the corner leading to the staircase, she overheard Lord Westcott speak to his mother.

"I would have a chat with you in the morning, if I may?"

"But of course, dear Drew. I shall be at your disposal first thing in the morning. Only, not too early," came Lady Westcott's reply as she, too, walked toward the staircase to go to her room and a well-earned sleep. Behind her, servants scurried about, setting things to rights.

Louisa marched up the steps, hurrying so she would be in her room before they entered the stairwell. Closing the door behind her, she submitted to Tabitha's ministrations before dismissing her. Then Louisa crossed to look out her window.

The moon would be setting before long. Stars in the sky were fading as pale gray crept into the east. Where was

Pamela's star, the one she spoke to each night? "Twinkle, twinkle, little star, how I wonder where you are," whispered Louisa against the soft silk of the draperies.

Was her heart broken? Hardly. It seemed it was far too durable a thing to shatter at the betrayal of her love. Was that too strong a word? No, she reflected sadly. But her faith in Lord Westcott—or Drew, as she had thought of him in her dreams—certainly had been damaged beyond repair.

He "didn't mind" if her mother had had an affair with his father! How it hurt to realize he believed such an unpleasant thing about her dear mother. Why, her parents had been so devoted to one another, it was unthinkable that they might have looked with covetous eyes at another. And to acccept such behavior for his father. Was it indicative of his own intentions? That was a curious thought Louisa decided it was better not to consider at the moment. And besides, there was hardly any point, was there?

The house remained quiet until a very late hour the following morning. Servants silently went about their work until all was restored to the state that had existed prior to the party. Even the breakables were back in place in the gallery.

Lord Westcott rose early to ride across his land, going first to the stream where he had observed Louisa and the children in their scandalous behavior. Or was it actually so terrible? Yes, he assured himself, it had to be. One must be proper. It was the very backbone of English life. Not for him was the ostentatious life of London. He disliked show, believing understated elegance and silent admiration to be the better choice.

Yet as he rode on through the fields he confessed that he rather liked Miss Randolph's ingenuous compliments regarding his home and land. With anyone else he might have been affronted. But, he admitted, he was finding it more and more difficult to see wrong in what she did.

Turning his horse around, he cantered to the stables, then strode into the house and up the stairs. He knocked at his mother's suite, then entered. Crossing through her private sitting room, he rapped on the door to her bedroom, then entered.

Lady Westcott was propped up in her bed, sipping her chocolate while she perused two letters.

"Mother, I would have that talk now," he said, with no preliminary to the subject.

"Yes," answered the countess with quiet dignity. She looked at the missive in her hand, then said, "I have had a letter from Cousin Eudora. It is as I suspected. Louisa is related to the Duchess of Emmerton."

"Splendid," he replied with a false heartiness. This meant Louisa would be leaving his house. Wasn't that what he had been wanting?

"Not so splendid, I fear," the countess disagreed, causing Drew to raise his brows in question. "The other letter is from the duchess's secretary. It seems the duchess desires nothing to do with the daughter of her wayward son. I suspect Louisa will wish to visit her, hope to alter her mind. I confess I do not know what to say to Louisa, nor how to persuade her to remain here. I fear that if she is rejected by the duchess, the dear girl will wish to set up her own household rather than return to us. She worries so about imposing on us." The countess cast a sly glance at her son before continuing. "As though another person made all that much difference. She has been such a great help with the children, I doubt I could have managed without her."

"What can you do?" Drew did not know what to say or suggest either. His earlier anger had evaporated.

"Her charming manner has quite won my heart. I have decided that I shall go to town for the Little Season and arrange a come-out for Louisa. I shall do all in my power to help her find a good husband. After all, my cousins Eudora, Matilda, and Millicent know everyone of worth in the city. It ought to be a simple matter to find just the right connection." She took a surreptitious peek at her son before dropping her gaze to the letter once again.

"But," sputtered Drew, rising from the chair where he had thrown himself, to pace about the chamber, "she cannot do that! The children. She must stay here to care for the children. They positively dote on her, and you said yourself how much better-behaved young Toby is now."

"You may have given her a fright with all your nasty charges. Oh, yes, she has told me about them. Pack of silly nonsense. I will refrain from saying the obvious. You must admit that to yourself without any assistance from me. I tell you here and now that I fully expect Louisa to leave our home as soon as can be arranged." That she held him partly responsible was clearly implied in her tone.

Drew threw her a fulminating look before stalking from the room, totally forgetting he had come to demand those blasted letters.

Down the hall Drew encountered Louisa as she left her room to go downstairs. He held up a hand to stop her.

"Good morning, suh," offered Louisa in a very quiet voice.

"Just saw my mother," he announced abruptly. "The letters arrived. You are indeed the granddaughter of the Duchess of Emmerton."

Louisa became exceedingly pale, then turned in the direction of his mother's room. "Do you think I might see Lady Westcott now?"

Drew nodded stiffly. "By all means." Then he paused before continuing on down the stairs. "What shall you do, Miss Randolph?"

"Why . . . I shall depart immediately." On this note she swiftly left him.

Drew watched after her a moment, his face a mask. Then he marched down the stairs to face his breakfast.

Louisa flew to Lady Westcott's bedside. Ignoring the contents of the lovely blue room, she concentrated on the figure sitting against the head of the handsome four-poster bed. "Can it be true?"

"I gather you have seen Drew. Yes. Cousin Eudora writes that it all pieces together. The name and date, the details. As well, your grandmother's companion has written in response to my letter." Lady Westcott gave a sympathetic look to the young woman she had come to love. "While she agrees you are most assuredly her granddaughter—your father wrote to inform her of all the births, you see—she has no desire to see you."

"No desire?" echoed Louisa, sinking down on the same chair Drew had occupied a short time ago. "I find that strange, ma'am. Could it be the companion who does not wish her grace to be disturbed?"

Lady Westcott gave a considering frown. "While it is possible, I think it unlikely. The letter was signed by your grandmother, not the companion. Few people sign what they have not read. I think you had best accept it as stated."

"I cannot," declared Louisa emphatically. "I am persuaded I must go to confront her in person. I thank you, dear lady, for all your help. Now I must make my way to those who ought to take me in," said Louisa with conviction.

"It gave me very great pleasure to assist, my dear." The countess paused, then added, "Promise me one thing. That if it does not go well for you at Emmerton, you will return to me. I have made a few contingency plans in that event. I dread to see you disappointed." Lady Westcott searched the sweet face so close to her. How much the girl had to learn about people. Certain people.

"Disappointments don't kill anybody," Louisa replied, thinking of that wondrous kiss and the disillusionment that had followed. "I shall bid good-bye to the children. Oh . . ." Louisa's hand flew to her mouth. "I am deserting you when you have need of me, and after your many kindnesses."

The countess shook her head. "Do what you must."

In a quandary, Louisa curtsied and left, then paused to instruct Tabitha before going downstairs to fortify herself with a sound breakfast. She must face Lord Westcott once again before she left. How to express the way she felt when she would like nothing more than to crown him, and not with jewels set in gold!

13

"I do not see why you must leave," Pamela said, trying very hard not to cry. "I shall miss my stories very much."

"Hush, dearest. I shall print them all in a book and send your mama a copy so you can hear them whenever you please." Louisa hoped that she would not break down in tears before she left. The children had become so very dear to her.

Seeming unconvinced, Pamela clung to Louisa's skirt as she prepared to depart.

Not wanting to remain under this roof another day, Louisa had blessed Tabitha's efficient ways when she had returned from a stormy breakfast to find most of her belongings neatly packed under layers of tissue. Tabitha had explained that her ladyship had lent her own abigail, a toplofty woman named Priddy, to speed things up. Within the hour, Louisa had her bonnet on, trunks packed. She took two along with her, leaving instructions for the remainder to follow when requested.

Now her nerves were nearly unstrung, what with Pamela clinging and Toby pouting.

Cecil and Cosmo appeared when she was about to walk down the front steps. Cosmo began, "Not that I believe you are about to jump from the frying pan into the fire, my dear, but have you considered what you are doing? The Duchess of Emmerton is known to be a crabby old soul." At a warning nudge from Cecil he shrugged, yet continued. "Well, and so she is. I mean to say, I know hope springs eternal, but dash it all, we shall miss you," he confessed at last.

"After all, dear girl, who else laughs at our little witticisms?" explained Cecil with a wry twist of his mouth.

"You are too generous, sirs." She had come to admire their cheerful, easy tempers, and appreciated the civility and kindness they showed her.

Lady Westcott joined her brothers and the children on the broad steps before the portico as Louisa and Tabitha entered the traveling coach the countess insisted they use.

Of Lord Westcott there was nary a sign. Louisa told herself she was quite glad of it. After all, the man had been perfectly odious at breakfast. Telling her she was making a mistake to go haring across the country to pester relatives that stated they did not want her presence. Nasty man. Never mind that he probably had the right of it.

Why she was so determined to see for herself, she couldn't have explained coherently. But her own grandmama? Refusing to see the only remaining child of a son who had fled years before and now was dead? It was too much to credit. So she bravely withheld threatening tears and climbed into the well-appointed coach, finding Tabitha already waiting for her inside. The flutter of her white handkerchief was the last they saw of her.

The journey was tedious in the extreme. The roads were abominable, she decided, unwilling to admit that the previous trip had had the advantage of Lord Westcott. Tabitha became ill from the motion of the coach, followed by Louisa when she foolishly tried to read. It had seemed such a splendid way to while away the hours.

"I fear I am a better traveler on sea than land, Tabitha," declared Louisa, feeling quite as green about the mouth as her abigail.

"Yes, miss." The maid was much pleased when the coach stopped for nuncheon, not that she wished to eat. She found a quiet place and leaned against a shaded tree while Louisa brought her a cup of tea.

Louisa ignored the stares of the other patrons, particularly a dandy who obnoxiously peered at her through his quizzing glass. However, she found the innkeeper to be most helpful once he caught sight of the crest on the side of the coach. All that she required was promptly provided for her.

And so the journey continued until they reached the garden-like area of Kent. Louisa stared out the windows at the lovely scenery. Oasts, fields of hops, such different and varied sights met her curious eyes.

Then they arrived.

Emmerton Hall was possessed of a magnificent parkland. Louisa could see horse-chestnut trees, tall beeches and lime trees, and a magnolia such as she had known in Virginia. The road ran along the mile-long lake until the coach came to a halt before the front of the house. The residence had turrets similar to Westcott Park's at the four corners, but there began the difference, for it was an enormous place. It was impressive, even considering the elegance of Westcott Park.

Louisa glanced at Tabitha, motioning the wan-looking maid to follow closely behind her. Crossing a narrow stone bridge, they walked through a passageway to enter a courtyard. The doors of the house opened with a majestic sweep, a distinguished butler appeared, looking down his nose at Louisa with hauteur. Naturally he had been informed of the crest on the side panel of the coach, or Louisa suspected she would have found herself standing at the door in vain.

"I am Louisa Randolph, granddaughter of the Duchess of Emmerton. I would see her, please." Louisa gave the starchy old butler her customary sweet smile, then sailed past him into the hall.

That he was not accustomed to such behavior was amusingly plain. Louisa stood with quiet dignity as he darted little glances at her, perhaps deciding whether to chuck her out on her head or not.

"Wait here," he intoned with basso solemnity.

Not daring to exchange glances with her maid lest she burst into giggles, Louisa composed herself on an oak settle. Not far from where she sat, the spreading double flights of a staircase winged upward. The butler had marched up to the left to find his mistress.

Louisa was on the verge of rising to explore the hall after sitting for what seemed an age, for waiting had never been one of her better occupations. About to get up, she subsided when a woman of middle years came down behind the butler. Beneath a plain muslin cap her hair was drawn back into an uncompromising bun at the nape of her neck. A drab gray muslin dress did nothing for a sallow complexion nor fine pale green eyes. She silently walked forward to inspect Louisa, then spoke. "I do not know why you are come."

"I wish to see my grandmother." Louisa rose to confront her, not wanting to be talked down to like some schoolchild.

"Did you not receive our letter? She has no desire to see you." Was that a look of pity in those strange eyes?

"But I wish to see her," repeated Louisa with all the conviction of one very young who is certain of success.

There was no mistaking the look of faint admiration that appeared on the faded face. Louisa walked forward to face the companion, as she judged the woman to be. "Will you give her a message?"

The woman shrugged. "I can but try. By the by, Miss Randolph, I am Miss Perry."

"I should like to refresh myself," stated Louisa, hoping to remove some of the fatigue of her traveling. "We have made a long journey."

The look returned plainly said that it was Louisa's own fault if she felt tired and mussed. "Come with me."

Motioning Tabitha to follow, Louisa trailed up the impressive oak staircase after Miss Perry. Ushered into a charming room done in pale gray and blue, Louisa found herself alone with Tabitha.

Louisa found herself wondering where the six grandchildren that Lady Westcott had mentioned were hidden. Undoubtedly they were kept in a remote nursery and brought down once a year at Christmas, such as she had heard was done in many cases. She would have liked to see them.

The maid set about unpacking the portmanteau she had carried up with her. "I don't know, miss. I can feel the nastiness about this place. Fair gives me the creeps, it does."

"I know what you mean, for I sense it as well. That poor woman, Miss Perry." Louisa shook her head as she stood by the window gazing out at the parkland. "My grandmother cannot be a kind person to permit her to be dressed in such a poor manner. My mama would never have allowed it. Our servants were always prettily dressed. Mama said it cheered her to see them bustling about the house in gay colors."

"I think the countess was right, miss. We ought to have

stayed at Westcott. My sister Biddy was due to come."

"I am sorry for that, but you must see I had little choice. I have no claim on the countess." Or her son, Louisa added silently. How it had hurt that Lord Westcott had failed to say good-bye. He had spoken those harsh words at the breakfast table, condemning her for foolishness, when he must have known she had no other path.

Nearly an hour had passed and Louisa was becoming hungry, wishing they had thought to stop at an inn before entering the Emmerton land. Could she be so bold as to order something brought to her room?

Then came a rap at her door. She hastily crossed to open it, and found Miss Perry again.

"Follow me."

There was no explanation. Louisa smoothed the pretty rose muslin gown she had put on, and walked behind Miss Perry. How strange to think of her papa living in this grand house. Not that their home in Virginia had been poor. Rather it had been opulent on a different scale. It had broad verandas with tall pillars in front of the house. Neat brick had been ornamented with stark white moldings about doors and windows in the fashion made popular during the reign of Queen Anne.

They passed through an anteroom, then into a large drawing room with tall many-paned windows draped with pale gray taffeta. There was a thin elderly lady seated by the fireplace, where even on a summer day a fire burned in the grate.

Louisa examined the woman who was her father's mother. She had something of his look about her. The eyes, Louisa thought. Those deep blue eyes ran in the family. Her soft gray silk sack gown was of a fashion set some years before. It had a square-cut décolletage covered by a white handkerchief, and short sleeves with deep ruffles ending just above the wrists. The single gray bow at the front of her bodice seemed almost frivolous considering the rest of her garb. Beneath the plain muslin cap was a much-lined face. The thin line of her mouth was compressed in disapproval.

Her face wore a displeased expression; even her nose was

pinched with disdain. The duchess had been equally busy examining Louisa. "You are a defiant miss. What have you to say for yourself?"

"My family in Virginia died of the yellow fever, ma'am. I believed it prudent to seek my family in England as my mama instructed," Louisa stated in firm tones.

The old lady gave no outward sign that the news of her son's death had affected her in any way. This was something the tenderhearted Louisa could not like.

"Well, I shan't take you," the duchess said bluntly. "I have enough, what with those others hanging around, waiting for my funeral. I'll fool them. Don't intend to die for a long time yet. Right, Perry?" The old lady cast a malevolent glance at her companion. Louisa could only pity the poor woman, so obviously despised.

"Yes, madam." Miss Perry rose to tug a bell-pull by the fireplace. In minutes a footman entered bearing a tray holding a rather sparse tea.

Louisa suppressed the desire to hungrily pop the dainty slices of buttered bread and tiny pastries into her mouth. Instead, she forced herself to nibble her way slowly through as many bits of food as she could sneak onto her plate without her grandmother catching sight of her. She just knew the old woman would make some unkind remark about Louisa's unseemly appetite.

There were no words exchanged while the duchess sipped her tea and ate surprisingly well of the food. The serving plates were empty when she signaled for the things to be cleared.

Nervously Louisa fingered the treble ruff at the neck of her gown, the ruffles on her sleeves falling back to reveal very dainty wrists. She was conscious again of the half-lidded stare from the old woman. It made Louisa wonder if the neat rose gown she wore was quite the thing. Did her petticoat peep out a trifle too much? Was the tucked hem overdone?

At last the duchess spoke. "You have been staying with Cordelia Shalford. She still pretty?"

It took Louisa a moment to realize that Cordelia Shalford was indeed the Countess Westcott. "I have, and she is. She is also kind and gracious. Her husband visited my parents in America. He was a delightful person. I was very sorry to learn of his death. I had hoped he would be able to help me locate you. You see,'' Louisa said with a deliberate care, ''my papa never mentioned you. Countess Westcott said he had written to you to apprise you of our births. I did not know that. I had nothing much to go on but Papa's names and the date of his sailing. I supposed my English family would accept me.''

''And now you know otherwise,'' said the duchess with a touch of asperity.

''As you say, ma'am.'' Louisa tilted up her chin. She would not succumb to the bereft feeling creeping over her.

''You are a very foolish girl.''

''So Lord Westcott informed me,'' Louisa replied dryly.

''It would have been better had you made a suitable marriage in Virginia, used that plantation your father owned to attract a man of wealth and position. Here you have nothing.''

''On the contrary,'' denied Louisa, a fire lighting in her lovely eyes. ''I have a sizable fortune and am not ugly. I suspect that with a sponsor I shall make a respectable marriage.''

''I shan't do it,'' declared the duchess. ''The duke won't either. Nor will that widgeon of a daughter of mine. Stupid enough to accept Selwick. She has a daughter of her own to launch.'' The words were snapped out in crisp order.

''I have met her,'' answered Louisa in a subdued voice. Her grandmama had known a good deal about her American son's family, it seemed. And yet she would have nothing to do with Louisa. The knowledge hurt.

In spite of the fire burning merrily in the grate, the room felt chilly. Louisa wished she had a shawl about her shoulders. Perhaps it was the gray atmosphere which lent its gloom, or the diapproving glare from her grandmama, or both. Miss Perry possessed no expression whatsoever that Louisa could detect. Her face was like a slate that had been wiped clean.

"It is too late in the day for you to leave now," barked the duchess, startling Louisa from her thoughts. "You may stay overnight. But you will leave tomorrow." Then, very softly, mostly to herself, the duchess added, "Jason was a scamp, but a good scamp. He would have been made, had he married that girl."

From those words, Louisa decided that his mother had never forgiven her son for not marrying where she wished.

The bedroom assigned to Louisa was quite comfortable. As the shadows lengthened, Tabitha rang for a dinner to be served. Louisa had accepted Miss Perry's suggestion that dinner in her room was to be preferred. The tray was placed on a small table near the window.

As she nibbled away at the roast chicken and boiled potatoes, Louisa considered her next step. It was so difficult to know what was best. Perhaps she ought to return to seek the advice of Lady Westcott. Could Louisa offer those cousins who resided in London payment of some sort to sponsor her? She knew that as the granddaughter of the Duchess of Emmerton and possessing a fortune, she would be accepted anywhere.

The sun was setting over the trees. Below her window, the artificial lake sparkled with ribbons of orange and yellow. A flock of birds rose to find an evening meal before night descended. It was beautiful, yet very lonely. Not one person could be seen.

Had it been hard for her father to give up his home? She supposed he had accepted that he must do so at any rate, since his brother would inherit this pile of stone. From what Cosmo had said, that gentleman, the present duke, rarely made an appearance here. Louisa could understand his reluctance if today was an example. The old lady could scarce have been less welcoming.

In the morning even the sky had turned an unwelcoming gray. Louisa decided she could not be unhappy to leave the house, no matter it was where her dear papa had grown up. How naive she had been to think that just because he had been so loving and kind, the remainder of his family would be as well. As Lord Westcott had said, she was foolish in the extreme.

Miss Perry greeted Louisa as she reached the lower hall, indicating that Louisa follow her to the breakfast room. Somehow Louisa was not surprised to discover the walls painted pale gray, with blue-and-gray-print curtains at the windows.

"Enjoy your meal. I . . . I am sorry things did not go better for you. I can imagine what hopes you pinned upon this visit. It was a waste, I fear. Her grace has become more and more the recluse." Then the companion clamped her mouth shut after catching sight of the butler near the door with the pot of tea. She whirled about and rushed from the room with only a hasty good-bye as she went through the doorway.

Following a breakfast of toast and tea, Louisa and Tabitha set out for the west and north in the coach. By the time they had left the property, a gray drizzle had begun to fall. When they passed through Royal Tunbridge Wells, the drizzle had become a downpour. With the roads less than excellent, Louisa decided to put up at an inn there.

Unable to tolerate the confines of her small, though clean room, Louisa donned a pelisse, took an umbrella, and strolled along the pantiles paid for by Queen Anne long ago. Louisa found she was able to avoid the worst of the rain by walking underneath the generous overhang of the shops. Espying a toy shop, she entered to buy Pamela and Toby each a surprise. A book about ships for Toby and a spinning top for Pamela were chosen with care.

She had missed them both. She had missed them all, she admitted as she returned to the inn after buying a bottle of honeysuckle essence plus a vial of the countess's favorite scent at the perfumer's shop.

Another morning saw drizzle once again, but Louisa was set upon resuming the trip. So they bypassed London, then drove north for what seemed like a month until they reached the village of Westcott in the midst of a rain.

Louisa glanced uneasily at Tabitha, who appeared to be

on her way to becoming a seasoned traveler. Rather than the pea green of the trip south, she was now a shade of gray.

"Well, we are nearly there. I am sorry it turned out as it did, but I am glad I went." At Tabitha's plainly disbelieving stare, Louisa said defensively, "I should not have accepted what manner of person my grandmama was unless I had seen for myself. And besides, it was interesting to see where my papa had been born and raised."

Tabitha merely sniffed and peered out the window as the coach entered the long approach to the house.

Louisa leaned against the squabs, reluctant to gaze upon the house. Where had all her girlish dreams gone? What had happened to that romantic idealist who was so certain her own kin could not reject her? Now she did not even accept the notion of a happy marriage. Rather she would hope that she might find an agreeable husband who would not spend her into poverty in a few years' time.

Of course, she considered, she might take a pretty house in the country and remain in single blessedness. Not that there was anything particularly good in the single state. But perhaps it might be the preferable course.

They had arrived. Louisa descended from the coach feeling travel-worn, and as though she had been away for a year rather than about two weeks. Although she was not expected, Louisa thought that at least Newton might have been there to greet them.

The door opened and Lord Westcott stood watching.

Head down, Louisa dashed through puddles, then underneath the portico, then again through the rain, cannoning right into him.

She raised her surprised face to look at him. "Good afternoon, suh."

He steadied her on her feet, then pulled her inside out of the damp after allowing Tabitha to scurry inside carrying the portmanteau that held the presents and Louisa's jewel case.

Watching her abigail disappear around the corner, Louisa wished she might follow her immediately.

"You came back. May I ask the reason?"

She lifted her chin a trifle and glared politely into his eyes. "I seek your mother's advice. Besides, the coach had to be returned at any rate."

"You seem a bit thinner," he said with a frown. "Did they not feed you while you were gone?"

Louisa took a few steps from his side, then turned. "I am not the best of travelers, I fear. And the evening I spent at my grandmama's house was not one to make Uncle Cosmo sigh with envy. I vow I longed for your cook's collops and Madeira cake."

The frown deepened. He was about to say more when Cosmo and Cecil entered the hall.

"Ah, you return!" declared Cecil, studying her with care. "I gather your trip was less than successful."

Louisa nodded. "The message was true. My grandmama cares not to have me near."

"Never too late to learn," declared Cosmo.

"You must be tired, my dear. Allow me to inform Cordelia that you are with us again. We shall see you later at tea," Cecil said after a dark look at his brother.

Thinking of the vast difference between Emmerton Hall and Westcott Park in the concept of tea, Louisa smiled. "I will be down in time, suh."

When Louisa had left the area, the three men strolled along to the library. Cosmo and Cecil walked to the window to look out at the rain-washed gardens and the graveled drive beyond.

"What will she do now, do you suppose?" queried Cecil of Westcott.

"My mother said something about taking her to London, but I cannot credit that. You know how Mother hates to travel." He shared an amused look with his uncles. His expression grew concerned as he considered the problem.

"Expecting guests, dear boy?" inquired Cecil as he observed a carriage coming up the drive through the drizzle.

"Not that I know. It may be someone for Mother." Lord Westcott joined them at the window to watch the coach draw up before the house. Rather plainly dressed servants, the sort one can hire complete with livery, hopped down to open the door. Westcott narrowed his eyes thoughtfully as he saw the tall thin man who exited. Where had he seen him before?

Behind the young man a similarly thin woman—most likely his mother—climbed from the coach, obviously complaining about something, judging her countenance and her companion's expression.

He swiftly left the room and marched along the passage to the entrance hall in time to hear a distinctly American voice inquire about the possibility of viewing the house. He sighed. Americans again. They seemed to make a pilgrimage of going from one great house to another, asking to be allowed to view the contents and grounds, happily paying the fees demanded by housekeepers or butlers while their owners were away. He walked forward.

Dismissing Newton with a slight motion, Westcott sought to satisfy his curiosity. He knew he had seen the man not too long ago. But where? "Please come in. Usually I do not permit the house to be viewed unless we are gone. But as that happens so rarely, I shall make an exception."

The woman now took notice of the heraldic emblem on the far wall, exclaiming, "That's it!" She pointed a dramatic finger. "I knew this would be the place. We insist upon seeing Miss Randolph. What have you done with her?" The woman's voice rose in volume and degree. She appeared on the verge of apoplexy.

"Done with her?" echoed a confused Lord Westcott. "I beg your pardon," he said with all the hauteur of a peer of the realm.

Giving his mother a long-suffering look, the gentleman spoke. "I am Aubrey Moss. My mother and I made the acquaintance of Miss Randolph on the ship traveling to England. We sought to protect her from the importunings of those less well-fixed on board. It is difficult for a wealthy young woman to travel alone. Her maid had failed to make the trip at the last moment, so Mother watched over her. She was not without chaperonage at any time," he declared, quite obviously feeling virtuous about the whole thing.

"Wealthy?" asked Westcott, his voice rather quiet.

"As a nabob. Came from a fine Virginia family, rich as

could be. Then they up and died, leaving her the plantation and all else, which she sold for a fortune. She said she was going to find her family." Now Mr. Moss cast an accusing look at Lord Westcott. "Where is she?"

"She found her family," said Cecil from the entrance to the hall.

"We desire to see the dear girl," simpered a hastily recovered Mrs. Moss. "She had such sweet manners. My Aubrey was quite taken with her."

Cecil and Cosmo exchanged guarded looks.

At that moment Lady Westcott floated into the hall. She wore a deep lavender gown of fine muslin with a silver-and-purple turban. Her eyes were sparkling with happiness. "Drew, can it be true? Did Louisa at last return?"

"Then she is here!" declared a triumphant Mrs. Moss. A significant glance was exchanged between her and her gangling son.

Lady Westcott moved closer as she gave Westcott a questioning look.

"Lady Westcott, Mrs. and Mr. Moss of America. They claim to know our Miss Randolph." Drew raised a brow that relayed oceans of information to his astute mother.

"How lovely. Do join us in the drawing room for tea while we find out all about your trip." She offered a regal nod of her head, then motioned them all to join her in the exodus.

Cecil watched the parade leave the room, taking careful note of the skinny Mrs. Moss as she evaluated every article in passing. "Looks like she's about to put it all to auction," he grumbled to his brother.

"He's a queer fish, if you ask me," said Cosmo. "Hardly of the first water, y'know."

"Hmm," agreed Cecil. "Best protect Louisa as we can. We shall keep our ears and eyes open, brother." Their gaze met in total understanding and they walked off to the drawing room looking very much like two conspirators plotting the downfall of Mr. Moss, not to mention his upstart mother.

They entered the room about the same time as Lady Westcott was announcing her plans.

"I intend to take Louisa to London and launch her with

great style. My dearest cousins have entrée simply everywhere, and my son knows ever so many eligible gentlemen. I mean to see Louisa suitably wed to a member of the *ton*." She bestowed a gracious smile on Mrs. Moss that had that dear lady in a state.

"But Aubrey . . ." sputtered the thin woman, resembling a gasping eel.

"I gather he has not spoken to her. For Louisa has become very close to me and she said nothing of any such affinity." The hauteur was now present in Lady Westcott's voice in full measure. It had intimidated far lesser persons than the humble Moss pair.

Not one of the assembled flock took notice of the pale girl who paused in the doorway. Her whispered "Oh, dear!" wasn't heard by anyone but Newton.

14

"Good afternoon." Louisa entered the room with a degree of caution. Not knowing what had been said by any of the parties present before she overheard the dramatic announcement by the countess, she decided to say as little as possible for the moment.

The group clustered about the tea table at the far end of the drawing room turned to see Louisa standing just inside the door, Newton directly behind her. At once a babble of voices broke out.

Mrs. Moss possessed the loudest. "Dearest girl, we have been so concerned. Mark my words, I said to my Aubrey, something has happened to her. Oh, the anguish I have known. The pain I have suffered." The good lady dramatically held up a cambric handkerchief to her forehead, looking ready to have a spasm at the very least.

Not wishing to appear coldhearted, Louisa reached out a tender hand. "Dear Mrs. Moss, please do not distress yourself so. For did I not tell you I would seek a solicitor and my family?"

Mrs. Moss drew herself up as stiff as a tree trunk and stared down that remarkably thin nose. "But, my dear, you ought to have known how very concerned we were for you."

Louisa wished she could cry out that she had not desired their protection, that she had detested their oversolicitous hovering. How maddening it had been to be required to sneak away from them for a few moments' peace. She was saved from a reply by Cosmo.

"I can see where it placed you in a bit of a cleft stick, madam. But you must know our dear Louisa is practically family. In a word, we could scarcely manage without her." Cosmo bowed his rotund form in the direction of Mrs. Moss, quite overwhelming the lady when she perceived the magnificence of his address.

"That is more than one word, brother," muttered Cecil, giving an annoyed twitch of his nose.

The countess had been observing the various faces. In particular, she had taken note of her son's unconcealed dismay when Mrs. Moss hinted at a connection between her son and Louisa. She had also noted the flare of dislike in Louisa's eyes as she viewed Mr. Moss. It presented an interesting opportunity for someone newly turned matchmaker. She seized it with both hands.

"We are pleased to see Louisa's friends," the countess announced in her most gracious manner. "I know it must be difficult to be a stranger in our land. Therefore I insist you visit with Louisa and us for a few days."

Louisa had strolled to the tea table to make a selection and was in the process of sipping hot tea from her cup. Only Cecil's presence of mind saved another precious bit of china from breakage.

"I am sorry," apologized Louisa in the ensuing fuss. "I must be more fatigued than I realized."

"Why do you not rest in your room, dear girl? I shall be up directly to see you." The countess beamed a sweet smile on her dearest guest.

Giving her hostess a puzzled look—one shared by Westcott—Louisa curtsied beautifully, then left the room. She wished she had taken a substantial plate of Cook's delights with her. Her stomach was protesting its neglect. As she reached the staircase, she heard steps behind her. It was not Cosmo, as she half-expected, but Lord Westcott.

He held a china dish loaded with delicacies for which his cook was famous. "I judged it ill of Mother to send you off to your room, even if she is right and you are tired. I thought you might wish to catch up on a few treats."

A pleased smile touched her lips. "How kind of you." She inhaled the aroma of the desserts with anticipation. "If that Madeira cake was not bad enough, those wonderfully rich Eccles pastries would undo me." She quickly took the plate from his hands before he could change his mind. "I shall savor them while curled up on the chaise longue by my window." She turned to go up the stairs, then paused, looking back at him, revealing her puzzlement.

"What is it, Louisa?"

"Does your mother often invite total strangers to visit, especially ones come to view the house, as Newton explained to me?" Her worried eyes sought his gaze. A small frown had settled between her brows and she nibbled her lower lip in her concern, something she rarely did.

"No, I'll confess that she does not. I shall try to find out what is going on in her mind, for I cannot imagine her purpose." He gave Louisa that smile she loved so dearly, then left to return to the drawing room.

With thoughtful steps she made her way up to the pink bedroom again. Setting the plate heaped with all those delectable morsels on the small table by the chaise, she plunked herself down. She proceeded to consider the matter of Aubrey and Mrs. Moss as she daintily munched her way through the Madeira cake. Why would the countess take it into her head to invite them to stay?

When not a single sensible solution came to mind, Louisa gave up trying and devoted her attention to the enjoyment of the crisp, buttery Eccles pastry. Spices with currants and bits of peel, combined in a wonderful light-as-air pastry, made too good a thing to ignore, mystery or not. Louisa could well understand why the cakes had once been banned by law as being sinfully rich.

A hesitant knock came at the door. Pamela peeped in. Upon seeing Louisa, she dashed across the room to where Louisa sat.

"Annie said you were sleeping but I knew you couldn't sleep at this time of day. I am very glad to see you back. It's been ever so long since you went away." She gave her dear friend a shy hug and a somewhat sticky kiss.

A fond smile from Louisa was followed by interesting words. "Go to that portmanteau over there and open it. I suspect there may be something of curiosity inside."

Toby poked his head through the opening left by his sister

and promptly entered the room as well. "May I too?" he said with boyish glee.

"You too," replied an amused Louisa. How their mother could bear to part with them for such a long, long time was more than she could see. Louisa was not pleased to see that Toby was again back in his skirts. How the boy must chafe at that babyish dress. Evidently Lord Westcott had had second thoughts about the skeleton suit.

"Thank you very much, Miss Randolph," they said in chorus. Both pairs of eyes danced with happiness.

Toby sat down on the floor to read his book, exclaiming what a jolly good one it was, while Pamela brought the spinning top to Louisa. "Show me?"

So it was that when Lady Westcott peeped through the open door, she discovered Toby near Louisa's feet, absorbed in his book on ships. Close by, Pamela was clapping her hands in delight while chanting, "Top go up, top go down, top go all around the town."

"Children, take your lovely presents and go off to the nursery. Annie must be frantic with wondering where you are by now." The well-modulated tones of the countess brought the children hastily to their feet.

Both moved to leave the room, though Louisa noted it was with reluctance. "I shall see you later, loves." Louisa rose from her chaise, watching the countess with interest.

Waiting to speak until the door was closed, the countess strolled to the window to gaze across the land to where the stream meandered in and out with capricious whim.

"Are you by any chance here to give an explanation for that extraordinary invitation?" asked Louisa, quite surprised at her boldness in daring to question Lady Westcott.

"I hope you are not upset by it. I have my reasons, which I will not divulge at this moment, however. Tell me, how do you feel toward Mr. Moss?" The countess turned from the view to face Louisa.

Louisa found herself subjected to silent scrutiny as she tried to find the most accurate words. "I suppose I ought to be polite and say I find him a pleasant gentleman. Actually, I think him to be a dead bore." Louisa's mind went back to the journey, recalling the long monologues from Mr. Moss on the subject of his mercantile pursuits. Had she been enamored of him, it might have been tolerable. She was not, nor ever could be. Decisively she added, "Were I faced with the choice of marriage to him, I should set up my own household immediately and never look at a man again."

"Hmm," murmured Lady Westcott. "What a pity. The poor man—or is it his mother?—seems most taken with you."

"I have the feeling his mother may be more desirous of fine connections than a bride for her son," stated Louisa, brushing the crumbs from her gown. "Somehow she must have learned of my relationship with the Duchess of Emmerton and thinks to get an entrée to society through me. Or," Louisa said with a sigh, "it may have been my money."

"Why, Louisa, you are becoming as cynical as my son," the countess said with a degree of surprise. "For a young woman who writes utterly charming children's stories, I must say you sound almost bitter."

"Do I?" Louisa said with a trace of alarm. Then she shrugged, adding, "I suppose I no longer believe in them. There is no prince to rescue me, you see." She smiled ruefully at Lady Westcott, toying with the fan she had bought while in Royal Tunbridge Wells. Then she crossed to rummage in the portmanteau to find the vial of scent for the countess, and gave it to her with no ceremony. "I know you like this scent, dear ma'am. My stop in Royal Tunbridge Wells was productive." Louisa waved her exquisitely painted fan in the air, much like Ernestine Blythe.

"You did not go through London?" The countess had been exceedingly curious about this failure to examine the cream of English cities.

"I was tired of traveling. I could only think of reaching here," said Louisa with a peculiar lack of logic.

"Surely a rest in Town might have been of benefit?" the countess probed gently. "Think of the shops to be seen, the curiosities to be observed."

Almost cross at this discreet prying, Louisa shook her head. "No, indeed not. Perhaps some other time. I was told London is thin of company in the summer, rather hot as well." She really did not care to examine her motives for haring back to Westcott Park as fast as the horses could pull the carriage. The coachman had fortunately shown no reaction to her request to spring 'em.

Lady Westcott moved to the door, preparing to go to her room for a bit of serious thinking. "I meant it when I said I would take you to London for the Little Season. I believe you would quite enjoy meeting my cousins. They are delightful ladies, and well-acquainted with everyone of importance. Consider it if you will. You might even find that prince of whom you spoke." She tilted her head to one side in a manner that reminded Louisa of a curious bird.

"Thank you, ma'am, I shall. However, I doubt there is a gentleman to be found there who would please me." She omitted the interesting fact that Lord Westcott would have suited her to a tee had he not been taken by the stupid notion about her parent.

Then, as Lady Westcott was about to leave, Louisa added a final word. "I do wish to thank you again for permitting little Biddy to come. My abigail is ever so cheered up, and from what Newton said, Biddy is working out quite well in the dairy."

"No problem at all, my dear. Only think what you will do when you leave here. Biddy and her sister will be parted once again." She placed her hand on the doorknob, then seemed to have another thought. "Oh, I almost forgot to inform you that I have sent off that collection of stories you left for me to read to a publisher in London, John Harris and Sons. Eudora wrote to me they frequently publish books for children." With that tantalizing bit of speech, the countess left the room.

Louisa stood still for several moments, considering those last words. The countess had mentioned Louisa's departure, sounding as though Biddy might have to go as well. Although Louisa had no intention of becoming one of those who examine every spoken word for hidden meanings, what *had* Lady Westcott meant by that remark? Then Lady Westcott had casually dropped the news that she had sent off Louisa's stories to a publisher! What an afterthought!

It was a perplexed young woman who curled up on her bed to take a short nap before dinner. The excitement she once might have experienced at the idea of being published was dimmed by the recent events.

Lord Westcott watched Mrs. Moss depart with the housekeeper, obviously anticipating the projected tour of his ancestral home. There were times, and this was one of them, when he found the burden of his estate onerous. He turned to Aubrey Moss, gesturing. "Would you like to see the stables, or perhaps the gardens?" He had found that American men leaned either one way or the other, never both.

"The gardens, by all means. I pride myself on the layout we have back at home in New York. Got the best gardener in the state, I vow. Can't take care of it myself, you see. Too busy." With that he proceeded to give facts and figures regarding his many mercantile interests in the city and state of New York. "Thinking about expanding. I could do it with a bit more capital."

"I see," replied Westcott, thinking that perhaps he saw a good deal more than Mr. Moss intended him to see.

They stood on a rise overlooking the landscaped park. In the distance could be seen the Doric Temple and the greenhouse. A corner of the stables could be glimpsed if you moved a trifle. Since Mr. Moss showed little interest in that area, Westcott omitted mention of it. "We have forcing gardens in winter, with special plants going into the greenhouse."

"What is the purpose of that little temple affair?" asked Mr. Moss.

Recalling the intimate scene with Louisa, Westcott was quiet a moment, then replied, "We have a few lemon trees in there at present. My mother enjoys spending an afternoon there during the summer." He steered the guest in the opposite direction. Somehow he could not bring himself to show the interior to the man Louisa might possibly marry.

"We landscaped on the principle that nature abhors a

straight line," Westcott stated, recalling a few of William Kent's words on the subject of gardening.

Mr. Moss displayed a satisfying curiosity about the unusual plants to be found. Then he darted a glance at Westcott, an admiring one that encompassed the tall form and artistocratic presence. "Miss Randolph visited her family?"

"That she did," replied Westcott, unsure just how much to reveal. If he told this upstart the Whole Truth, he might insist on dragging Louisa away with him, demanding the right to "protect" her. Or her money.

They came to the edge of the ha-ha, where Mr. Moss stood in total puzzlement as he gazed into the ditch.

"It keeps out the animals—deer and the like—while not disturbing the view from the house with a fence," explained a patient Lord Westcott.

"Capital, capital," answered Mr. Moss, while absently looking about him at the trees and shrubbery.

"You came to know Miss Randolph well during the journey, I take it?" Drew led his guest toward the rose garden and the artificial lake.

"Very well, indeed. She was most kind to minister to me when I had injured my head, you see. Comes from a very fine Virginia family, as I suppose you know. Very top-of-the-trees. Had an impressive house, I understand. She was too modest to say much to my mother about her fortune or home. Ran into a fellow from that part of the country just the other day. Told me of the sizable plantation her father had owned. About eight thousand acres, all told, he thought. He knew about the sale. Said she kept the finest pieces of furniture, storing them in Alexandria until they could be sent for. Her father had always bought the best of everything."

Westcott decided that Mr. Moss sounded as though he rather relished getting his hands on that precious furniture and the mementos that Louisa had retained of the family. Lord Westcott was not of a mind to make it an easy task.

"How interesting. She told my mother that she plans to settle here." He gestured about him so Mr. Moss might be forgiven if he believed Louisa to be remaining at Westcott Park.

"How so? Do I gather the visit with her family did not go as she hoped?" Mr. Moss leaned over to smell one of the flowers in the garden. As he stood upright, he observed a white, black-spotted puppy gamboling about the feet of a little boy coming toward them.

"Toby," called Westcott, thankful for the distraction, "come show the gentleman your pup. I'm breeding them for coach dogs, possibly hunting as well."

"Unusual mutt," murmured Mr. Moss, mindful of the lad's feelings.

"Louisa is quite fond of them. Do you like dogs, Mr. Moss?"

"Well enough," came the answer, but it sounded as if the man who voiced the words cared about as much for the animals as the plague.

"She dotes on the children too. Takes them fishing and for donkey rides. Tells them stories by the hour. Even goes wading in the stream with them and sails little boats. Do you enjoy children, Mr. Moss?" Westcott was taking great delight in enumerating these charms Mr. Moss hadn't known about, for they seemed to dismay the man no end.

"She brought me a jolly good book on ships, Uncle Drew," piped up Toby, not to be outdone with kind remarks about his dear Miss Randolph.

"There, you see? Excellent young lady," offered Westcott with a hearty manner.

"My mother does not care for the patter of little feet, gives her the headache." Aubrey Moss strolled away from the boy and his pup as though fleas might soar through the air to settle upon his fine pantaloons.

"Pity, that," murmured Westcott in a falsely sympathetic voice. He motioned Toby back to the stables, while directing Mr. Moss toward the lake.

"Louisa has a great many interests. She plays the pianoforte extremely well. Were you aware of her talent? No? A most accomplished musician. I hope the pianoforte does not give your mother the headache as well. Louisa tends to practice a good deal. Cuts silhouettes, too. Devilishly clever girl. I told her she ought to sell them, you know, like artists do their paintings. Those silhouettes have been all the crack for some time now.'' Westcott hoped the gentleman didn't know that silhouettes had been around for donkey's years. Louisa was gifted at them, and it was a point to use with this punctilious man.

''Sell them?'' While it might be fine and well to have a mercantile interest, one's wife hardly entered into the business of selling anything. ''Wouldn't be proper.''

Westcott hid his amusement. A man might think Moss the aristocrat, given his disdain for the very notion of Louisa selling her silhouettes. Not that Westcott would have approved of such a scheme, but Moss did not have to know about that.

As they walked along the graveled path, Mr. Moss turned his head to look at his host. ''I am certain that once I explain my plans for Miss Randolph's future to her, she will see things my way. We could use the remainder of our trip to England as a sort of honeymoon, visiting the sights, taking in the Season in London. Mother looks forward to that, you must know.''

''You plan to be here so long?'' asked Westcott, clearly dismayed at this news.

''I can well afford the trip'' Moss said stiffly. ''And once Miss Randolph gets all this nonsense out of her head, she will properly return to New York and settle down with Mother and me.''

Lord Westcott thought that sounded like a rather grim prospect for the delightful girl he had come to love. ''Her parents knew my father, you know,'' he said suddenly, his mental wanderings leading him to the topic that bothered him the most.

''Really,'' replied Mr. Moss, sounding totally uninterested. The two strolled up to the house, where Lord Westcott begged his guest's pardon and went up the stairs to his mother's suite.

He charged into her room like a bursting dam. ''Now, see here, Mother, I won't have it. That Moss is an utter . . .

fool," he finished. He had been about to say something more deadly, but refrained after considering his mother's sensibilities.

"I know," the countess replied.

"Then how can you possibly allow him to remain where he can try to lure Louisa, that is, Miss Randolph, off to America? She belongs here." Drew began to pace the floor in a most agitated fashion, reminding his mother of a frantic dog who has misplaced an only pup.

"I believe Louisa intends to set up a household west of London. Perhaps in Richmond. Someplace rather pretty, I think she said. I doubt she will write fairy tales any longer. You must have infected her with your cynicism, for she says she doesn't believe in them now. You see, there is not a prince around to rescue her." The countess inspected the state of her nails while announcing this bit of news.

Westcott halted in his steps to give his mother a look of consternation. "What the devil does she mean by that? You are quite certain she does not desire to marry that pompous ass?"

"Well, we had best wait and see. Keep your eyes open, is my advice." Lady Westcott buried her face in a dainty handkerchief and blew her nose ever so gently.

"Be assured I shall," muttered Westcott as he slowly strolled from the room.

With an immensely pleased expression on her face, his mother reclined on the chair where she had been waiting for him.

Westcott entered the library, hoping not to discover either Mr. or Mrs. Moss inside. When he surveyed the interior to find himself quite alone, he breathed a sigh of relief. He strolled along the polished oak floor with slow, considering steps. In the center of the room he paused to lean against his desk.

He did not wish to see Louisa wed that man. How best to accomplish his goal? He turned his head to stare at the painting above the fireplace, Sappho writing odes dictated by Love. The figure of Love was that of a young man, very well-formed, with discreet draperies preventing the picture from offending the sensibilities of women such as Agnes Turner or the Dunstables.

Would that Love might tell him what to do and say. He certainly seemed to make a hash of things whenever he spoke to Louisa. Then his countenance brightened. He had called her Louisa earlier and she had not objected at his being overly familiar.

She had bought a book for Toby. Thoughtful woman. He had nothing for her return. He was about to leave his sanctuary to order flowers from the greenhouse for Miss Randolph when the door inched open.

"Oh, Lord Westcott. I am sorry. I simply wanted to avoid those . . . that is, I thought I might select a book to read." Louisa paused just inside the library door.

"Am I correct that you were about to say that you wished to escape the company of the Americans?" Drew inquired, momentarily overlooking the interesting fact that Louisa was also an American.

The pink blush that spread across her cheeks was utterly bewitching. "You have caught me out, I fear."

"What errant rubbish. I have no notion as to what Mother's intentions are in this, but the invitation surely does not require that you sacrifice yourself to their amusement," he firmly declared.

"Thank you for that," she replied, her face softening into a smile.

"But?" He noticed a hesitancy of manner, a distinct wariness on her part that seemed to have nothing to do with her fellow Americans.

"I am quite vexed with someone around here." She gave him a pointed look. "Since I do not know where to place the blame, I can scarce make accusations, can I?" Louisa clasped her hands before her while trying to meet his eyes. They seemed to hold a tender regard in their beautiful brown depths, but that was absurd.

"What sort of accusations, may I ask?" Drew left the support of his desk to amble in what he hoped was a non-threatening way toward Louisa.

"I bought those skeleton suits for Toby. You know how he adores exploring and wants so to be grown-up. Fancy how he must feel wearing that babyish dress and trousers. Even I can see how foolish he feels while astride his pony."

Lord Westcott stood looking down at the delightful young woman, wondering how she always managed to throw a damper on his intentions. He clasped his hands behind him lest he reach out to give her a shaking. Really, she was provoking.

Yet, was his position regarding Toby and that dratted suit so terribly important? Was it worth an argument? If he wanted to drive her into that upstart American's arms, might this do the trick? He had best squelch his ire.

Drew smiled at her and chuckled. With chagrin, he observed her swift lightening of expression. Did she really think him such an ogre? Why, he was the most mild of fellows.

Her relief revealed in her voice, Louisa said, "Then we may put aside his dresses, let him be his age? He so wishes to be an explorer—even if it is the park."

When Drew nodded his agreement, he was charmed by her quick hug of delight. She stepped away from him as she realized the impropriety of her action, a blush again staining her pretty cheeks. "Oh, what you must think of me."

Watching her put her hands to warm cheeks before she whisked herself from the library, Drew murmured, "If you but knew, Louisa. If you but knew." Then he wished he had been able to read those letters.

Surely she had brought them back with her, for he knew they had departed in her trunk when she left Westcott Park. In a way, he had been angry, yet curiously relieved. But he must face the truth, and soon. He set off to consult with his mother.

15

*I*t was two afternoons later that Aubrey Moss managed to corner Louisa. Not corner, precisely, as she was in the rose garden at the moment, but she certainly felt cornered.

She carried a basket full of roses picked at Lady Westcott's suggestion, although both she and Louisa knew full well that morning was the best time for plucking flowers. Louisa held the wicker basket before her in a gesture of near-defense. "Mr. Moss, I trust you are enjoying your visit to a true English estate. You often mentioned on the journey from America that you wished to do just this."

He glanced about him at the beautifully managed gardens and the serene lake beyond, and nodded with what seemed to her reluctance. "That I did."

"I expect you will be off to Scotland before long. There is much to be seen in this lovely land. I thought the scenery in Kent to be most beautiful."

This was exactly the opening Mr. Moss had been waiting for, a mention of her family. "I gather the visit to your grandmother was not all you hoped it would be."

Sighing, Louisa shook her head. "I fear not. My grandmama is rather distant in her manner. She is not at all the sort of loving relative I had hoped to locate when I traveled to England. I suspect she believes her entire family is awaiting her death like a flock of vultures—ready to descend on her fortune. Although I have no need for her money—indeed, I care naught for it—she is persuaded otherwise. Poor lonely old woman."

"How can you pity one who has rejected you?" exclaimed Mr. Moss, clearly affronted at this peculiar behavior.

"I have my life ahead of me, one I hope to fill with joy. She has nothing save her gold. She rejects her family, and even her memories cannot please her." Louisa strolled over to one of the marble benches placed to view the garden and seated herself, unwilling to remain standing for what she surmised was to come.

It seemed Mr. Moss was completely unaware as to how transparent his intentions might be to others. He paced about, bending over to examine a rose here or there, hands clasped behind him, looking as uncomfortable as possible.

"Ah, regarding your future, you intend to remain here? Or do you think to return to America?" He paused in his perambulations to peer at her where she perched on the edge of the bench.

"I have nothing left in America. My future lies in England." Louisa studied a lovely white rose in the basket, a cabbage rose with tints of pink along the edges of the petals.

"May I suggest an alternative plan?" He looked immensely pleased with himself. This appeared easier than he expected, it seemed. "Why do you not marry me, travel about for a bit in England, then return with us to New York? Mother and I would be pleased to have you join us at our home. I feel sure that you would be an asset in my life, and do credit to our name."

As a proposal, it had all the romance and enthusiasm of a business merger between two solicitors. Mr. Moss was overly obvious in what attracted him the most—her assets. Somehow, she did not feel those included black hair and blue eyes, nor a pleasing person. While Louisa had lost much of her cheerful optimism, she had not totally given up her dreams. Castle-building might be left to others more utopian. However, she felt her plans to write were on solid rock, and her fortune would enable her to live as she pleased. She was not about to finance Aubrey Moss's expansion in the mercantile world.

Her lack of an instant acceptance of his most generous offer seemed to upset him. Mr. Moss frowned at her. Perhaps he was wondering if he ought to have gone through all that nonsense of getting down on one knee, or spouting silly words of love. Louisa felt sure that love would have no place in his marriage. Rather, it would be based on family and money, not necessarily in that order. Perhaps more like the merger she had thought of minutes ago.

"Sir, you do me great honor . . ." She paused, noting with annoyance the smug expression on his rather plain face. "But I fear I must decline. Not that your prospect is not interesting. Indeed, I should wonder what your mother would say to sharing the duties of the household when she has been accustomed to rule for so long. Most curious. But, as I said, my life is now here. I have no desire to return to Virginia or to settle in New York."

The very idea of sharing a roof with Hannah Moss was depressing. Louisa associated that lady too closely with the zealous Hannah Moore. Mrs. Moore sermonized. The heroine of her own novel was a priggish young shadow of a girl; dull, domestically dutiful, and dependent, with not a thought of her own. Mrs. Moss appeared to embrace that philosophy wholeheartedly.

"But you cannot remain here," Mr. Moss declared. "Lord Westcott is a single man. Even though his mother is in residence, it is not quite the thing for you to remain at Westcott Park. You would be better off in a land you know."

"New York is as foreign to me as England, for that matter." His statement of what she knew to be the hard truth had not endeared him to her, nor made her wish to ease the pain of rejection. "I have quite made up my mind." Then, thinking to convince him, she uttered what was, as far as she was concerned, a lie. "I shall accept Lady Westcott's most kind offer to travel with her to London for the Little Season."

"I see." His reply was almost amusing, for it was quite plain that he did not see. Or if he thought he did, his conclusion was incorrect.

"Perhaps you were unaware that the Countess Westcott has sent in a collection of my stories to a publisher? She expects they will be accepted. I can only hope she is right. I should very much like to have them printed."

Off to one side Louisa could hear a song thrush singing rather saucily from up in the branches of a young Turkey oak tree. The scent of the late-blooming roses was delightful. Most of the bushes had burst into flower early in the summer. Now only a few of the newly developed roses had color. Countess Westcott enjoyed having the very latest of hybrids in her garden, although she did not make a great fuss about them.

In the distance she could hear Toby chattering to Jack, his beloved pony. She could only pray that either this rather painful interview would be concluded by the time little Toby rounded on the scene, or that something else would bring it to an end. She rose to her feet, hoping to assist the talk to this conclusion. "Now, if you will excuse me, I must get these roses to the house before they wilt beyond redemption." She curtsied as best she could while carrying the basket over one arm, then turned to walk to the house. She could almost feel the annoyance emanating from Mr. Moss.

"Well, I scarce know what to say." But he did. For the entire ten minutes it took to walk into the house, she heard his views on women being permitted to decide their own destiny. He announced his intention to seek Lord Westcott's assistance. Surely his lordship would be anxious to have a *writing* female removed from beneath his roof!

"Of course, you must understand that this nonsense about writing stories will end," he stated, with the assurance on one who is always in the right.

"Even if they might be improving tales? Sarah Trimmer and Mrs. Sherwood write such," murmured Louisa with tongue in cheek. "I believe even Mrs. Moore approves of them, along with her own moral tracts. 'Tis felt they help to keep the decent working folk happy with their lot and teaches the young their proper place in the world."

She had paused in the entry hall, conscious that Newton hovered not too far away. What that venerable gentleman might think of such talk, she did not know, but she suspected he was far more supportive of the status quo.

"Well," Mr. Moss said with some hesitation, "I suppose those might be well enough. But I should not wish you to be public with them. 'Tis not at all seemly to call attention to yourself."

Louisa gritted her teeth lest she say something nasty to this prosy bore. She had listened for hours to his plans to promote his mercantile interests with a good deal of publicity. Apparently the standard was vastly different for a merchant than for a writer of children's stories.

Turning to Newton, Mr. Moss inquired, "Where might I find Lord Westcott?"

"In the library, sir. Follow me." Newton led the miserable Mr. Moss across the expanse of the hall while Louisa hurried to the housekeeper's stillroom.

Here she calmed herself by arranging the roses in a lovely old crystal vase. She took a good deal of comfort in knowing that Lord Westcott could not force her to wed Mr. Moss. She felt that his mother was on her side as well.

When Newton opened the tall oak door that led to the room Lord Westcott considered his private sanctuary, Mr. Moss was met by the sight of a frowning gentleman. It was hardly a propitious beginning. He got straight to the point with no roundaboutation.

"Sir, I would that you persuade Miss Randolph of the folly she intends. I cannot see how attending the Little Season with your mother will be of benefit to her. It will only serve to bring the fortune hunters buzzing around. And this utter rubbish of her story-writing ought to be quelled as well," pronounced Mr. Moss with the determination of an oracle from on high.

"Turned you down, did she?" Lord Westcott could not manage to acquire a suitably sympathetic face. The best he could summon was a neutral expression. "Never know what she might do. Delightful girl, though. It won't do to tell her not to write. Stubborn little thing. She'll keep right on with it behind your back. I believe you are well rid of her, Mr. Moss. Best thing for you to do is go home to America and find yourself a girl just like your mother. Easier to train, you know."

Drew walked toward the window lest his widening grin betray his true sympathies. "I expect that with this blow, you will want to be on your way. I've heard tell that Scotland is a wondrous place to soothe the wounded soul."

Mr. Moss shifted from one foot to the other, clearly unsettled by Lord Westcott's failure to champion his cause.

"But, Lord Westcott . . ." he offered in a faltering voice.

"I know you appreciate my advice, old fellow, no need to thank me. It has been good for Louisa to get this straight in her mind, I feel certain. Poor girl might have been confused regarding her loyalties, otherwise." Drew wondered if he was beginning to reason like his uncles.

There was little for poor Mr. Moss to do but agree with his host. Murmuring words regarding the imminent departure of himself and his toadeating mother, he left the library.

It was well the American could not hear anything through the heavy oak of the door, for the elegant Lord Westcott was whooping with laughter.

The following morning saw the departure of Hannah and Aubrey Moss. Among the group clustered about on the broad steps descending from the portico, there were solemn faces that looked like they wished to smile. Certainly Louisa tried to refrain from a pleased grin. As the hired coach rattled down the gravel drive, faint sighs of relief could be heard.

Louisa had noted that Hannah had refrained from words with her. Indeed, neither of the Moss pair had much to say, thank heaven. Louisa had been given all the advice she cared to receive for a good time to come. Now she must settle a few things before she left.

Once inside the house, Louisa placed a slender hand on Lady Westcott's arm to detain her, then looked to where Lord Westcott stood watching. "I should like to speak with you both, if I may?"

"Goodness, but that sound ominous, my girl," replied the countess. She strolled along to her sitting room, where the beginnings of a pair of slippers were strewn about on a table.

Louisa took comfort in that homey disorder. Putting her hands behind her back, she walked slowly toward the window that looked out onto the gardens. Turning to face the others, she swallowed carefully, then spoke in a small, brave voice. "I must leave here as well. You have been excessively kind, but it remains that I have no claim on your hospitality, nor do I any longer have the excuse that you are helping me to locate my family."

She dropped her hands to her sides, fingering the soft India mull of her gown with nervous fingers.

"What do you have in mind?" inquired the countess in a deceptively mild voice.

"I shall explore the environs of Richmond, as you once suggested, ma'am, and settle there." Louisa most carefully refrained from meeting Lord Westcott's gaze. She had no idea as to what she might see there, but she feared that his expression might be one of pleasure. She did not believe she could tolerate that at this moment.

"That does not sound like a particularly good plan, Miss Randolph," he said. "Indeed, if you intend to leave us, I would feel much better about the thing if you had a definite goal in mind. Why do you not permit me to make inquiries on your behalf? Once you get a list of suitable properties, we can decide which might prove the best for you." His voice was kindly, rather disinterested, and most disheartening.

It was a pity Louisa was not watching Westcott, for she totally missed that wicked gleam in his eyes. However, his mother had not failed to note it. For this reason, she murmured, "What a praiseworthy notion, dear Drew. Not even Cecil could have done better."

Westcott gave her an affronted look, then caught the meaning behind her words and coughed, lest he laugh and ruin the entire thing. He was pleased that his mother joined him in his desire to keep the lovely Miss Randolph at Westcott Park. Of course, their motives were undoubtedly far apart. He surmised that his mother desired a companion. Drew had other ideas.

Cecil paused at the door to the sitting room, his coat the same blue as the walls, and with a cream waistcoat embroidered with tiny blue forget-me-nots. Louisa thought his attire quite remarkable.

"Brother, do help us persuade Louisa to remain here until we can get her future sorted out," pleaded the countess. "The dear girl says she wishes to travel to Richmond to search out a small home where she might settle."

"Set up her own household? 'Taint done, you know. She will be proclaimed either a bluestocking or an antidote." Cecil looked to his sister for confirmation of his assessment.

"Louisa most assuredly is not one of those," insisted Cosmo in horrified accents as he entered the room. "Why, she has the loveliest of manners. I enjoy her playing of the pianoforte, for she plays music I can recognize. And she is wonderful with the children." As far as Cosmo was concerned, this seemed to be all that was necessary in a young woman. "I would not be surprised were she to prove to be accomplished at watercolors."

"It seems I owe Louisa an apology," inserted Westcott at this point. He bowed slightly in her direction. "Mr. Moss kindly explained to me that you are an heiress, and far from being in need of a job as a governess. And you write, as well," he added, as though her talent was another asset to be counted.

He had been so certain that Louisa had taken the letters with her. When he had mentioned them to his mother upon Louisa's return, he had been astounded to find they had sat in his mother's drawer the entire time. He desired to speak with Louisa, tell her how wrong he had been about everything, but not in front of his mother and uncles. There were a few times when a man must have privacy, and this was one of them. For now, he merely did the polite and waited.

Just as Louisa was sorting out the various comments that had sprung to her tongue, the countess picked up a paper from among the litter on her table.

"Oh, Louisa, I received a missive from London this day, and what with the excitement, I have not had the opportunity to tell you. Mr. Harris has accepted your stories for publication! He offers a fair payment, though not what I suspect you deserve. He also wrote that he has engaged someone to illustrate the book—a Mr. Cruikshank. Fancy!

Before long your little book shall be on the shelf of a juvenile library."

"Oh, dear," replied Louisa, groping for the back of a chair. "I am delighted, needless to say."

"You really don't sound delighted," said Cosmo, frowning at his dear girl. "As a matter of point, you don't sound the least happy. The laborer is worthy of his hire. Harris ought to pay you more."

"I quite assure you, sir, that I am—"

Her defense was interrupted by Toby and Pamela entering the room to politely wait for attention, having apparently escaped Annie for the moment. Pamela stepped forward to claim Louisa's arm, tugging on it earnestly.

Putting aside the concerns that hovered over her head, Louisa knelt beside Pamela. "What is it, love?"

"Toby says he is going to be an explorer like the ones in the book you gave him. Only I said we ought to ask you first. He wants to have an adventure, like Robert." Pamela searched the face of her admired Miss Randolph to see if consent might be given for such a daring expedition.

Glancing first at the countess, Louisa gave Pamela a considering look. "I tell you what: why not a little outing just for the three of us?"

"And Pepper," inserted Toby, anxious to have his puppy along.

"And Pepper as well." She smiled fondly at Toby, then turned to face Lady Westcott. "Does that meet with your approval, dear ma'am?" Louisa rose to stand with one hand resting on the blond curls that tumbled over Pamela's head.

"With my daughter and her husband likely to show one of these days, judging from her latest letter, you may as well take them. Heavens knows when they shall have another opportunity for such a jolly little trip very soon."

"I had not realized they would be arriving shortly," Louisa said slowly. She would miss the children terribly. Once they departed, there would truly be no need for her to remain at Westcott Park.

At the moment, she might delude herself that she was

performing a service for the countess. In her heart, she knew full well she stayed because of Lord Westcott. When those brown eyes gazed at her with that delicious sense of warmth, she felt near to melting. And he had looked at her like that this very morning. And yesterday. It was as though he reached out to touch her. And she well remembered his touch.

Cosmo coughed, then said, "Well, I hope your daughter has managed to keep her husband's eyes off those blond Danish beauties I have heard about. It is well she went with him, I believe. I doubt it is a good thing for a man like Bromfield to be left to his own devices. It stands to reason that he might stray. He was never one to let the grass grow under his feet."

Cecil, with an eye on his sister's distressed face, countered, "Do not make a mountain out of a molehill, Cosmo. While Bromfield is a man of parts, his talents are directed toward his country."

Not taking his brother's hint, Cosmo murmured in an audible voice, "For the moment. No need to look daggers at me, Cordelia. I have never been one to mince matters, and you know it. You ought never have permitted your husband to haring off to America if you felt that strongly about the subject." He bestowed a nod in her direction, then strode from the room.

Cecil shrugged and followed after his brother.

"Oh, dear," murmured Lady Westcott, and forgetting Louisa and the children, she rose from where she had seated herself, leaving in great haste.

"I hope she will be all right," said a concerned Louisa.

"It is time and enough she faces the past, I believe." Drew looked down at Pamela and Toby, who stood with enormous wondering eyes.

"Are Mama and Papa truly coming?" said Toby at last, a trifle anxiously.

"According to what your grandmama said, yes." Louisa wished she might reassure the boy that his mama would look kindly upon the changes that had been made during her absence, but she could not. For all one knew, Felice might not like the skeleton suit, or the puppy, or the pony. Louisa could only hope that Lord Bromfield would show more tolerance.

"Then let us go at once. Mama will stop anything that is fun." Toby earnestly tugged at her hand.

Louisa turned her head, meeting in Lord Westcott's gaze a rueful acceptance of young Toby's assessment of his mother. She turned to the children. "Get your bonnet, Pamela, and wear something sturdy, both of you. I shall ask Cook to pack a little picnic for us."

"Jolly good!" shouted Toby as he ran from the room, totally forgetting that his dear mother would have a spasm if she could hear or see him.

Louisa was left facing Lord Westcott. The silence grew as each sought the words to be said. Neither managed to utter one of them at first.

"I had best get to the kitchen, or the children will return before I have left the room." Louisa took a step toward the door, then paused. "You see now why it is imperative I leave?"

"I see nothing of the kind. Would you listen to gossips?" He could have kicked himself at her look of alarm.

"You have heard gossip about my staying here?" Her suddenly pale face was worried. "I could not bring myself to accept the offer Mr. Moss made . . ."

"And rightly so. He was plainly seeking your fortune. You deserve someone who desires you for yourself," said Drew, hoping she might take the hint. "I have heard nothing." Cosmo had, but that was beside the point.

"But I would never bring dishonor to your mother." Those exquisite gentian eyes were large and troubled.

Drew hadn't read the remaining letters, yet he felt it unnecessary after perusing a few. His eyes were opened to the truth. Louisa Randolph was incapable of the conduct he had accused her of earlier. She was a rare woman, totally honest as well as very desirable. He wanted to take her in his arms, tell her how he felt. Yet any moment those dratted children would come tumbling into the room, and his entire efforts could be ruined. Even now he could hear the patter of little feet on the staircase off in the distance. He sighed.

"Nothing you could do would ever have that effect. I applaud your efforts at writing, Louisa."

At that crucial moment Toby came bouncing into the room. "No picnic yet, Miss Randolph? I say!" exclaimed the disappointed boy.

Louisa threw an anguished look at Lord Westcott. What else had he been about to say after those remarkable words? "I shan't take another moment, dear. Permit me to speak to Cook, then I shall fetch my bonnet. You may talk to the groom about Jack if you would. And organize something to carry Pepper. Pamela and I shall require the donkeys."

Drew frowned at those words. "You ought to have a pretty little mare to ride. I should have seen to it before."

Surprise clearly written on her face, Louisa shook her head. "I do not mind, for the most part, and Pamela likes that we ride the same sort of beast." Louisa made a funny little face at him, then hurriedly left the room.

Drew turned to Toby. "See that you look after her. Where do you think she will take you?"

Toby proudly stood a bit taller, and considered this question a moment before answering. "She promised to show us the view from Blackwell Hill once. There is a parting in the woods where you can see ever so far, according to the groom. When Miss Randolph heard that, she said it would be lovely to view such a sight. Perhaps we could go there?"

Drew wanted to forbid the outing. Part of that hill had been cut away for gravel, leaving a pit of sorts. The idea that Louisa might get hurt if she strayed off the path bothered him. Normally it was the most easy of outings. The hill was not terribly steep, and if the weather was good, quite a charming place. "You be careful, and stay on the path at all times." Best not to inform Toby about the gravel pit, or the boy could be off to explore, with disastrous results.

When Louisa entered a few minutes later, bonnet neatly in place, a light pelisse over her arm, Drew wished he had the power to keep her here, close to him. "I trust you will have a pleasant outing. Lovely day to go on a bit of a jaunt."

Louisa wished she could beg him to come along. She

wanted to share with him the view, and the laughter, and the joy that the children brought to her. "How true," was all she said, taking one last look at that sculptured face before she accepted Toby's hand and left the room for the kitchen.

Drew stood at the library window watching as Louisa, Toby, and Pamela, followed by the nursery maid and the groom holding a wiggling Pepper, ambled on their mounts down the path toward the hill. The donkeys were being especially good. He wondered if Louisa had become clever at offering carrots to them at propitious moments. There were so many things he wished to know about her, so many times they were interrupted or disturbed. He turned away from the window as they disappeared from sight around a bend in the path.

The house was quiet for several hours. Cecil and Cosmo were in the gallery perfecting their game of billiards. Of Lady Westcott, nothing was seen or heard. Newton was in the entry hall, polishing one of the heraldic emblems on the wall by the front door, when the distant rattle of carriages could be heard.

He had the door open and was at the top of the short flight of stairs when the Bromfield carriage pulled up before the house. Behind him Lord Westcott strolled to the portico. "Felice! And Bromfield! Well, as I live and breathe. Mother said something about you showing up one of these days. I trust you had a pleasant journey?"

"Tolerable," declared a handsome Lord Bromfield. He gave his brother-in-law a grin, then accepted a jovial clap on the shoulder.

They entered the house together, Felice chattering about the delights of the Danish court, Bromfield listening with good humor.

Lady Westcott bustled forward from the door that led to the staircase. "Felice, my dear. I trust all is well?" There was the barest hint of a question in those words.

"Quite well, Mother. Where are the children?" Felice looked about her with mild curiosity.

"Louisa took them on a little picnic. It will give us a chance to visit before they descend upon you. I am sure they have missed you both quite dreadfully.'' The countess gathered her daughter into a fond embrace that had Felice looking wide-eyed with surprise.

''Well,'' added Drew, ''you know how boys are. Toby wanted to explore a little on his pony.'' He gave his sister a wary look.

Bromfield spoke before Felice could fly up into the boughs over the thought of her baby on a pony. ''Excellent. I have wanted to buy a pony for him for an age. Glad you took it in hand. And Pamela?''

''A donkey at present. She does rather well on the beast. Louisa keeps a close eye on her, while the groom is teaching Toby the niceties of riding.'' Drew exchanged a grin with his brother-in-law. He couldn't recall feeling quite so in charity with him in the past.

They settled at one end of the drawing room to converse, if having a delighted Felice chatter on about the fashions, the interesting people, and the sights to be seen could be called conversation.

The day had grown dim, the sun slipping behind low clouds. Felice glanced out the window, then at the pretty watch pinned to her bosom, and declared. ''I believe the children ought to be here by now. I hope nothing has happened to them.''

Drew looked out the window, and thought of the gravel pit.

16

It was a lovely morning, the air fresh and smelling of summer flowers and newly scythed hay. Louisa's fat brown donkey trotted along beside Pamela's with great goodwill. At least for the nonce. Louisa had utterly no illusions about that animal. He had a will of his own and did not hesitate to insist on getting his own way if he so pleased.

Ahead of her, the groom instructed Toby for what might be the last time, if Lord and Lady Bromfield returned shortly. Poor little lad. He wanted so much to grow up, as Louisa supposed all small boys did, but rather than being encouraged, Toby was being forced to remain in those horrid skirts and trousers like a baby.

"Will you tell us a story, Miss Randolph? I should like to hear more about Robert and his dragon," announced Pamela in her wispy voice.

"I thought that story was just for Toby," teased Louisa.

"No, indeed," answered Pamela soberly, sounding remarkably like her grandmother. "I like him too."

"Since you have been such delightedly good children, I shall finish the tale today." Louissa decided she might as well. Even if the children remained for a week or so longer, Louisa knew that the sooner she left here, the better for her heart. That fragile object could take only so much battering.

They plodded along the trail, winding along the stream for a bit before entering on the country lane. At the crossroads they passed the Rose and Crown, waving to the innkeeper, who paused outside his door to wave back at them. They jogged along until they could see the rise to Buckwell Hill. Even with the sun shining down to bless the day, it was not as cheerfully warm as yesterday. Perhaps the state of her heart had a bit to do with her chill.

It seemed the seasons were not quite as predictable as in

Virginia. Here, if the wind blew from the northwest, you were certain to get cold, usually wet weather. An east wind brought very cold but dry skies, while a wind from the south supposedly brought mild, cloudy, and wet days. A southeast wind was said to be rare, and could bring a hot spell. However, it seemed to Louisa that rain could occur at any time, no matter what direction the wind was from. She sighed as she thought of her accusation thrown at Lord Westcott—that he was the type to carry an umbrella on a sunny day. Now that she knew the vagaries of English weather, she could well understand such caution.

It was a pity they had been so at odds from the moment she had fallen into his arms. Still, he had seemed such a lovely man when first they met. Only when he set foot on his ancestral grounds did he become the pompous Englishman. And when he got that maggoty notion about his father's letters, he had turned impossible. What a sad state of affairs, to be sure.

"Frightfully lovely, isn't it, Miss Randolph?" piped up Pamela in her high little voice, recalling Louisa to her duties.

"Lovely," Louisa echoed in agreement. She glanced behind her at Annie, plodding along on the donkey Toby had first ridden. She was a good sort of girl, and amazingly agreeable about riding on the beast.

A pleasant clearing seemed just the right place to stop for their picnic. Louisa urged her animal to a halt, the one thing the beast knew well how to do, and slid down to the ground. She helped Pamela from her donkey while Annie took charge of the puppy, then went about removing the picnic hamper Cook had carefully packed for them.

Toby surveyed the clearing, then announced, "Once I've had a bite to eat, I shall explore."

Louisa glanced at him, trying not to permit her trepidations to show. It would never do to allow him to think he actually disturbed her, and she supposed little boys had a natural inclination to explore. Best attempt to try to curb him a bit.

"Well, you should, I expect. First let us taste the treats Cook sent along. Then I can tell you another episode about

Robert and his dragon. Did you know they started a business together?"

Intrigued at this bit of nonsense—for whoever heard of a dragon in business!—Toby permitted himself to enjoy the feast set before him by Annie, feeding tidbits to Pepper.

Pamela sat close to Louisa as the story, the last of the series, unfolded. It seemed that Robert was worried about his good friend the dragon. Robert's parents were determined to ship him off to school. What would become of the dragon? So at long last, after a good many wrong turns, he persuaded the local baker to give the dragon a job starting his fires every morning, and they were in business.

Toby clapped his hands with delight. "Jolly good, Miss Randolph. It will be nice to think of the dragon starting the baker's fires of a morning." He jumped up from where he had intently listened to the improbable story. Pepper wagged his little white tail and ran around in circles to get some desired attention.

"You know," said a confiding Toby, "my Papa said I might go off to school one of these days." His face grew wistful, and he added, "I expect Pamela would be lonesome for me, but it would be jolly good fun to be with other boys, wouldn't it?"

"Yes," said Louisa calmly, "I expect it would. Perhaps you could leave Pepper to watch over Pamela. He would be good company for her too." She wondered just how long things would be "jolly good" for Toby. She hoped it was for a long, long time.

"I shall learn to sew and do sums, and write with a neat hand, and play the pianoforte like Miss Randolph. I should be very glad for Pepper," Pamela said earnestly to her brother, knowing that if Papa had said Toby was to go to school, it was a fact. Papa seldom issued statements. When he did, it was a good thing to pay attention, for he had a habit of doing precisely what he said.

Toby nodded sagely, much cheered by his sister's acceptance of what he hoped to be true. He rose, then studied the path that wound gently upward out of view. Woods and brush lined the way beneath the trees. It was an appealing sight, luring him to explore.

"I believe I shall go now. Will you come along, Miss Randolph? And Pamela?" It was clear to Louisa that Toby did not want them along. Like any little boy, he really longed to explore on his own, with his little puppy for company. Girls tended to be squeamish about silly things like spiders and bugs and snakes.

"No, I thank you. I believe Pamela and I shall stay here. I promised to help her weave a daisy chain." Louisa beamed him an encouraging smile.

Pamela gave her adored Miss Randolph a happy look. The notion of making a chain from the ox-eye daisies growing abundantly about them was clearly pleasing.

Toby whistled to Pepper and the two set off up the hill with only one backward look along the way.

Louisa watched him leave, smiling at his gallant march up the hill. "Stay on the path and come back soon," she called. Perhaps she ought to send the groom with him? She checked on that worthy character to see he was tending the pony at the moment.

Pamela ran about the little clearing, plucking daisies with sufficient stems so as to make the promised chain. Absorbed in creating a double chain of daisies, Louisa failed to note the passage of time. When she did, it was with concern. Many minutes had flown by.

The weather had suddenly changed, peculiar and disturbing. Louisa grew alarmed. She had never seen fog in the summer, though this was late summer, and she supposed that a change of wind could bring it about. Either the clouds were lowering or there was a fog creeping in about the area. She shivered in the dampish air.

The groom voiced her thoughts. "We'd best be getting home, Miss Randolph." He paused, then frowned. "I hope the lad ain't gone near the gravel pit. Nasty place for a fall."

She looked at him in growing horror. "I had no idea such a place was near here. Had I known, I'd not have permitted Toby to go off by himself." She glanced up the path, then back. "You pack up the things and prepare to leave while

I look for Toby. He'll not hide from me." She knew how Toby loved to play tricks on the groom. The boy might not realize the seriousness of the situation, and act silly. She felt he would come to her with no argument. At the moment she did not wish to even think about an accident.

"Pamela, wrap that shawl about you and help Annie. I shall be back in a trice." So saying, Louisa put on her light pelisse, then on impulse picked up the tinderbox included in Cook's basket in case they wanted tea. She tucked that in her reticule along with a supply of cakes and biscuits. Little boys were apt to be hungry after climbing about. Toby's sturdy spencer jacket was in a heap where they had eaten, and she gathered that up as well. Her heart was beating rapidly as she prepared to leave.

Pausing at the edge of the clearing, she turned to face the three, hoping to reassure. "I ought to be back quite shortly. Keep Pamela occupied and warm. This is most peculiar weather we are having today."

"Yes, miss," agreed Annie to everything.

The walk would have been lovely on a sunny day. Now the trees dripped with moisture and the path was slick where stones paved it. Louisa's well-made jean half-boots made short work of the rough, slippery ground. She wove in and out of the trees, concerned as the path grew fainter, less well-marked. When there were barely signs that another person had passed this way recently, she became apprehensive. What if she was following, not Toby, but the track of some animal?

"Toby! Can you hear me?"

She thought she heard a faint reply and hurried on. Shortly she paused and repeated her call. Once again she heard the reply, only this time stronger, clearer. It most definitely was Toby.

Bursting into a very small clearing, she discovered the boy sitting on the ground, his face pale and rather crumpled-looking. He was obviously in pain. Beside him crouched a subdued Pepper. "Toby, love, what happened?" She knelt at his side to check him over, then found his boot pulled off and a badly swelled-up ankle.

"We saw a little brown rabbit. Pepper wanted to follow

it, and so did I. We were running along very well when I tripped on a nasty old root and fell down a bank. There were a lot of rocks, and it was hard to climb up, but I did," he said with modest pride. "My ankle hurts very much, Miss Randolph. Can you fix it?"

"I shall try, dear. I shall try." With that, Louisa tore strips off her white petticoat and began to bind up the ankle so it would be kept still when they moved. Once she was finished with that, she wondered how to get Toby back down the hill, when she realized there was a much worse problem. She couldn't see a thing beyond a few feet.

"I say, it's a bit thick, isn't it?" said a wobbly-sounding Toby.

"Perhaps if I build us a little fire we can keep warm. After a while it may improve and we can go down. This fog ought not last too long. Does that seem all right?" said Louisa in a bracing manner.

"Good show," said Toby, trying to sound encouraging when he suspected the fog might last all night.

"I have a tinderbox. If I can find twigs to begin, we can keep the chill away. What a pity we do not have the dragon to help us with our fire," she said in an attempt to cheer him. She kept the cakes and biscuits a secret for the moment. There was no telling how long they were to remain in this place. She hoped the groom would come to find them or get help.

"I believe we have waited long enough," announced Drew. "With the weather changing, I find it impossible to believe Louisa would not bring the children home immediately." He sought his mother's confirmation.

"You permitted a stranger to take the children for the day?" cried Felice, a slightly hysterical note in her voice.

"You forget, dear. Louisa has been here all the while you have been gone. We have become quite fond of her." Placing a comforting arm about her daughter, Lady Westcott gave Drew a significant look. "I am certain they have paused at the inn for a cup of chocolate. But just to be safe, perhaps you ought to check on them."

Catching her look and knowing her well, Drew nodded. "I will leave at once."

"I believe I shall ride along with you, old fellow. After being in the carriage all day, I would welcome a bit of fresh air." Bromfield joined Drew with a casual nod to his wife.

Felice studied them with suspicious eyes, but did not object to their departure.

Within a short time the two men rode from the estate. Drew, as decided, went toward the crossroads. Bromfield was at his side until they reached the stream.

"Louisa often takes the children down along the bank. She reads to them and they play. Go along for a distance. Perhaps they have paused there. If they are not to be seen, then come after me."

Bromfield agreed, and they parted company. Drew rode along until the crossroads, stopping before the Rose and Crown. When he questioned the innkeeper and found that Louisa and the others had passed this way hours ago but never returned, the worried frown on his forehead became deeper.

He almost missed the turnoff where they had had the picnic. Had it not been for the braying of a donkey, he would have ridden past, lost to them by the increasing fog.

Pamela was huddled against the nursery maid, eyes wide with fear. She said nothing, merely watching as her uncle approached. The groom stepped forward to greet Westcott.

"Sir, I'm that glad t'see you. Master Toby went explorin' and failed to come back here. We thought it best to leave for home, so Miss Randolph went after him. She hasna' returned, and it's been some time now." The worried groom stood by the pony little Toby had ridden, clearly unsure what he ought to do. "Sir, she didna' know about the pit."

Concealing his growing concern, Drew said, "You had best take Pamela and the animals to the inn. Should Bromfield arrive, bring him along back here to join in the hunt. 'Tis growing dark, however. It will not be long before we won't be able to find them until daylight. I fear lanthorns will not be of much help in this fog." He exchanged a look with the groom, one that urged silent caution.

"Aye. I'll tell his lordship." The groom looped the pony's

reins over one hand, then climbed up on the mare he had ridden out.

"If it becomes too dark, return to the estate and come at first light." Drew took a step toward the path.

"Aye." This time the look was commiserating. A stout coat and warm blankets helped, but fog was insidious stuff. The groom cast a glance at the maid and Pamela. "Come along. We'd best warm oursel's and soon."

Drew watched them depart, giving the uncomplaining child high marks for courage. Snuggled against the maid, she had ridden off with no objections, only a plea.

"Please find Toby and Miss Randolph," she lisped. The tears trembling unshed in her eyes had been far more eloquent than a storm of crying.

Drew set about studying the situation. Since the trail appeared to be a narrow one, one he suspected grew worse as it rose, he tied his horse to a tree, then gathered the supplies under an arm and set off up the hill. Before he had gone very far, he heard a call, muffled through the fog.

"Westcott, old fellow, wait up." Bromfield rode into the clearing, then jumped off his horse to dash up to Drew.

It took considerable persuasion to convince Bromfield it would be better if he took Pamela home to her worried mother. Drew assured his brother-in-law that he would have Toby home in no time. Privately, Drew felt that calming a likely hysterical Felice would tax his mother too much. His sister needed her husband at a moment like this.

Once he was alone again, he set off up the hill, gazing with intent eyes at every sign that someone had passed this way recently. As he walked, he reconsidered his feelings toward Louisa. He had been in love with her for some time, he knew. Hadn't wanted to admit it. But he did now. He could only hope that she felt something more toward him than indifference. Her eyes had told him she cared, but then, he might have interpreted that gaze wrongly. If only they had not been interrupted, he might know now rather than wonder.

Was she all right? Toby might be hurt. That might be the reason they were delayed. He didn't want to cosider that

Louisa might be harmed in some manner. His cynical attitude had been shed some hours past. Now was the time for hope, some of her customary cheer. Drew clasped his bundle more tightly, then marched upward. And worried as he inspected the ground ahead for clues.

He had climbed for what seemed an age when he smelled wood smoke. Searching about, he thought he detected a speck of color through a patch of brush. He wound his way around a cluster of whitebeam. He had found them.

"What the devil are you doing here, Louisa?" he scolded gruffly with relief as he quickly ascertained it was Toby who had been hurt, not his dear girl.

Calmly Louisa rose to face him, extending her hands to clasp his. "Toby hurt his ankle and cannot walk. Poor soul that I am, I could not manage to carry a great strapping boy like him." She cast a fond look at the little lad. "Besides, I fear that the fog has made traveling nigh impossible. However did you find us in this soup?"

Ruefully compressing his lips, Drew shrugged, thankful for the warmth of her hands. "I followed your trail like a pup with nose to the ground. I am glad to see you are all right." He longed to pull her to him, kiss those lips.

"We would be worse but for this little fire I started. Perhaps you can help with a bit more wood?" She dug into her reticule to find a biscuit for Toby. "I expect we had best settle in here for the night. I cannot fathom how we could reach the road in this awful fog." She handed the treat to the boy, who hungrily munched away at it.

"I suppose you did not have such in your dear Virginia?" he teased, glad to see she had not fallen to pieces at the crisis.

"Oh, we had fog, all right. I was wise enough to be in the house at the time." Her voice was saucy, but her eyes revealed her inner worries.

She shivered, and Drew impulsively pulled her against him, enfolding her in his greatcoat to give her warmth, he told himself.

"You are cold. As soon as you stop shivering, I'll build up the blaze." She smelled of smoke and honeysuckle, an odd but precious combination at the moment.

Louisa nestled against the lean strength of his body. How in the world was she supposed to stop trembling while held this close to him? Yet she treasured the moment. It was one she would never know again, once they left this spot. Sanity asserted itself and Louisa hesitantly pushed herself away from Lord Westcott. Drew.

"I feel better now"—she managed a little smile for him—"especially since I have you to lean upon. It is disturbing to be alone, and with such a responsibility." She nodded to where young Toby sat hunched by the fire, poking at it with a stick to help keep it going.

Drew's look was all admiration now. The scolding she had received, she guessed to be worry-prompted.

"Of course." He motioned her to follow him, ostensibly to hold the wood he found. Once they were a slight distance from the boy, he said in a low voice, "Bromfield and my sister arrived shortly after you left. I persuaded him to take Pamela to her mother. I also felt Felice would have need of his support. She has always been a worrier. He's to return at first light with help. I don't see how we could find our way to the bottom of the hill now, with it nigh dark."

"I expect you are right. While I doubt we might stray into the pit, there is no point in taking a chance, is there? I was not told about that pit. I'd not have permitted Toby to leave my side had I known, you can be sure." She accepted more wood, then turned toward the fire once again.

His mother had said Louisa showed great good sense, and she did now. She need not fear the gossip. He would see to that. Nothing would be said once they married. He sought to reassure her. "I know now you have our best interests at heart. Know that I have yours as well."

Louisa had worried before about putting Drew in a compromising position, not wishing to trap him into a marriage he did not desire. She was determined not to do so now. "Please, do not concern yourself over such. Once I leave Westcott Park, this will be forgotten."

"There may be talk." He didn't like to hear words of her leaving. "Don't you know that even if you settle in Richmond, this story might follow you? This is a strange world, where an innocent girl can be tarnished easily by an equally innocent happening."

"I refuse to worry about it now." Louisa gave him a steady look, then turned to place more branches on the fire. Westcott had found a half-decayed log, and she watched as he dragged it over to push one end in the flames.

It was not long before total darkness closed in upon them. Not even an owl was about to offer a mournful to-who.

Toby happily munched on the bread and cheese from Drew's pack, then tucked into a cold chicken leg with the enthusiasm of the very young who firmly believe in adventure. When he'd had his fill, Drew held him up so Louisa might wrap a blanket about him, then cover him with another. She pillowed his head on his little jacket. It was not long before sleep overcame excitement and hurt. Pepper wiggled beneath the covers as well.

And she was alone with Drew, Lord Westcott.

Picking up a stick from the whitebeam tree, Louisa traced patterns in the dirt. "I suppose we ought to get some sleep as well."

" 'Tis early yet. No need. Unless you are tired, that is. You must have worried about the boy." He edged closer to her, offering the shelter of his greatcoat. He had tucked the remaining blanket about her legs, up to her waist. Shared warmth would be a practical solution to the damp cold. He tossed more bits of wood on the fire, watching the smoke spiral up into the overhanging branches.

"True. But I doubt I could sleep, either." She avoided his eyes at first, then said, "I do not know what to say, at this point."

He tried not to smile and failed. "I have made a royal mull of things, haven't I?"

"You?" She was startled enough to look up, then was caught in the warmth of those brown eyes. How beautiful they are, she mused. Especially now in the soft light of the fire.

"I ought to have trusted you from the beginning. I should have known that any woman with such honest eyes could never have planned to write about my father and her mother." He covered her lips with his fingers as she opened her mouth to protest. "Especially, I should have realized such an event was unlikely to have occurred in the first place. I fear I did not know my father very well. And your mother not at all, more's the pity. I am sure she must have been lovely, if you take after her at all."

Clearly bewildered, Louisa twisted about so as to study his face. "You mean that, don't you?" she whispered. She shook her head slightly, as though to understand what she had heard. "What changed your mind about me, and the letters?"

"My heart kept telling me that I wanted you, and my stubborn will resisted the gentle appeal from your eyes, your sweet nature. Little by little you crept inside my mind, joining it to my heart until I knew for certain that I loved you. Then I began to read the letters, and I found the truth." He tenderly traced the curve of her jaw. "Such petal-soft skin you have, what time we have wasted." His eyes now held more warmth than the fire blazing not far away from where they huddled. "I foolishly tried to build a sort of wall between us. I was so satisfied with my life and I was so determined that a pretty young colonial had no place in it. I was wrong. Totally, utterly wrong. Louisa, my dearest girl, can you ever forgive me?"

"Is there something to forgive?" whispered an enchanted Louisa as she offered her lips for another one of his most wondrous kisses.

"I should like to do something with those letters."

Louisa gave him an alarmed look. Warily she inquired, "What?"

"Publish them . . . with a title like *Conversations with an Osage Chief* or something similar. They are delightful and you were correct to bring them to my mother. They have given her something infinitely precious—memories to treasure."

Louisa's face was wreathed in a misty smile. "How lovely. I'm very glad." She nestled against him.

"You *will* marry me, Louisa," he announced with a trace of his old pomposity. Then, before she might object to his bold assumption, he added, "And we shall have a lovely bridal trip. I intend to take you someplace where we can wade in a stream, perhaps walk in the rain, and relax together, just the two of us."

Toby stirred by the fire and Pepper let out a little yip. Drew kissed her gently, adding, "And no children for you to governess, or puppies." He held her closer, wondering how he was to manage to remain near her for the night without yielding to his desires. "At least for the moment."

"For the moment," she echoed, quite charmed by all he said. She had come to England to find her family, and although it seemed they did not want her, she had found far better. She had found true love.

She snuggled closer in his arms and watched the smoke spiral upward, then turned up her face once more for a kiss. Morning was a ways off and she suspected there were more interesting things to do with their time. There were.

Only a crashing through the brush as Lord Bromfield staggered up the trail to join them brought a halt, a most proper one, to their lovemaking. The tender looks exchanged between Louisa and Drew promised that the day was coming soon when there would be just the two of them.